A Death at the White Camellia Orphanage

MERCER
UNIVERSITY PRESS

Endowed by
Tom Watson Brown
and
The Watson-Brown Foundation, Inc.

A Death at The White Camellia Orphanage

A Novel

Marly Youmans

Mercer University Press
Macon, Georgia

MUP/ P467

© 2012 Mercer University Press
1400 Coleman Avenue
Macon, Georgia 31207
First Edition

Books published by Mercer University Press are printed on acid-free
paper that meets the requirements of American National Standard for
Information Sciences—Permanence of Paper for Printed Library Materials.

Mercer University Press is a member of Green Press Initiative
(greenpressinitiative.org), a nonprofit organization working to help
publishers and printers increase their use of recycled paper and decrease
their use of fiber derived from endangered forests. This book is printed on
recycled paper.
Library of Congress Cataloging-in-Publication Data

Youmans, Marly.
    A death at the White Camellia Orphanage / Marly Youmans. -- First
edition.
        pages cm
    ISBN-13: 978-0-88146-446-7 (paper)
    ISBN-13: 978-0-88146-271-5 (cloth)
    ISBN-13: 978-0-88146-364-4 (e-book)
    1. Boys—Fiction. 2. Orphans—Fiction. 3. Death—Psychological
aspects—Fiction. 4. Runaway children—Fiction. 5. Voyages and travels—
Fiction. 6. Depressions—1929—United States—Fiction. I. Title.
    PS3575.O68.D43 2012
    813'.54--dc23
                            2011050845

To Howard Bahr

The gods gave you a new chance every day, he thought. Trouble was,
you pulled the old days behind you like a long freight train.
H. B., *Pelican Road*

Also by Marly Youmans

Thaliad

The Throne of Psyche

Val/Orson

Ingledove

Claire

The Curse of the Raven Mocker

The Wolf Pit

Catherwood

Little Jordan

A Death at the White Camellia Orphanage

Pip

1

Death comes to White Camellia Orphanage;
A savage laugh, a riddle and reply.

Pip Tattnal woke in the dense warmth of an Emanuel County summer at 4:17 a.m., a fact that he would learn much later when he became acquainted with clocks. For the rest of his life he would jerk from sleep at that very instant, his body refusing to sleep through the stroke of darkness. He did not open his eyes. He did not need to open his eyes. He knew where he was—the same place he had been for almost a year. He was on the farm sharecropped by the Hooks family, although the land was always called by another man's name as if to remind Mr. Jimmie and Miss Versie that they owned not much more than debt and the clothes on their backs plus a spare change for Sunday, a clutter of ironware and dishes, and a few clanking enamel chamber pots. For the last several years it also had been known as The White Camellia Orphanage or The Cottage because of the doings of Mr. Sam Truetlen, owner of a nearby cotton gin and the far-off Gen'l Notions Store, who had traveled all the way to New Orleans and on to Dallas once upon a time, and there, on the outer edge of the known world, had toured a cottage-style orphanage intended for destitute white children and run by the Klan. Being a man prone to fits of "projecting," he later backed his own orphanage, though most of the children still claimed at least one parent on some played-out, ramshackle farm. Wherever his kind had sunk so desperate and low as to scoop up the red clay to eat, Mr. Sam would arrive on muleback and plod away with one or more children riding pillion, some to stay at The Cottage for a month, some longer. It got so that people for miles around could recognize Daisy Belle, the white mule, and Goshen, the soot-gray one. As for the name of the orphanage, that was the influence of the Klan, with its Knights and Dragon, its

Cyclops and Nighthawk and Kamellia—and Mr. Sam's tip of the hat to the city of Dallas. So that was where Pip had been lodged for almost a year, in The White Camellia.

It was high, hot summer in Emanuel County, Georgia, and not one soul was saved from the day's blaze or from the night's smother of warmth. Up and down the county, the only sleep was a restless sleep, and near Lexsy, one or two old people woke in a fright because the air was just about too dense to breathe—their trembling hands reaching for funeral-parlor fans printed with a portrait of Christ and some luminous, faintly green sheep—and on some gully-shattered sharecropped place, an infant who had been fighting for air yielded up the ghost on his mother's naked breast. Mr. Sam, next door to the cotton gin, returned to bed and dreamed his nightly dream of being weighed in the scales and found wanting. At The White Camellia Orphanage, the bone-tired children slept without dreaming, all but one, who dreamed about a lost penny.

When he woke, Pip knew something was off kilter. He did not know more, neither whether the hour felt wrong or right. There was a faint slippage of coolness on his back where his half-brother Otto normally slept. The kinship bond between them was tangible, such that the children seemed inseparable, a blood brotherhood of commingled beings. Loss and grief had only made their physical need and ache for each other more clearly manifest. The musky smell that belonged to the little boy was ebbing away, and Pip could detect only the presence of the two others in the bed and the four across the room. The brothers always slept together, with a careful space between themselves and their bedmates, an act that demanded they cling to their perches even in sleep to avoid tumbling down into the deep valley of the bed. Now Pip lay breathing in the scent of near-naked boys and the stink of the chamber pots. These were smells he did not find disagreeable, just as he did not dislike the fumes of kerosene from the lamp or the odor of Miss Versie, unwashed and marked with a faint whiff of blood.

Where was Otto?

As he slipped off the ticking, Pip felt coolness against his legs; then it was gone, absorbed into air, until his feet found a trace of it on the floorboards. Coolness was the thinnest covering of all, so frail it would tear and tatter under the press of a body. Although he knew it was no use, he knelt and looked under the sway-backed iron bedsteads. Occasionally one of the orphans would climb out of bed and collapse against the floor on a hot night. But now there was nothing but a pair of sentinels, enameled chamber pots with their headpieces firmly set, waiting for a child to tote them behind the kitchen house and dump the contents onto the singed ground.

Ducking under a fly tape, Pip paused at the window. A length of gauze had been tacked to the frame to make a screen, but through the billowy gaps between nails, he could peep at the world. As the constellations vanished, piece by piece, the night was beginning to absorb bits of light, to become subtly paler as if the stars were being ground in a mill and were shedding fine bright flour over the whole sky. He could see nothing but a gloom that must be fields of cotton, tobacco, and corn, and a distant low horizon that meant swamp and pines and a grove of wild plums, flattened under the height and heft of temperature and sky.

Unhooking his overalls from a nail, he slipped them over the once-white shorts stitched by the ladies' circle of the Emanuel Primitive Baptist Church. Pajamas and underwear at once, the eight sets of homemade nightclothes were meant to provide modesty to the boys in the front bedroom.

Leaving his room, he crossed the parlor where the girls slept in matching gowns, their beds only slightly less hammocky than those of the boys. The front door was flung wide open, and even the new screen door provided by Mr. Sam was ajar, letting in mosquitoes, moths, and long-legged gnats. The ratcheting night song of katydids and frogs in the creek called *come out, come out* to Pip so that he stepped to the screen and peered at the porch, barren except for the glowing moon of the enameled basin resting on a cross-slat between two uprights, its big dipper dangling from a nail. Nothing more.

Passing by the girls' beds, he glanced at the chimney jutting between the two windows and then continued into the winter eating room with its tin cabinet of gaudy mismatched dishes and its wooden table, the legs propped up at one end with stacked shims of wood. The chamber was so slant-floored that it gave Pip a sensation of vertigo. He felt his way along the wall but stopped when he heard Mr. Jimmie's laugh and a screeching of bedsprings from the back bedroom. Knowing he would be whipped if caught, he nevertheless halted and listened to Miss Versie's muffled cries until he suddenly lost interest and tiptoed away.

Now he was sure that Otto was nowhere in the four simple rooms that lacked both halls and closets. Objects and sparse furniture were beginning to stand forth in the dark as he headed past the sleeping girls. The screen door made a faintly luminous rectangle. While he hesitated on the threshold, coolness brushed his face and he stepped out. Oh, it was too sweet there on the porch with the dipper and basin and the huge gleaming mounds of shrub that Miss Versie called *hedge* and Mr. Jimmie called *gardenia*. It was not what his mother had called gardenia, for though these leaves shone in dark or light, they were starred with tiny insignificant flowers that poured forth a cloying honey that caused Pip to sway, half-sick from the scent. The shrubs made a towering outer wall to the porch and kept the air whirring with bees and hummingbirds in the day. As green and glistening as camellias, they might have been an inspiration for Mr. Sam when he set his mind to naming.

The boy looked as if he might take flight, leaning forward above the steps. The smell had worked into his throat, and it seemed to be filling his belly, making him nauseous and faint. Scent pinned him to the floor as if to strangle him with sweetness. It rolled through every inch of his frame, spilled into his skull until he could hardly remember why he had risen from bed or where he intended to go.

Pip shut his eyes, concentrating, and the words from one of the three books he owned as a legacy from his father, his only treasures, drifted into his mind:

The King's horse, with a kind of contempt of the enemy, charged with wonderful boldness and routed them in most places, till they had left the greatest part of their foot without any guard at all of horse. But then the foot behaved themselves admirably on the enemy's part and gave their scattered horse time to rally and were ready to assist and secure them upon all occasions. The London train-bands and regiments behaved themselves to wonder; and were, in truth, the preservation of the army that day. For they stood as a bulwark and a rampire to defend the rest; and when their wings of horse were scattered and dispersed, kept their ground so steadily that, though Prince Rupert himself led up the choice horse to charge them and endured their storm of shot, he was forced to wheel about.

Eyes still closed, the boy leaped from the steps into the sand yard, plunging through the heavy odor of hedge. "When I get to be a man," he thought, "I will go to England and see the battlegrounds, and I'll be a titled *Childe* of noble and gentle birth, and I'll know what a *train-band* is and what a *rampire* is. I'll ride on wings of horse." It was a part of the boy's strangeness that he could draw to mind great swaths of the words in the three books that had belonged to his dead father even though he hardly knew what some of them meant or who Prince Rupert or the writer, the Earl of Clarendon, might be. His teacher at school had been no help, scorning his questions—did not like any of the pupils in overalls with no shirts whether they were from the orphanage or not.

Had he been born some seventy years later, even an orphan boy with oddities of memory and behavior might have been diagnosed and his syndrome named. At school he would have been "classified" and made to learn by rote the laws of conversation, the rules belonging to social commerce, and the expressions of the human face. Instead, he was born to strangeness and the need to fit into the world as it was.

While hanging on to the handles of a cut-down plough, Pip often recited passages aloud, repeating them over and over. In this way he conjured a realm very different from his own—and from the one described in his father's books, for there was much he could not grasp even if he knew the words by heart. A squat, diminutive tower that must have been used to store water long ago was his castle. Before a wade in the creek, he and Otto would act out scenes of "foot" and "horse" along the bank, pelting one another with rotten plums.

Otto. Where was Otto?

Dust from the bare yard powdered his toes. He stepped carefully, watching for Miss Versie's rusty cans of zinnias, cautious as he bent to swing under the half-downed cedar wrapped in trumpet vine. Beneath its cavernous side were short-fused, tiny scorpions, firecracker hot and eager to pinch and sting a bare heel. To the west Pip could see the unlit hulk of the kitchen house, beached in white sand. Rats from the corncrib crisscrossed the floor at night, or so Miss Versie claimed. Mr. Jimmie said only, "Haints." Neither one of the Hookses would go in there after the girls scrubbed supper dishes on the back step. Come morning, the pots would be overturned, and black grains left by rats stippled the contents of the meal bin.

The boy shivered, his eyes moving from the kitchen to the crib to the barn the boys had built with Mr. Jimmie earlier that summer, and then to the shelter piled with rust-pocked tubs where the chickens nested. A dim blur by the fence was the sow, asleep with her litter flung close to her teats. Some runty pomegranate trees leaned beside the fence, along with the doorless ruins of a kitchen stove where the girls would bake mud and juniper berry pies after a rain, first prodding the innards of the oven with a stick to oust a drowsy hen or sometimes a snake. Copperheads and rattlers would be dozing now: no need for a cudgel.

The fence in front of the yard was Miss Versie's pride, made of heavy wire elaborately crimped and looped, with scallops along the top and a matching gate and latch. It had been donated by Mr. Sam, along with a stamped tin sign: *The White Camellia Orphanage. Mr. Samuel Truetlen, Founder & Benefactor.* The gate must have been unfastened for a while; Pip noticed an escaped chicken nestled between rows of cotton but decided that just now "the foot" had more important business than charging after hens. Miss Versie kept the children in a constant skirmish with the poultry, which were to be kept out of the fields and off the porch.

Furious resolution, Pip recalled, his eyes on the furrows of pale cloud, their bolls hardened and split by sun. He liked the sound of the two words together. The Earl of Clarendon did not talk like anybody at the orphanage.

He started down one of the two ruts that passed for a road and sliced the farm into halves, walking slowly and then more quickly toward the woods where Mr. Jimmie had slashed the trees to collect pine gum.

Otto.

"The king was fearless in his person," Pip blurted out, his words loud, the sole human utterance for miles around in fields mastered and held by the whining saws of insects.

He was beginning to feel uneasy. What did it mean to be fearless *in his person,* Pip wondered. He swung around but could see nothing except rows of cotton, becoming distinct as more and more flour from the stars sifted across the heavens. He did not like being abroad in the night. He did not like missing his brother Otto, as near and essential as his own cast shade. He did not see how a king could be anything *in his person.* Could the earl say that the king was fearless *in his chicken? In his plowshare? In his sword?* It made no sense. Pip danced up and down in the road, his hands fluttering. *Where was Otto?* Tears pricked at his eyes.

"Too dry and too durn hot to cry," Miss Versie would say.

Waving his arms, he raced down the lane, shedding his panic like the tufts of fur that floated and then snagged on the cedar and barbed wire fence Mr. Jimmie and the older boys had wrestled into place during the spring. The darkness hid his awkwardness, how one leg almost crossed the other, how his hands flailed at the air. Pip worked hard at running, harder than it seemed anybody could ever need to work. When he stopped a hundred yards east of the house, he leaned over and spat, tasting the fragrance of hedge in his mouth. The sky was appreciably lighter, and the plants and fence posts and wire had become more clearly defined, though the world still hunkered in gloom. Soon sunrise would be upon them, rending the air with heat. Pip knew how the dawn looked. There would be a burning knife—surely the magic, gold-red weapon of a king—hanging sidewise in the air, the blade turned toward the farm. Around the edge would float jags and flecks of gold as if it moved in a furnace and, fresh-forged, brought the hot spirit of a heavenly tempering in its metal. He leaped and spun in the air. He would find Otto, and they would rout the lone chicken under a molten daybreak. Afterward, he would recite the list he had made, lying in bed, of the weapons used in the Rebellion.

"Fearless," he repeated, "wings of horse."

Cutting through the press of heat, Pip galloped farther.

Suddenly reined in, he halted so quickly that he toppled to one side and had to catch himself.

"Fearless," he said softly.

He craned his head, looking at the thing that had stopped his flight.

It was the body of a boy, perhaps a year younger than Pip, arms lashed against the topmost strand of barbed wire, legs bent and tied to a post. Although his cotton underwear flapped in a hot breath of wind, he was otherwise quite still. His head had fallen over to one side as if the neck might be broken. A strand of barbed wire haloed the hair, arcing across the brow, and a few jewel-like drops of deep red beaded the skin. Some half-healed sores and scabs pocked his arms and side, suggesting that he had been malnourished. Despite these and if only he had been alive, he would have appeared a child of notable beauty, with his curly hair spilling onto one cheek, long eyelashes, olive skin that had been protected from the sun by overalls, arms and neck and face burnt darker. Pip squatted and tilted his own head to one side. It seemed he could not take in the sight.

For another boy, the grasping of this image would have been more immediate. Here was a brother, bound to a post, dead.

"Otto?" His voice was drowned by the keening of insects.

Pip rubbed his forehead. The smell of the hedge was still clinging to his arms and face, pushing into his lungs and belly. He dropped to his knees and retched, bringing up a gruel-like spit, greenish with lady peas. Head bent, he watched the vomit be taken by the dust.

He let his eyes follow the legs, let them travel along the wired arms, up the bruised neck to the cheekbone. Pip had never liked to look anyone in the eye. He had learned to focus on the temple or the bridge of a nose because there were people who did not like it when he would not meet their eyes with his own, who would welt him with a strop or a branch if he did not. What did it matter whether he looked straight at them? He could see them well enough, his eyes resting in middle distance where he could dream of horse and foot without disturbance. He heard their words all the same. He noted the talk, slack and empty of interest compared to his own urgent thoughts. He felt their presence, flinging a shadow across his mind. He did not need to nod, to answer yes or no, or to look into their naked eyes. He disliked the pale blue eyes that tingled against his skin. He loved only brown eyes, his brother Otto's eyes, but even those he rarely met with his own. He knew Otto, felt him. He did not need to look. Now he let his own gaze inch along the hoop of wire orbiting the forehead and creep to the eye.

"Fearless," he muttered.

There was something big in his chest, mounting up, as in a landscape just before the sun rises. And there was something else, narrow, slicing him across the throat, like the knife of dawn. To neither of these feelings could he begin to put a word.

A tinny insect voice, like the sound of the preacher, kept insisting at his ear: Who shall deliver me from the *body* of this death? Who shall *deliver* me from the body of this death? Who shall deliver me from the body of this *death*? Who *shall* deliver me from the body of this death?

Pip knew whose voice it was! It belonged to the little King James from the frontispiece of a Bible, too short to peep over book and podium, his boot heels clicking as he rose and sank.

His stare rested on the curled eyelashes of the image that was like his half-brother Otto. Centimeter by centimeter, it moved eastward toward the sun, toward the other eye, and there his gaze halted. He detected, tame and small, the flames of morning shimmering on the iris. He shifted his glance. Pip's eyes fixed on the iridescent green backs of a pair of flies, piggybacked on the curve of an eye.

The big thing in his chest stirred and shook itself. For a long time, maybe fifteen seconds or more, the boy could pull only the faintest tendril of air into his lungs, could not breathe out. The something that had seemed to be garroting him across the neck now gashed at his flesh, his windpipe, freeing his voice and breath so that he shuddered, spitting milky fluid onto the earth. That other, bigger knife, hammered from the iron of daybreak, vaulted into view, shedding flakes of fire above the horizon.

"Otto!" Pip cried, his voice returning with an "O, o, o" as he shouted the name over, and the dagger in the sky came nearer, searing the furnace of the cotton fields with its heat as the boy bounded up, yelling his brother's name, and laughter with a fragrance of hedge sprang from his mouth. His voice pulsed out of his throat like blood, and merriment battled out of his chest like the beating cry of a war drum. And the helpless roar that from the distance of The White Camellia Orphanage sounded so like a scream seemed to involve the very skies in its clamor, as in a rhythm of call and response. The sun swelled and soared to become a rosy "O" burning above the plum trees, and the heat waves of its solar outcry aroused the tobacco leaves and the rosined pines and the snake-dripping swamps like immense but unheard mirth.

2

Eclipse endured; Pip meets the eyes of men.

All morning the children from The Cottage kept going into the yard where they had been forbidden to go, and looking down the dirt lane where several trucks and cars could be seen. They had been wakened by Mr. Jimmie's shouting; then he had gone off in the wagon while Miss Versie herded the children to the board table near the kitchen house. The riven table with the lichens that the girls called "doilies" was loaded with milk and hominy and fried eggs, a better beginning to the day than usual. Perhaps because of the breakfast, or because of the missing boy and the other one sequestered in the kitchen, or because of the way Mr. Sam Truetlen jolted too fast up the lane—he dragged a great swirl of dust behind him—then stomped on the brakes and shouted for Miss Versie, there was a feeling of dread on the farm. It did not stop the children from playing as they did their chores.

The girls were calling responses to a game called "When I am Queen" while they sat on the front steps shelling heavy cobs of corn, their thumbs working busily. It was what Mr. Jimmie called *horse corn*, huge ears with dented, yellow-orange kernels that were difficult to force from their sockets. When each seed had been popped from its place, the remaining cob, stiff and red, was still massive, a good weapon for the little boys, who yelled and hurled them at one another until Miss Versie came out with a twig broom, shooed them away, and swept the ground in front of the house, catching up a litter of fallen needles, spats of tobacco, and bird droppings. Her eyes rested on the huddle of vehicles. A little before nine in the morning, she gathered the children together and paraded them through the fields toward the plum grove and the stream. A sand bar had formed near an elbow in the channel, and each child would fetch home a pail or bowl of fine sand to empty on the yard. Miss Versie marched in front, a cudgel resting on one shoulder. She was a wonder against snakes, and the barefoot children trusted her to clear the path of copperheads and rattlers. If they behaved, she had promised to boil green peanuts in the laundry kettle next to the kitchen house.

Pip remained at the shack. Miss Versie had comforted him as best she knew how, giving him a glass of warm water and a slice of the tender peach pie made for Mr. Jimmie's supper.

He had eaten the pie like a dog, snapping it up, his mouth low to the plate, and it was gone before he tasted anything more than sweetness, something custard-like on the mushy bottom crust. Looking at the table, he felt faintly surprised that the treat was gone so swiftly and that it had not pleasured him more. After a minute he took the dish and licked it clean.

Then there was nothing for him but to wait. Already it was hot in the house. Small biting flies crawled along his arms and cheekbone and tested the entrances to his head. When one bit, he slapped at the spot, his face unchanged. For a while he dreamed about the English Rebellion, plotting out attack and counter-attack, planning where he would arrange his horses and his men and how he would surprise the enemy. Letting his eyelids fall shut, he imagined an elaborate map decorated with a park of magnolia trees and low elevations; he added stick figures and brushed the air with arrows. There was no paper at The White Camellia Orphanage, not unless you counted the yellowed sheets of newsprint glued to the rough-cut siding with flour paste. They were meant to stop the drafts of cold air on a winter night. He would have liked a tablet and a pencil, and he would have cherished a few penny soldiers and horses of lead or stamped tin. To handle them would have been deeply satisfying to him. But not one of the children who had come to The Cottage over the past few years could be said to own a toy. Nuts and an orange and a piece of candy were the heights of a Christmas gift for them. They made frog houses and animals from pinched mud when the rains came, and one of the girls, Nonnie, whose mother had been trampled by a bull and crippled past mending, carried about a cypress root swaddled in torn strips of yellow cotton. The part she called a face was curiously modeled, boasting a nose and cheeks and chin. The root doll was so ugly that it made Miss Versie laugh. Nonnie's "Buh" was the closest thing to a toy on the whole farm, and Pip, who was already ten, would never have a plaything, not in his whole childhood.

After a while the heat and the stillness poured into his mental battlefield, bringing the Rebellion to a halt. Briefly, with a single jerk of the head, he felt panic, remembering the angle of Otto's neck. Then the image subsided, and he sank to sleep. The next he knew, Mr. Jimmie was squatting beside him.

"Wake up, boy. Wake up."

Pip woke with another spasm, sliding his glance around the room until it rested on the farmer's shirt, faded by sun and sweat and repeated boiling in the wash pot. Mr. Jimmie was talking, but there was a buzzing in the room. The boy yawned and rubbed his head. His cheek was sticky where it had been pressed against the oilcloth. *Otto. What were they going to do with Otto? But maybe it was a nightmare. Maybe he was heat sick.*

"Come on out in the yard." Handing him a brimming glass of water, Mr. Jimmie stood up and looked through the open door of the back bedroom. Miss Versie's nightgown lay puddled on the floor.

"I sure am sorry about your brother," he added.

So it was true. Otto was dead. He drank at the warm water, but it gave him no relief.

The boy pushed back his chair, scraping it along the floor, and the farmer swung his gaze around. Pip rose to his feet and forced himself to look the man in the face. The raw stare of the other burned; he had never felt Mr. Jimmie to be so unfamiliar. The head, had it always been just so, almost wedge-shaped? Were the eyes paler than before? The cheeks were pitted, stubbled with black filings. The nose looked broken at the tip.

"Dadburn fool thing. Why they had to go and put him here, I don't know," Mr. Jimmie's mouth was saying.

"Did you do it?" Pip heard the question before he knew that he had spoken.

The sharecropper shook his head.

"Gol-durn. You know me, boy; would I mess with a thing like that? That ain't nothing a man like me could do. That there's the devil's handiwork."

The child paused, stumped. He did not know. And he could not read the face: for him, the narrow-honed head might as well have been the Rosetta Stone. Was Mr. Jimmie telling the truth? Twice, three times he met the eyes that seemed to crackle with their heat, singeing his skin. He remembered a handful of broken blue and white marbles he'd seen once, beautiful and useless for play. Withdrawing his gaze, he looked at the man's feet. They were dusted with whitish-grey sand just as fine as a town lady's powder. He wondered why a woman would want to put dirt on her face, wondered what the men in the trucks had done with Otto and whether Mr. Jimmie would say. Maybe he would not if he'd been the one who had done something to Otto. Hurt him to death. Killed him dead. It seemed to the boy that he could never again follow Mr. Jimmie to the fields, jumping the rows and singing.

Just yesterday, everything had been different. Otto had held the tub while Pip stirred chemicals for the fields with his arm, churning the pale stuff until clouds rose and coated their cheeks. They had laughed out loud, making faces and spitting the bitter specks from their lips. Afterward they went off, still ghostly, to hunt for late blackberries, walking a mile to the lane's end where the wild fruit ripened in snarls near the swamp. But there had not been any, nothing but dried knots.

Mr. Jimmie was still talking, and after a while the boy blundered through the doorway and the shadowy front room.

On the porch the men stopped rocking when he came out.

"C'mon over here, son," one of the fellows said.

But Pip had frozen, his eyes on the deep shadow next to the hedge at the far end of the porch. There was something lying on the boards, covered over by a length of loose-woven fabric. He thought the cloth might be one of Nonnie's diapers that Miss Versie was always folding. From the bottom protruded two legs, one pulled up and barely visible in the gloom. He could feel the men at his back, watching him. Their eyes caught at his skin like ice. There were four of them.

"Son," came another voice.

"It stinks." He did not turn around.

"He don't cotton to the smell of gardenia," Mr. Jimmie told them.

And now there were five. The boy felt their stares like the weight of a hand between his shoulder blades.

"I ain't walking in no sun, no sir," the first man said, his voice testy.

The smell hurt Pip's nose and throat. Shifting on his feet, he turned far enough to glance at the men. He did not recognize any of them but Mr. Sam Truetlen, who was fanning himself hard.

The one with a gun on his hip leaned forward in his creaking chair.

"See here, son, we just want to help. See can we find out what's been happening around here. Who would go and do such a thing."

Such a thing. Who would go and do such a thing.

Pip cocked his head to one side and looked at the men. It was the first time in his whole life that he had paid attention to fellows in a group, had bothered to pick them out separately and try to fasten names on them. It often took him a year to learn a new name because it did not matter to him. The word was not significant, not an important part of being with someone. When a name came along, fine. Otherwise, what did it matter? Now he was unmoored. There was Mr. Jimmie. There was Mr. Sam Truetlen, wiping his upper lip on an immense handkerchief and then stuffing it back into his pocket. And there were three others, whom he examined as closely as he could. He did not know how to go about it; he started with the feet and worked up. The gunman wore broken shoes with his uniform.

He was a lean, withered man with a sunken jaw who looked like all the old farmers on the Saturday bench outside the dry goods store in town.

Squinting, Pip looked off toward the kitchen to see if the big iron kettle was on the boil. He could feel it coming on, the thing that he called his *eclipse. A clips, bay flips, ray thrips, flay whips....*

The air was darkening. It was now the color of smoke from the fire below a pot, though there were no flames. The kettle was still lying on its side in weeds, near the depression where slop jars were dumped out in the morning. The smell of the hedge was at him again, thrusting its tendrils down his throat. Shivering, he turned his face from the men, who now were arguing among themselves; he winced as Mr. Jimmie touched his arm, wrapped a hand around his forehead. The roar of bees and the beating wings of hummingbirds jammed his head. A haunted color came over the porch and the yard with the downed cedar: the tint of glass he and his brother had found in the ruins of a burned house near the swamp. They had looked through a shard, and Pip had recognized the landscape of his eclipse. Stumbling forward, he trembled, his eye snared by the floating white rectangle on Otto's body; then he vomited over the porch rail that held the basin, Mr. Jimmie's hands coming to rest on his temples.

"Sweet Jesus." That was the grating noise of the man with the gun.

Mr. Sam Truetlen was praying out loud. The name of the Lord had been taken in vain, and it was an act the children knew Mr. Sam could not abide.

The air was close to black now, as dark as tobacco spit gone deep in the can, with rotten bog shapes floating in the murk.

Gasping, the boy clutched the handle that Mr. Jimmie tendered him, his teeth chattering against the bowl of the dipper.

"Go on," the man urged him, "spit it out."

He could smell the vomit, as strong as if flowers of hedge had been compacted and distilled. Obediently, he sloshed the well water around in his mouth and spat. It tasted of pollen, and he vomited again. This time Mr. Jimmie led him to the steps and forced him down, pushing his head onto his knees. The warmth and pressure of the man's hands alarmed him, so seldom had he been touched at the orphanage by anyone but Otto. What did it mean? Pip let the question rest, hearing the feet on the porch and the voices of men fading away. They were shambling down the side steps, rounding the house, past the spot where lay some rusted-out cans and a pair of ruined paintbrushes that he and Otto had found in back of the school. Only yesterday they had been painting the house with water. The thirsty gray boards sucked in the liquid almost as fast as they could brush it on. Their game was to see how much they could cover before their first strokes vanished into the air. The activity had pleased them both, the repetitive, senseless motion and the defeat of their work by heat and air and devouring wood. When the sound of the men died, he could hear the puttering hunt of the bees and hummingbirds again, less loud this time. The eclipse was starting to ebb.

"You boys are fools for work," Mr. Jimmie had called out the day before, ejecting an arc of tobacco juice over the side of the porch. And Otto had laughed, his arm moist with sweat and the rivulets of "paint."

If he moved his head, he could see the rectangle of white where Otto was lying. But not Otto; Otto was gone, slipped off like Pip's mother, dead after childbirth. Nothing was any use with the life gone out of it. *Mommer.* He could barely remember her in a white shirtwaist and a plum-colored skirt, stacking canned figs and peaches in a big cupboard. Her sleeve had caught on the edge of a lid, and three of the jars had fallen, and his mother had cried out once, *Oh!* Like the sunrise, bouncing Otto's name. The picture lodged in him, the smash and the chunks of glass shooting across the floor, syrup pooling around the figs and the halves of white and yellow peaches.

He had forgotten the taste of peaches until he licked the plate. Miss Versie had been given a jar of yellow presses by the preacher at the Primitive Baptist Church. Pastor Bell had a tree that bore yellow presses in his bee yard, and he knew that they were Miss Versie's favorite peaches. Small, cling-seeded, bright, with speckles of black on the skin, they were the best for making pickled peaches because of their flavor and firm flesh. One jar was not enough to share with the children, so she had baked the fruit into a pie that made the whole kitchen house fragrant. And he had been given a piece, but he had hardly noticed, had hardly tasted it. Really he had missed it somehow. Because his mind was not on it, had gone off somewhere else. His mother would never have let him miss that pie. "You *et* it," Miss Versie said when he had asked for another slice, her voice rising.

He wondered whether Mommer had washed those peaches and figs and canned them over again or whether she had sighed and thrown the whole mess away. Georgianna Jo would not have let this happen. Had she said anything to her husband when he brought Otto and his older brother Chach home? A moment must have come when she knew that Gilead was not just her husband and father to Pip and the others but also something more—when she saw his own mouth and nose and crooked eyebrow on those two boys and knew they were his but not hers. Mommer would have kept them safe, even the ones that were not rightly hers except by feeding and sewing and scrubbing. She was dead with her baby though. That was a way mothers went.

After she died, there were only five of them left, and then the oldest two left to help at farms sharecropped by elder brothers. Nobody was home to shell field peas and butterbeans, to shuck corn, to peel and preserve tomatoes or beans or vegetable soup. As if Georgianna Jo were still there, the little boys kept on retrieving peach windfalls, though no one washed the fruit and cut away wormy flesh and canned the precious remains. The squashed and browned ones they hurled at the pigs; the others they ate. No Mommer prevented them now.

Meanwhile, Daddy was—how old? sixty? seventy? more?—as old as Father Time on the December calendar page at the feed store, and with a beard as bountiful as the one in a picture of Moses tacked onto the boys' bedroom wall. Gilead kept on traveling about, constructing bridges over Georgia gullies and streams, until he dropped dead on a sand bar in the Ohoopee River. The loss was not real to Pip, not even when he reached in the box and squeezed a fistful of beard. It was not until dinner came and nobody remembered him and Otto and Chach that he realized everything had changed. Then he wanted his daddy to tell them a story in the evening, and he cried, realizing that the old man would never read to them again, sitting in the Morris chair with his glasses pulled down to the end of his nose.

After that Chach was sent to his mama's sister like a C.O.D. parcel, a bill for transport and the name and address of the woman pinned to his overalls. Nobody offered to take the youngest boys, who clung to each other and shrieked if anyone tried to pull them apart. It was a bad year for Mr. Gilead Tattnal's twenty-four known offspring, and no doubt for a certain number of his unidentified children as well. The bridge builder was dead. All unbridged gaps remained uncrossable. No one objected when Mr. Sam Truetlen put the small brothers pillion on his second-best mule, Goshen, and jogged away to The White Camellia Orphanage.

Pip shoved a thumb against his eye. Had it been just when he remembered the smash of glass against floor that the ache had started? He was used to pain, the vise and screw of migraine that came on in the field when the summer sun bored down at mid-afternoon or when the smell of hedge grew intolerable. Otto knew not to speak when his brother's head was hurting, but Mr. Jimmie did not know and kept on talking. The boy could not make out the words, could not latch on to syllables that kept getting lost in the blur of hummingbird wings and in the orbit of flame that rounded his eye and streaked into his brain. A searing and throbbing always followed eclipse.

"Feeling peart enough to walk?"

Pip heard the question, and his gaze wobbled unwillingly to Mr. Jimmie's face. The shadows were draining away, but to his sensitive eyes, an aureole seemed to pulse around the farmer. In its light the wedge-shaped skull appeared predatory, the watery blue eyes luminous.

"What you staring at?" When Mr. Jimmie slapped him on the back, something that felt like sparkles and shanks of fire tore through Pip's head.

"Dadburn." The older man sighed, getting to his feet and tugging at his charge. "If this ain't the worst I ever seen."

Wrenching away from the arm gripping his, Pip staggered across the sand yard, his eyes on the man's bare heels. Mr. Jimmie kept murmuring as he passed the corner near the chimney. Somebody had kicked the rusty "paint" cans under the house, and the boy quelled the urge to crawl underneath and fetch them out. If he bent over, he would throw up again, and right now all he wanted was to be somewhere quiet where he could still the shards of metal and glass that kept shifting and forming fresh patterns inside his mind.

In the rear yard the visitors were talking water, standing around the well. A foolhardy source for an orphanage, it had sides made of slats of wood, a flimsy board roof, and a bucket of mottled gray enamel on a chain. Although forbidden to do so, the younger children liked to get a toehold and climb up. From the well's top one could look into a magical tunnel that was like nothing else on the farm of dust and clay and sand. Ferns pearled with drops of water held motionless until a bead rolled away or until a droplet struck a frond that would then droop and spring, trembling on its tether. Mounds of moss clustered along the walls like prickly-backed English hedgehogs from a realm of fairy tale. At the bottom appeared the sphere of another world; it had tempted more than one child to dive, though none had ever done so. Gleaming with filtered light and lustrous, like the largest and most perfect pearl, it seemed a dimpling door to a moony land under the earth and was what had floated into Pip's mind when Pastor Bell intoned, "Lord God Hisself shall grant us that perfect peace that passeth the understanding of mortal men." Peace: for the child, it came down not as the preacher's mighty cataract but as the slow, thoughtful gathering of an enormous orb of dew, meant to lie in earth and reflect on all that went on, the works of men and the labors of women who were dead or dying in childbirth or who would be bound to do so some day.

Around the well he sensed only more unrest. The strangers were jawing again, with Mr. Jimmie trying to quiet them.

"Hush up, hush up. Y'all trying to swamp this boy."

Pip lifted his face and squinted at the jagged edge of sun surrounding the talkers. He listened to Mr. Sam, who was naming the party. Mr. Willie Swain, the gaunt one with the gun, was in charge. The boy wondered what he was—a detective, a sheriff, a policeman? He and Otto had played at being New York City dicks, looking for missing jewels near the cow pen and in the hen's nests. *Otto should be here,* he thought, for an instant forgetting that a breathless Otto lay more still than peace under a rectangle on the porch. Mr. Willie Swain's voice rose; Mr. Willcox, a short, barrel-chested man, would be helping him. A younger man, a Mr. Collins, had been placed in charge of writing down notes. Winking against the blaze of sky, Pip raised one hand to shade his brow. He needed to look at their features, but it was hard when his eye ached and longed for nothing but night.

"That boy's Daddy—same as yours?"

Pip nodded, his eyes feeling their way across the mass of men toward Mr. Willie.

"Yes sir," Mr. Jimmie instructed him in a whisper, prodding his arm.

"Yes sir."

"But not the mama."

"He's asking," Mr. Jimmie explained after a moment in which Pip made no reply.

"No sir."

"What kind of a woman was his mama? Can you tell me that?"

The boy shook his head.

"No sir, he can't do that," Mr. Jimmie added.

"I'll ask the questions. I'll thank the boy his own self to answer. How's it to look in the record book, without that? Unnatural. Won't make a grit of sense."

"Usual thing is, we can't shut him up." Shrugging, Mr. Jimmie looked at Pip. "This just ain't the usual—"

"You call to mind her features?"

"No sir."

"Seems like she'd be some kind of Injun. Dark-complected. A Spanish girl, maybe. Or Portugee."

Pip looked at the questioner, dumb to reply.

"Boy does not know," Mr. Willie said. "That's for the record, Johnny Collins."

The young man waved a pencil back and forth above his notebook. His greased cowlick had sprung upward, and now, as he combed his free hand through the hair, it parted into furrows and sprouted up in every direction.

"What about the part, 'that's for the record, Johnny Collins,'" he began hesitantly. "Is that in, or is that out?"

Pip and the other men stared at him and then at Mr. Willie, who appeared to doubt what he had just heard, his mouth agape. He closed it, shifted from foot to foot, slapped his gun.

"Of all the durn cotton-picking—"

Mr. Willie tore off his hat and flung it to the dirt yard. After a moment in which he glared first at Johnny Collins, and next at the hat, he stomped on it.

Pip took one giant step back.

"If that ain't the veriest foolishness," Mr. Willie intoned, "I don't know what is. It don't pay to try and bring along this next generation. Nothing but the purest kind of moonshine fools. One hundred proof distilled addlement. Bad enough we don't have no photographer or no artistic renderings of the crime scene, but we got to be saddled with this—"

Johnny Collins ducked his head and began scribbling frantically in the book.

"Just a bale of cotton-picking eejits. Where was I?" Mr. Willie settled the hat back on his crown, where it emitted a puff of dun-colored motes. "You been pondering, boy. Can't help but be. You got any concepts, any big ideas? About who done such as this?"

To Pip, the man with the gun looked like the very devil, his head smoking and smoldering with powder. He retreated a little farther from the group, his stare fixed. One by one, the eyes scorched him. Even Mr. Jimmie's encouraging smile felt false, his lips pale as the lining of a cottonmouth's open jaws. The glaring corkscrew of light hooped around their figures like a crooked lasso declared that they were all the same, all in the same hellish circle.

Without speaking, he gazed at a second puff that escaped from under the hat as Mr. Willie scratched his pate. His own head was burning, suffering torments of pitchfork and hellfire. He remembered holding aloft a teacher's homemade kaleidoscope to see a jumble of busted glass, cobalt and rose and green—"Turn it to the light, and you'll see something beautiful," she had said—and how a star of sun jabbed through the crazy scene and speared him in the eye, shooting an ache into his head that would not leave for days. He felt the same way now, as if a picture would not fall together and make sense, as if he had been pierced through the brain. Lifting one hand to shelter his eyes, Pip again forced himself to sweep his glance across the men's faces. Their irises, a shattered blue and green, sparked in their skulls.

He wanted to veer and flounder away, lurching through the overheated atmosphere. But he could not leave Otto—what was left of him—under the white rectangle that could not protect a body from the prying bees and hummingbirds or the hands of strangers. When he felt better, he would be able to sense whether his brother's ghost hovered in the air, rested in the dead arms, or was jailed and swooning in the perfume of the hedge. Mr. Willie's question came back to him as if in echo.

Yes, he suspected someone. Who would do such a thing. Yes, he feared their guilt. Could see it shining, cracked and loony, in eyes.

"Speak up, boy," Mr. Willie said testily. He swung around to hawk and spit, and Pip saw blotches of perspiration on his shirt.

Oh, for the day a day ago, with his gaze sliding over a man's shoulder, resting on his nose like the metal bridge to a pair of glasses, lighting on a mole below a cheekbone. Those hours were swallowed up. From now on, he would have to look everywhere and always until he found out what he needed to know. He would be scalded in the hog barrels and boiling kettles of men's eyes. He would have to learn to read the terrible enigma of their masks. It was difficult; its mystery might take a lifetime to master unless he already knew all that there was to know—for now, all he grasped was that men were confessing some guilty secret. He could see it shining out of sweat-slick features, out of irises that crisped his skin. They were each found wanting. As the preacher had shouted to them on Sunday, "We are every last one fallen short of the glory of God. Every one! All fallen away from that righteousness!" They were lacking: Mr. Jimmie, Mr. Sam, the man with the gun, the man's companion, and the purely foolish one. Somehow they were bound up with the killing of his brother; he was sure of it, as sure as if he had seen the act. And now he knew that wherever he went for the rest of his life, he would see a kind of burning in the faces of men, and that until the day he died, he would never be able to look away from their eyes or from their secret knowledge.

3

The Earth as a blue eye; and Pip, bereft,
Goes searching for Otto among the dead.

The *spang!* of insect cries, fused into a single vibrating note, soared into the sky. Pip thought perhaps he could see its shrillness when he looked straight into the burning sun and saw something like a rope made of gold, its frizzled threads on fire. The sound and the light jabbed at his eyes, and he ducked his head.

For three days now he had understood nothing except that confession gripped the glances of men. On the farm he had known it for the first time. When taken into town to make a deposition, he had seen it again. From one cast stone of wrong, the circles ran outward forever, widening to hold the world, which was itself like a single blue eye decked with green and set in a socket of darkness.

What could a boy do about such evil? Pip thought about the chain of days, spaced through the summer, daybreak to sunset spent in mopping cotton to kill cotton worms and boll weevils. At dawn his right arm had been powdered white from lead salt, what the feed store men called *arsenic of lead*. For weeks in early summer, he and Otto had trailed down the rows, smearing molasses laced with lead on the stalks with cloth-tipped sticks. Later on it was the young blossoms and then the bolls that needed mopping. Gangs of honeybees and wasps and what seemed a thousand different insects clouded the air behind them, pursuing sweetness, bumbling into ears and lashes as if the boys might be molded from sugar. In the morning they would have to scrape flies and wasps from their overalls. At the end of each round of poison when the work was entirely done, Miss Versie would plunge the children's clothes, coated with sticky residue, into her boiling pot, skimming dead bees from the water with a ladle. Mopping cotton was a job that sickened Pip, with his hatred of sweet odors, but it had to be done. The bucket was too heavy for Otto, so it was Pip who had to heft and swing its weight, the stink of hot molasses in his nose. At least it was not as cloying as the smell of hedge.

Was there a medicine good against a man worm, against the weevil at his core? What a job it would be to mop every boy in the world, dabbing poison on his arms and head so that he could grow right without that look of fire in his eyes.

On the afternoon of the killing, two men came with a wagon and took the body of his brother. Miss Versie held Pip's wrist so that he could not get free while he strained away from her, his face set like a dog's against the leash. The other children were filtering into the rows of cotton, their cut-down sacks sagging, but they stopped to watch, fingering the fleece with its dark seeds in their hands. The shape, almost covered by white cloth, was borne on a wide slat to the wagon bed. Pip growled, his face scrunched, but only when the wagon was an invisible seed inside a cotton-head of dust did Miss Versie let go of his arm and the clump of overalls she had seized in her fist.

He flung himself out the gate, making Mr. Sam Truetlen's nameplate shiver in the air, and dashed down the road, his feet pounding on the packed dirt and the runty, dark-red stones that Miss Versie called *garnets*, though they were not real jewels or of use to anybody. They were just pellets of rust-colored ore, liable to crumble into grains when squeezed between fingers. From the house the woman might have seen that he ran with a kind of stagger as if one leg wanted to cross the other. The sun melted against him, slicking his skin with gold. He chased the oxen the quarter mile to the farm gate, lurching first through puffs of blowing dust and lead, his mouth open to pant in the shape of a grieving O, and then in a stinging cloud of grit. What was in his mind he did not know: nothing except the getting back to a living Otto, the getting somewhere that seemed as long and arduous a passage as being born—a process he knew well and knew that it too might end in death.

When the men in the wagon rounded the corner with a lurch, they stopped and waited for Pip to catch up. Collapsing onto the wagon boards, he gasped, feeling the pain of running so far, so fast like something torn inside. Copper-tasting saliva trickled from his mouth. He reached out and took hold of his brother's ankle as if he would deliver him from the wagon bed.

The man who had swung down from the seat surveyed the boy.

"You know me?"

Looking away from the limb in his hand, Pip's eyes scaled the stained shirt and the face. He liked brown eyes.

He nodded; it was Tobbie Jones, a black tenant farmer from a 30-acre place about a mile off.

"What you want with this boy?"

"My brother—Otto's my brother." He clung to the foot.

"Sho." Looking toward the shack beside the chinaberry trees where a blue dot that was Miss Versie could still be seen in the yard, the older man perched on the tail of the wagon, letting his legs dangle.

"Here," he said, reaching to pull aside the white cloth. "Ain't nothing to do but pay respects. Nothing wrong with that."

Pip let go. He climbed aboard and sat on his heels, studying Otto. Hard drops like nubs of garnet studded the forehead though the face had been washed. The insects were gone. He felt a sudden impulse to witness to a bond of blood that predated words and persisted beyond explaining.

"He's all I got," Pip whispered, leaning forward. Someone had filled his eyes with tears that wavered down his cheeks and splashed onto his brother's face.

Tobbie Jones bowed his head.

"Then you the saddest boy in the world," he said slowly.

For a long time they stayed like that, the child kneeling with his eyes on his brother's features, the man with his face lowered. The other man hunched motionless on the board seat, the reins held loosely in his fist. His head was cocked, as though he might be listening to the silence and waiting for words to be spoken.

"You got to go back," Tobbie Jones pronounced at last.

"What about him? What about Otto?"

"They's people to bury the body, down by the old Tattnal graveyard."

"Can I go?"

"I be afraid to venture."

When the ox-wagon toiled on, it was without Pip. Tobbie Jones had promised the boy that somebody would take him to Tattnal cemetery. He would speak to Mr. Jimmie. It was the best he could do. Before jumping down, Pip had closed his eyes, feeling his brother's forehead with one hand, reading the message of the hardened dots of blood. Then he bent to kiss the cheekbone. It was an act he was unsure about—he couldn't remember receiving a kiss, not at the orphanage and maybe not even before. He supposed Mommer had kissed him, only he had forgotten. Tobbie Jones lifted him and set him down in the dirt, and even that seemed surprising and like something that had never before happened. Pip had hardly been touched by anyone in his years at The Cottage—by nobody but Otto and now and then one of the little ones who might have to be cleaned or helped over the stream at Miss Versie's say-so. Not until today unless he counted whippings.

Tobbie Jones studied him.

"Listen," he commanded, "they's them can take what you got, but they can't never take away the love of God. You hear?"

Intent, Pip looked at the man, searching to know whether he could be trusted. In the end, all he was certain about was that the eyes were brown, like Otto's.

He watched the wagon pull away, faint streamers unfurling from the wheels. Once he raced after his brother but stood still when the two men slowed again. He followed in flying silt, from time to time rubbing his watering eyes, until the oxen heaved to the left and vanished with their burden behind a wall of scrub. After that he was alone, the world gone suddenly shut and silent, the road to town invisible, and the farm obscured by a windbreak of nettles and blackberry shrubs. He listened. He heard cicadas and the distant *bob-white!* call of a quail. Down the lane, he could hear birds fluttering inside the shelter of a ti-ti thicket. For the first time it occurred to Pip that he could just walk away, that no one would know for hours, and that no one would really care.

"For they stood as a bulwark and a rampire to defend the rest," he murmured. Where was his bulwark? Nowhere. He sighed and remembered that Miss Versie had told him that a sigh was just the silent way a poor helpless sharecropper had to let out a screech.

"I could. I could just go. Skedaddle."

Eventually his brothers and sisters would hear about it, but they were scattered across Emanuel County and beyond, most with broods of their own to feed on farms that were too small. And they had done nothing to stop what had happened.

But Tobbie Jones had promised that someone would take him to the Tattnal burying grounds, and that was, right now, where he wished to go.

When he swung his gaze toward the farm, he could feel the air between him and Otto widen, growing loose, Otto going one way and he another. It made sense. Hadn't he seen strong cotton fibers give and separate as a nest of tight-knit seeds was torn asunder? They would never lie down together again as they had before, to wake cheek against chest or backbone to backbone like double clingstones in the heart of a peach.

He trudged by the blackberries with their stripped twigs, the few remaining fruits burnt and shriveled, and on past the glossy leaves of the ti-ti thicket with the birds rattling about inside. He would never again hunt in there with his brother, nor would they pick wild plums beside the stream, nor lean on the top of the well and reflect on the pearly eye staring at them—a thousand doors had slammed, a thousand fences and hurdles and gates been set between them. The walk to the farm seemed a journey. The ruts of the road were like scars, and the faux garnets like scabs of blood.

Weeks of heaping a croker sack with cotton passed away, and though he woke every morning with the thought of Otto first in his mind, no one offered to take him to the Tattnal cemetery. A callus developed on his shoulder. The strap of the bag dug into the skin, the hard burrs pricked at fingers and made them sore and red, and bending strained the back and the belly. As a picker Pip was a fanatic, cleaning the bolls and moving more swiftly along the rows than any of the other children.

Through the hot September days, he could not rid his mind of the thought of Otto. When he tore the lint from the pods, feeling the seeds inside, he sensed Otto just behind him with his smaller sack dragging on the ground. Sometimes when he was in tall cotton, shielded from the other children, he talked to his brother, asked him where he had gone, whether it was nice where he was, and was it true that he had plenty to eat and no work? Because that's what Miss Versie had promised.

"What you care?" one of the older boys, Durden Pooler, had asked him one day. "He ain't nothing but a nig—"

"Hush your mouth," Miss Versie had hollered. "Cut me a pomegranate switch, and cut it long and limber, a good whistler. I'll have you know, we ain't never had such as that living on this place. Not right along with the children."

Miss Versie's favorite switch was pomegranate, with Elberta peach running a close second.

"It's what the fellow with a gun said, right here in this yard," Durden had protested.

She had whipped the boy behind the barn, the younger children pausing in their play to witness and Pip feeling his heartbeat trip and rush in a panic.

The next morning Mr. Jimmie offered to take him to the cemetery. "Set you down there, get you coming back," he explained, spitting a stream of amber into some weeds beside the house. Two streaks of juice had seeped down the dry creases beside his mouth and made him look angry, but the boy nodded.

He sat beside Mr. Jimmie with a view of the backbone and slowly joggling head of Old Ridgetree. The wagon jolted down the lane, following the path that the prone, unbreathing body of Otto had taken with Tobbie Jones and the other man. Over his shoulder Pip glimpsed the farm, the abandoned water tower and shack and outbuildings looking crude and small, their unpainted sides blending into the background. The fields and road were white in the sun, a pearly gray under the hedgerows of saplings and blackberry bushes, and only where the lane was sprinkled with iron ore and shadowed by leaves did it seem pinkish. By the gate, the deep-cut earth showed itself red with clay.

Pip felt himself subtly enlarged in importance as if the boles of trees and the clouds of dust and the birds breaking the blue with the sudden black *crack!* of flight were acknowledging his status as a mourner. The world was looking at him, resting her gaze right on him. The route to the cemetery was along piney woods, featureless save for ditches in which some yellow-green pitcher plants still held out against the coming fall. He began to feel sorry for himself, for he was the bereaved pivot around which the globe turned. Even the grains of dirt and the soaked blots of flies lying in the vases of the pitcher plants must feel the pull of his grief! For a while he even lost sight of his errand, thinking about himself as the moving center of the landscape, with the sun following as the wagon crawled between the pines and fields.

Near the cemetery he noticed ladies' hatpins, white and dry, rocking on brittle stems, and he remembered why he had come. He had a can Miss Versie had given him, full of red zinnias and water, and when Mr. Jimmie stopped to relieve himself at the edge of the woods, Pip jumped down and picked some hatpins to add to his bouquet. They were too tall for the other flowers, so he spent time breaking the stems until they were just the right height, their pale buttons hovering among the zinnias like floral punctuation marks.

"There." He sighed, holding out the can to inspect his handiwork.

"Looks nice." Mr. Jimmie nodded, spitting to one side. "A pretty lady on Sunday morning."

The boy glanced at the two streaks of tobacco by his mouth.

"I can't do no better." Pip rolled the tin between his hands, puzzling over how a rusty can of flowers could be a lady. The white and red together was eye popping, and the whole thing tidy, the neat disks of the hatpins next to the zinnias that themselves looked almost like hats, their petals tight and mathematically precise, the centers crowned with pollen. Maybe that was what Mr. Jimmie meant—the Sunday hats of ladies. He wished that Otto could be there to see how pretty it was, the way Mr. Jimmie had said.

He did not trust the man anymore but would measure him by what he did. The ride to the cemetery was an inch in his favor. His liking the flowers—maybe that was another inch. If he did not look in Mr. Jimmie's eyes, he could pretend that the blue fires were not burning, and he could get along.

"That's it." The farmer clapped the boy on one shoulder as Old Ridgetree came to a stop. It was not hard to get the mule to halt. Out in the fields, the hardness had to do with starting him again.

"Thanks, Mr. Jimmie."

Pip slipped a hand up his arm, wondering what the man had meant by thumping him. It was all right, though. Everything seemed to be all right.

"You ain't scared? Not likely to be bothered by haints in broad day."

"No sir." Pip shook his head, eyes on the bouquet. There was something satisfying about the rich red of the zinnias, a tint he could almost feel. Even the white flood of sun could not wash the color away, make it drab. If he saw a ghost, he would give it a flower. He would not be afraid, not when it would be a shade from his own kin. It would not look at him with fiery eyes. He would be glad to sit and talk with Otto's haint.

"Be two, three hours before I get back again," the man called. He clucked to the mule, slapping the reins against the knobby spine. Old Ridgeback sagged and then plowed forward, and Mr. Jimmie waved the hank of rope that he called a whip for a goodbye.

The boy did not answer but stood witnessing until the mule walked the wagon and the man out of sight.

He did not turn around until there was nothing to be seen, not even a discoloration in the air from the dust kicked up by hooves, because he did not want any taint from The White Camellia Orphanage to infect this place, which was a Tattnal spot where he could do what he liked with his own people even if they were nothing but bones.

The sun was blaring down on the burial grounds. Somebody had come with a hoe, and bunches of weeds and grass were lying beside many of the graves, dry and wrung out like rags that had been left to stiffen in the heat.

"Who did that?" He looked around to see if anyone would answer.

Whoever it was had trimmed and swept only half the cemetery. A pile of blackened leaves and needles was heaped outside the blocks of marble that announced the four corners. The graveyard was as stark as a corpse, its nakedness raw and pale in the noon light. Although he had been here when his mother was lowered into the earth, and later his father, Pip had no memory of its bleak expanse. Mr. Jimmie might as well have dropped him on the moon, so bare and brilliant and unfamiliar did it seem, the tablets ablaze and unreadable in the brightness until one came close. Snake holes pocked the soil, and the boy made a wincing face as he imagined where they might be nesting—in some cave of ribs, sheathed in stays and silk. Pip set his can of flowers on one of the four boundary stones and began searching the names. Stooping, he collected the weeds that had been hoed by somebody who was maybe a Tattnal and might know his name—*Pip, Pip Tattnal*—while he worked his way through the inscriptions. There was not a one he knew until, close to a second boundary stone, he found a marker for Gilead E. Tattnal, with the dates 1847–1933.

"I know you," Pip said aloud. "You be—you *are* my daddy. Gilead E. Tattnal. What's the *E.* for? Emanuel County, maybe." He could not feature a man's name that began with *E.* At the foot of the grave, already slightly sunken, was a square stone with *G. E. T.* inscribed on it.

"G. E. T." Pip pondered the mystery of it. He felt the cut marble with his hand, flicked some black ants off the T. The letters stayed themselves, intractable. *Get what? Get.* "Get dead," he said at last.

Strewn across the mound were conchs, bleached by the sun. He knew what those were for. *Catch the haints.* He picked up a shell, dry and pale as an old bone, and peered inside. Could anything live in there like a Georgia ghost crab in its hole, skittering along sideways and ducking into the dark? He'd read about them in a book. Someday he'd go to the ocean and see a crab, he promised himself.

"You in there, Daddy? Mr. Gilead, you at home?" A gust of wind sawed through the conch, sounding a single sonorous note. *That's not what my daddy sounded like.* The boy rested the warmth of the shell's side against his cheek, and after a minute he raised it to his lips and blew. The sound was awkward as a fart, unmusical, stubbed off.

"I shot him out if he was home," Pip murmured. *Go on now, Ghost, fly where you want. You're free, Daddy. Sail up high where the shells and the glass bottles stuck on branches can't catch you.* A tree all decked with cobalt medicine bottles and clear flasks and jars that had gone amethyst from being in the sun was a splendid sight, but Pip had always felt sorry for the ghosts if they were there, trapped and swirling behind walls. It would be pure pleasure to smash the glass and unloose the haints, to see chunks and shards glitter in the dust.

Smaller conchs lay on the graves of Gilead's two wives, and one by one the boy blew lightly on the shells.

"This one's mine. The young one, the pretty one." The image of a woman drifted into his thoughts—moving behind the sheen of heat, her hands gripping a Snowdrift shortening bucket heaped with peaches. *Who was that? Mommer? Some forgotten neighbor?* He traced the name with his fingertips, embedding it in his mind. He had not been sure how to spell it, or even of the whole of it: *Georgianna Jo Tattnal.* The old one had been born way back yonder in 1863, had been a baby when Gilead was young. The stone claimed that she'd borne nineteen children. Gilead was gray when he married Georgianna Jo, but he still had a lot of nature left in him. That's what folks said. People still talked about how the bridge builder had traveled over the state and into the western Carolinas. Sometimes they said that nobody knew how many children he had sired around Georgia. But the known brothers and sisters had let Pip and Otto ride off to The Cottage with never a thought for what could come.

The boy lay on his mother's grave, waved his arms in the dirt, and then jumped up to inspect his creation. He felt disappointed. It did not look much like an angel.

"Mommer," he whispered, outlining the faint impression of wings with a stick. There was an infant in the grave with her, one of his brothers or sisters, but no name was chiseled on the stone. Nobody had remembered to put a tiny shell on the mound. Probably the baby haint was flying free, playing with stars at night and the reddish grains in the road by day. He wondered how the conchs had gotten here from the ocean, or maybe from the wild islands where alligators and castaways lived. Their furled shapes, porous and pitted, looked to be of great age. Maybe the Indians had traded them inland. Or maybe slaves had passed them west, plantation to plantation. Maybe that belief about shells and ghosts had sailed as cargo from Africa; the slave women could have told ghost stories to their children.

"Mommer," he repeated, and again, "Mommer. The peaches fell and the glass broke and we stood back. Somebody was bleeding. You had on a white shirt, and your face was like an angel's, shiny." It was all he could remember of that day. On the belly inside the angel's wings and skirt he wrote the word, *BABY*. It seemed wrong to him that there was no reminder.

But where was Otto?

The ratcheting of insects jagged from the dry ground and trees, mixing with a shimmering noise that Pip thought might be the anger of snakes, their rattles shaking in hidey holes among the bones. *Where was Otto in this fearsome place?* That was Miss Versie's phrase. "A boneyard is a fearsome place at night," she would say.

Standing, he looked across the square of graves. He did not notice that the angel had powdered his clothes as if to say, *Dust thou art.*

"I'm not afraid of anything," he said.

It was not until he gave up, letting his eyes pass beyond the cemetery's borders, that he found what he was looking for. A grave mounded high with white river sand lay some fifteen yards from the boundary, directly across from Gilead Tattnal's grave. He peered at the too-radiant pile for an instant before crossing graves to the edge of the cemetery.

Was this Otto? Why was he here, not safe inside the four corners?

Flowers had been stuck into the mound of fresh sand, but the leaves and heads now curled downward, scorched by the sun. An unpainted cross had only the misspelled word *Oto* scratched on it. That meant Otto was there, under the ground. Already someone had left a conch shell, one so small it could hide in Pip's fist. Another conch lay in the shallow depression next to the mound, and Pip picked it up and blew softly. Maybe the low place was the grave of Otto's mother. After she had passed on, Gilead came home with Chach and Otto in his arms, and Georgianna Jo took them in.

Running awkwardly, Pip went back to fetch his can of flowers, carrying them slowly so that no drop of water would slosh from the container. Moisture would not last long, not in September heat. But zinnias and hatpins would endure a while, stiff and severe as they were, not like frailer flowers, morning glories or the sprigs of tiny wild orchids in ditches. Next April he would bring some of those; he knew a gulley where they never failed to bloom. He planted the bouquet right in the center of the mound.

"For you, Otto," he whispered, plucking out the dead stems left by somebody—Tobbie Jones? the silent man in the wagon?—and flinging them into the weeds. With his finger he wrote "Otto Tattnal" in the soft sand, and the dates: July 7, 1927–Sept. 6, 1935. He was good at dates. From a pocket he took a handful of the garnets that were really only compacted particles of iron and a faceted black bead and buried them near the cross.

By accident, his fingers closed over the half-sunken shell, and he withdrew it from the mound. Not yet bleached white, the conch was pale pink and peach, a horned thing with a thin jagged lip.

"I got you," he whispered.

"Pip!" came a voice from the road. "You done? It was a trip for nothing—nobody home. Let's go!"

The boy looked at the spiked curl of calcium in his hand, thinking to set the spirit free with a puff of breath. But wouldn't Otto be afraid, catapulted above the piney woods and into the sawing of insects and the whirling of ghosts? Otto was just a child, younger than he. Although part of him felt sure that no ghost was lost and confused in the windings of the shell, something stopped him from blowing into the hole at the end. He was reluctant to put it down as though the small object were somehow mysteriously connected with his brother. Pip gripped the conch, letting the sharp points press into his hand before dropping it into his bib pocket and turning to run.

4

The locomotive song gets in Pip's blood;
He runs away, and Southern Serves the South.

In the January following Otto's death, Pip turned eleven. No one marked the date; in fact, he got a beating that afternoon. He had not chopped firewood for the stove or remembered to slop the pigs.

He remembered. After all, he was good with dates.

"It's my day, Otto." He held the shell to his ear, listening to its echo. "I'll be gone soon. I'll be taking you with me. Funny the way the sea is. So big. But a ship can fit in a bottle and an ocean in a shell." He pressed the sharp edge against his skin. "Is that how the dead talk, Otto? Like the sound of the waves?

"We'll sail away. Follow this little creek to Savannah, Otto. Never stop until we find our rampire and bulwark." He squatted, leaning against a plum tree and fumbling in the dirt. Then he began to flick pebbles into the stream.

Earlier that month he'd begun thinking about leaving The White Camellia Orphanage, and his mind was already roving elsewhere. There was nothing for him at The Cottage. As the months passed, he realized that no one intended to find out who had murdered Otto. When he tried to consider who might have done such a deed, who had put his particular set of hands around that neck, and who had crowned Otto in wire, fog seemed to fill his brain. This non-thought and non-answer made a kind of sense. For him, the murder never felt like an enigma. Pip always felt that the plain and simple answer, the killer, was the evil flaming in eyes.

But how could he adjust his world to that fact and the absence of Otto? There lay the real mysteries of the event. The men who had questioned him visited once more, milling aimlessly in the yard. While picking velvet beans back in December, he had glimpsed the man with the hat as he climbed into a pickup and jounced away, the white dust ballooning behind. It seemed to him that in the end Mr. Jimmie had shown a longer concern when his hound went missing. Miss Versie got quiet whenever he brought up the search for the killer.

Pip remembered the games he had played with his brother and how when they were city dicks, they never failed to find the missing treasure. It was always the same one, made from the pebbles in the road that were rusty and dark as blood drops, with the addition of a single jet bead Otto had found in the dirt near the train station. The boys considered the glittering, diamond-cut sphere their greatest jewel, sheared from a lump of compressed coal, liable to smolder and burn and be lost. The game was very clear: the riches were always recoverable, the thief would be unveiled, and the reward presented.

But Otto was not to be found, and the eyes of men were all the same. At night Pip lay staring into the dark, his back chilled where once Otto had pressed against him. It took him a long time to grow drowsy and close his lids, and on waking he felt dead tired.

Although he seemed to have absorbed them more through his pores than to have reasoned them out in any way, the boy understood matters now that he had not grasped earlier. From the jeers of the boy Durden, he knew that Otto had been a *nigra*, in Miss Versie's word, or a *nigger* in Mr. Jimmie's—scorned for his skin. Perhaps it was because Pip had what was called the Tattnal eccentricity that he'd never thought about the color at all, had not paid any attention to the shade of pigment or to the curly hair. Now he guessed that the reason Chach, the older brother, had been sent away like a parcel was that he was dark, his hair too tightly kinked to pass in The White Camellia Orphanage.

Had somebody been angry that Otto Tattnal was often fed three times a day, sometimes with donations from stores in town or the Primitive Baptist Church? But plenty of times they had been hungry, with nothing to eat but a scraping of cold grits or the songbirds that the orphans hunted with bow and arrows in the ti-ti thickets. Maybe somebody thought that Otto shouldn't have been sleeping in a bed with white children—not that that was so unusual since younger children all played with their neighbors without much regard to color. When tired, they sank down together on the nearest floor or under a tree and slept.

Maybe it was simple, Pip thought: Otto was just the same as the others until somebody noticed that maybe he wasn't. Like an okra spine under a fingernail, maybe that difference and how it had fooled him worked at the killer until he was maddened and ready to tear at himself to get it out.

These ideas were difficult for Pip because of his Tattnal nature; it was hard for him to see and understand what other people thought to be important and why it was so, but after his brother's death the effort became nigh impossible. Otto was Otto, himself. It could not make any sense to hurt Otto. He had been one thing, one self through and through, the same at the beginning and the end like a circle. Like an O. Otto.

"Childe Tattnal the Younger is dead," he told Old Ridgetree's hindquarters. "The rampires failed—whatever they are."

Why hadn't their grown brothers and sisters thought of the risk? Or had Otto been too minor a child to care about, the youngest of them, illegitimate, child of a yaller woman that surely their daddy was way too old to touch?

During chores he would often pause, thinking about his brother, hand reaching to touch the pocket where he liked to imagine that Otto's ghost curled inside a shell. Already he had wrapped his books in a sheet of brown paper filched from school and tied them with a discarded string, writing with the stub of a pencil: *Property of Pip Tattnal. He will come get them later. Do not bother!* Afterward he shoved the package on top of a chifforobe where nobody could see it unless they climbed on a chair and looked.

He was primed to go and would be leaving just as soon as he had all he needed. So far he had collected a five-cent piece that Mr. Sam Truetlen had slipped him on the day Otto died, some sweet potatoes packed in pine straw, and a worn-out cotton blanket, a mere net of holes, its edges raveling.

In the fields he would let Old Ridgetree stop, and boy and mule would listen to the far cry of a passing train. For years now he had seen strangers, sometimes carrying a hoe, jump aboard the Southern Railway for a free ride. Not far from town, the trains often paused at a water tank; travelers waited in the nearby thicket. At the station, too, he'd seen hobos as the freight trains slowed to a standstill or to a pleasant clacketing sway, the engineer waving as he passed. They looked mighty set-up and easy, those fellows, their legs dangling from an open boxcar door. Many of the trains were longer than the hamlet itself, their weight dragged forward by a double-header. One day he had seen a fellow hop a fast-moving freight, throwing himself onto a short ladder at the rear of a boxcar—he had been hurled between cars and mangled. Pip had gotten a good look. If to live was luck, the man was lucky, for it seemed he would survive. He had lain moaning on the ground, his legs crumpled, the hoe beside him snapped into three pieces. The injured worker had kept enough presence of mind to grab at the blade, his bit of livelihood.

"Gimp," the boy had muttered. "Strike out wrong, and you'll be nothing but a gimp forevermore."

The sight was not so terrible to him, for Pip had seen much uglier-looking damage from knives and razors outside Rud Johnson's shack where moonshine was sold, but it was a lesson just the same. You had to be careful around the iron wheels.

Sometimes on Saturdays he would be around when a locomotive came in if Mr. Jimmie had spent a long time in the feed store or hunkered on the bench out front, swapping stories with other sharecroppers. After Otto's death, the farmer always took Pip along as if to make amends to the boy.

The scene was like this, give or take a detail: in every season, the sun shone on what was the merest excuse of a township, its mutts rolling about in the dust and not even bothering to roust themselves out of the roadbed for a nap. Occasionally it rained on a Saturday but never for the whole day, and when it rained the mud was as bothersome as the dust had been, and in summer the earth steamed afterward. The downtown was a sleepy kind of place for more than dogs. Not much happened in the winter, and come late spring, it was nearly too hot to move. The flies butted against the windows and crawled into corners all year round, and in warm weather the earth showed her infinite fancy for insects with kissing bugs, damselflies, bees, wasps, and gnats. Come a burning afternoon, the air slowed to treacle, although dragonflies still proved mettlesome enough to flash through its heaviness.

On the platform bench outside the office, the agent might be slumped, his cap tilted over his face to ward off bites and Special, the station dog, stretched underfoot. Gaunt but ever hopeful for handouts, she seemed perpetually to have six or seven pups squeaking at her long teats, their eyes mere crescent slits. Now and then a child would be forced from one of the nearby buildings and go coasting down the walk to the general store, coming back more slowly, shoulders hunched against the heat. Everyone else was out of sight, somewhere in shade, men from nearby farms congregating under the feed store's three ceiling fans.

Pip would plant himself on the edge of the platform, his feet swinging lightly above the cinders, taking in the smell of coal, which he liked, and the sights—piles of switch ties, some greasy rods, a pail of dried "Tuscan Red" paint, mysterious rings and valves that must have come from the bowels of a steam engine—all magical to him, like the hoard of a fire-breathing dragon in a fairy story. A far-off whistle sounding, the boy would lean forward, straining for the first trace of smoke in air already rumpled by heat mirage while the agent stirred, got to his feet, and headed into his office where he could be seen to wipe his forehead, put on his glasses, and rummage through a ledger. Minute by minute, he took on importance, a depot boss busying himself with bottles of ink and pens and blotting paper. The next child sent on errand halted, staring, mother and peach switch forgotten, summoned elsewhere by the tossed lonely wail. Filtering onto hardpan, farmers in overalls hacked, spat, and scanned the horizon.

Soon the shimmying air would show the palest smudge of smoke. Some older children and a few women materialized in doorways, peering out. Special crooked up one ear. From his post by the track, Pip caught sight of the train, a dark emphatic point in the low landscape, swelling as if an unseen pencil were scribbling, pressing down, circling, and widening its movements until finally the round mark was seen as something that actually came forward, pushing out of the flat scenery with its windbreaks of scrub between farms. The whistle sang out again, and smoke spouted, boiling into the sky—looking as dense as cotton candy and as complicated as the canopy of a tree close to the engine but loosening as it trailed away, becoming merely a magician's impression of smoke. At last it was lost in the blue. Staggering to her feet, Special trembled and stretched her hind legs, first one and then the other. It was 2:15; there was hope for a bone.

The cry got into Pip's marrow, and he scrambled to his feet and jumped with pleasure when it whooped again. Although never very coordinated, he leaped high, and he sang a daffy little song of his own making: "Doodley-doo, doodley-doo, I'm gonna ride on the big choo-choo, I'm gonna dance, I'm gonna prance when I get to ride on the big choo-choo."

In the street a toddler in a white dress and trailing sashes was inconsolable; his mother, who even when she smiled still looked harried, thrust him under one arm like a half-tied parcel and headed to the station where, heels clicking out a thousand pressing messages, she bustled into the little office with the telegraph man and banged shut the door.

Beside the rails, Pip drew himself to his utmost height, balancing on his bare toes, feeling the coming palsy of earth in his feet and legs as the locomotive bored forward through the molasses-heavy afternoon, tearing away the tethers of sleepiness that held the town until, like the suddenly freed inhabitants of a pent-up anthill, men spilled from stores and children skipped to the brink of the rails and a woman in a local milliner's hat that resembled something grown on a tree, fungal and yellow and decorated with green piping like a caterpillar parade, rushed full tilt toward the station, her husband carrying a shiny silk bag that was not a valise but would do.

The metal face of the train with its bright Cyclopean eye and its smokebox and clanging bell thrust itself into Pip's sight, and again he was as astonished as if he had never seen such a vision in all his born days and forgot everything but the hurtle and rising aria of the train that made his own chant seem silly and childish. He did an awkward half-split, jumbling his hands in the air. The monster took no notice but plunged, vaulted, and dived over the slight rolls of the land, shaking the earth as easily as a hound shakes a kitten, spewing cinders and smoke, drive wheels pounding and somersaulting over Emanuel County, so swift and thunderous that it seemed nothing in the world could cry *halt!* to such an extravagance of force. High as a house, the engine swooped down on Pip, hissing and hooting in his face, in his very being, turning him inside out, ringing him like a bell. The sun clanged in the sky, the earth quaked, and the pistons of the train shot out steam as they rhythmically proclaimed the company motto—*Southern Serves the South, Southern Serves the South, Southern Serves the South*. Who could stand against such a beast or rein it in? But there they were, the aloof, cool kings of the cinder-trail, the fireman and engineer, as calm as if they had not been handling the mysteries of coal and power and locomotion but had been helping set up a board table under a rustling tree, getting ready for a Sunday supper after church.

Brakes sparked the air, and the long squeal of metal against metal signaled a stop as boxcars and tank cars and engines and caboose swayed on the tracks, straining at couplings. It was like trying to keep a town on a steep hillside from plunging pell-mell into avalanche; like holding down an epileptic string of stores and houses that were starting to seize. The whole long street of the train wanted to crash together with a roar and a magnificent smash-up and a

Jericho clash like ten thousand cymbals. The cars wanted to roll sideways, doors shooting open, hobos cannonading circus-style through the air, and those riding the rods beneath the boxcars screaming bloody murder as the brakes screeched and let off fireworks.

With an irregular clanking, the train slowed and its rocking gait lessened. Here and there a face looked out from the gloom or a young man leaned from an open door, his eyes searching for a signal from somebody that here was a job, some food, coins to be had. More hisses of steam, a glide, a proud pulling up: the train stopped, and the woman with the funny hat got on at the single wooden coach—an arch-windowed remnant of the last century—because this was no passenger train with Pullmans and a baggage coach, a dining car with steam trays and cloth napkins, but a freight local. A black man dressed in stripy overalls and no taller than Pip got off the back of the train with a crate of chickens, vanishing in the direction of the feed store, and somebody threw a sack of mail onto the freight platform.

The engineer clambered back out of the dog hobble and blackberry scrub where he had made a quick hunt for berries, with no luck. Throwing a bone from his pocket to Special, who chomped and snapped until it broke, he climbed aboard and began to pick burrs from his pants. The brakeman stood on the caboose steps and gave the highball signal, waving mightily: every child in town and round about knew the signal to the engineer. Brakes off, the locomotive coasted backward. A hobo shrilled two long notes on his harmonica, grinning at Pip as he threw a Tootsie Roll straight into his hands. The boy stood, mouth ajar, staring at the paper twist of candy as if he did not know what to do with it. Drive wheels struggled to rotate, grinding against the track, slinging the train forward slowly and then faster, and the children sprinkled along the rails began to dance as the rhythm worked itself into their marrow: *Southern. Serves. The. South. Southern. Serves. The. South. Southern Serves the South. Southern Serves the South, Southern Serves the South, Southern Serves....* Short bursts of the whistle told them that some poor fool of a cow was straddling the rails up ahead; the notes rose over the cry of the harmonica as the train highballed out of town, hips swaying, shuddering, swinging the big Mama tank cars and the wide-mouthed boxcars, and the caboose went shaking its tail into a febrile distance that was wavering with summer heat.

That'll be me, Pip thought, *rattling across the fields.*

A girl kept hopping long after the others quit, a transparent pink wave of dust washing over her, stinging her eyes.

The farmers lounged outside the feed store until one by one they ducked inside or wandered off. A woman hollered for the son who had never come home from Hooper's grocery, and he went, scowling, the cube of yeast gone sweaty in his hand. The man with chickens banged open a screen door, crate in hand and a burlap sack over one shoulder, and started trudging east toward home.

Chin lifted as if she'd personally been involved in flinging the locomotive out of the station and as if its vibration and rumbling thrust and ejaculations of hot steam had something intimately to do with her, the telegraph operator's wife popped out the office door and hurried toward home. Her little boy was tiptoe on a chair, and Pip could see him pointing out the dingy window, his father standing close beside.

After surveying the rails and the unchanged gullywashers of the dirt street, the agent sank onto the bench where he had been snoozing, just at the moment when Special flopped onto the cement floor at his feet, gnawing at the remains of a bone while mewling puppies struggled toward her, eyes fast shut. Veils of powder drifted across the station and into the road, over doorsills and windowsills. Something perhaps imagined, the miles-off song of the locomotive pricked at the air.

When the train was entirely absent from the town and yet so recently departed that it was still remembered and even mourned, the wraith of it hanging over the scene like a heat mirage, Mr. Jimmie trudged over to the station, detaching himself from where he had been jawing with a knot of farmers from the feed store. As he approached, Pip would be thinking that Saturday was over, all the fun dragged out of town, but his mind would still be working over the details of that particular day: the sweet eager squeaks of the puppies, the brakes biting down like a fang onto the wheels, the rare, impossible-to-believe surprise of the Tootsie Roll. Still, he did not like candy, did not like the taste or smell. But Otto did. He put the Tootsie Roll inside his bib pocket with the tiny conch.

Each Saturday in town furthered his resolve. And it was not just a determination to walk away from this life—itself an orphaned thing, castoff and poor. It was also a kind of itch, the desire to be going, kicking his legs with the free-as-a-bird fellows in the boxcar door, letting the world slide by.

How fine, he thought, to see a mountain, to see a canyon, to see the ocean. He might wash that shell in the waves. What else was out there beyond Georgia, he hardly knew. He had some knowledge of math and science, tares gleaned from school, and he had read a good deal of poetry and history in his father's books, most especially some accounts of a certain English rebellion. But all his knowledge was a child's, a piecing together of a world based on insufficient information. He longed for a land beyond The White Camellia Orphanage, the swamps and ditches and fields, the seven-house hamlet at the crossroads, and even the town with its stores and depot.

Toward the end of that June, he borrowed a box of matches out of the kitchen house. He reasoned with himself that he would pay Miss Versie and Mr. Jimmie back when he returned for his father's three books, stored on top of the chifforobe. Even though he'd worked for them and never received much more than an occasional penny from a visitor, he had a hard time convincing himself that this was all right. After bathing in the creek, he made a hobo's bindle from his blanket and a few sweet potatoes. His five-cent piece he dropped into his pocket next to the shell and the Tootsie Roll before heading toward the water tank.

He did not say goodbye. If he had said the word, they would have stopped him. Or Mr. Sam Truetlen would have galloped after him and brought him home pillion as though he were no more than

49

the little boy who had clung to his brother on the mule that took him to the orphanage.

From a ways off, the train idling by the tank did not look so big. And he had practiced for this, grabbing a vine and swinging his legs up and onto the fork of a tree, over and over, until the jump to his "boxcar" was easy. Grey smoke vented from the stack at intervals, barely staining the air. But when the train began to move, it accelerated rapidly, the whistle crying two notes about a tug-of-war meant to budge tons of metal, to hurl wheels along the rails. Smoke geysered from the stack in jet thunderheads. As the engine loomed up, Pip began to lope, his gait crooked, his bindle swinging from one hand. Stumbling, he almost tripped and dropped beneath the iron wheels, and with a lurch of fear he leaped at and seized a handle.

The powerful sweep of the train jerked him from his feet, banging him against the side of the car. Cinders and stones pelted his bare soles. *Up—out—legs away from the wheels!* The thudding and pounding brought on an ache and then an eclipse, the landscape darkening steadily as he was flung against metal and across the open doorway. He reached for another grip with the hand that held his bindle and failed to find it. The pain in his head blotted out everything except his need to find safety in his grasp. The locomotive rocketed on; hot air gusting from the wheels spewed against his ankles. Jabs of anguish in his head wanted him to go sailing into the puff briars and berry bushes beside the train. He could not. Could not hold. Could not keep battering the flank of the boxcar and swinging his legs toward a security he could not find, the handle digging into his fingers. Hollering against the vibrating metal and a skull-caged star that sprouted new spikes of pain, Pip let go.

But something had seized his wrist, held him a moment like a flag, flapping outward and threatening to fly, and then hauled him inward and flung him onto the floor of the car where Pip lay panting, saved, alive, his head speared by migraine, his ears deafened by the galloping noise of the wheels, and his whole frame shaken and racked by the clamorous train.

Pip, picaresque

5

Pip Tattnal, free and easy on the rails,
And Otto in his bib; he meets a pair
Of blue forget-me-nots—eyes of a bull.

Never was travel so noisy as in a boxcar. It creaked and shivered, groaning as it slowed. And though these were smells that the boy rather liked, it stank of creosote and oil. After sleeping off the worst of his headache, Pip sat in the open car with his legs dangling down, and it was as fine and sweet as he had imagined. He remembered crashing onto the floor. "You just about joined the birds," his rescuer had joked. But now all fright had receded. He felt peaceful and safe, sitting beside the spike that kept the heavy door from sliding on its track. On waking, he had emptied out his story to his new companions in one rush of incidents, holding back only Otto. Although he had already been warned that this was as easy as a ride ever got, the crew showing a little sympathy to a fellow hoisting a bindle, the new traveler was already picturing himself crossing the prairie and climbing the Sierras in the same style.

The freight train crawled east toward Savannah, stopping frequently. Once they halted to shoo cows off the tracks, and the engineer ordered a boy to jump from one of the cars, sending him down the track at a lope. Dodging back and forth, he managed to herd three toward a gate, but a fourth one charged him, her udder and loose skin jostling. Her show of mettle was contagious, and a bull chased the kid as far as the engine, where somebody caught him by the collar and hoisted him; Pip could hear the trainmen laughing in front. After a while the would-be cowboy came sauntering past, and everybody cheered.

At another spot the fireman jumped down and dashed toward an unpainted house under some cedars. He came back more slowly, pursued by a pair of girls and a woman—his wife, Pip supposed—wiping her hands on a checked apron. Whether the children were yelling because the fireman had taken off with the pie that had been cooling on the windowsill of the cookhouse, it was impossible to tell. Maybe the mother was not his wife; maybe she was just famous for pies. It looked to be egg custard, ringed by golden crust. That's what somebody on the lookout said—he had tramped by the doorway and stopped to tell them as if they would be sure to take an interest. Gnawing at a raw sweet potato as the car rocked back and then forward, Pip remembered licking the plate with the remains of peach pie back at The White Camellia Orphanage.

The train shook, increasing speed.

"I worked there once." The man the others called *Gandy*, the one who had hoisted Pip inside the boxcar, nodded his head in the direction of a crossroads. "Ain't nothing but a little old sawmill town. Worked at the next place over, too. A big grease-rendering plant. You could get all the hog rinds you wanted for free."

A man in the shadows laughed.

"Crackers," he jeered, grinning, but the others paid no mind. He was drunk, leaning against the rear wall, legs splayed, the holes in his boots showing grey and brown cardboard. Pip had avoided him after seeing what he was up to—squeezing a ball of jelled alcohol wrapped in a rag and catching the drops in his mouth as the liquid soaked through the cloth.

"Don't you go drinking that canned heat," Gandy told the boy. "That stuff'll kill you, for dead certain."

"I'd never do that," he said. "Gives me the shakes just to think about it."

"He's a good kid." The girl named Fayella, the one Gandy called "Cinders," sat up and buttoned her shirt. She stuck a corner of a diaper packed with sugar into her baby's mouth.

"Talks too damn much," the drunk shouted. "Can't get a word in. Who needed to hear all that about a cracker orphan and his crack-assed cracker daddy and—"

"Shut your mouth," Cinders drawled without rancor, and the bum turned on his side, hacking and gasping for breath.

Pip liked her because her eyes were near-black, as was her hair. Next to that inkiness, her skin looked as pale as could be, the kind that burned and peeled with a migrant's life.

She talked to him about riding the rails to the Pacific Northwest, six months pregnant. When she and her brother found the husband she had not heard from in a year, he told her to go back East. He had no money to feed a wife and a baby and wanted no part of them. Had not known there would be a child and could not even keep himself, he informed her.

She shrugged. What else was there to say? And what had he thought came of a man lying in bed with a woman? She and Bobbie had harvested eastward, following the rails from hops in the Northwest to haymows in the Rockies and on to corn and wheat in the middle of the country. Now they were almost home.

The drunk began cursing, kicking at the wall of the car.

"Don't pay no heed to that fellow," Fayella told Pip. "You're all right."

"Sure, he's a good kid." Gandy nodded. "We're all nice kids, even Mr. I-Suck-Heat over there in the corner. Just looking for a fellow human to love us enough to give us a damn job, that's all."

He leaned back, searching his pockets until he found the stub of a cigarette, which he lit and dragged on until it began to scorch his lips.

"Well, I just want—"

Pip stopped, unsure. He wished that he belonged to somebody, the way the girl did. She looked no more than seventeen, but she had a brother, and she had a baby, born in a barn somewhere in Colorado. At home there was a mother. He did not belong to anybody, but he had started listening to these new companions as if they mattered; there were things he needed to know.

"You want to go to the Rockies, see the country," Cinders told him. "Then on to Texas. Maybe west to Arizona. In winter there's lots of cotton to pick. That's what they say. And it ain't real picking. Down there they just pull it, so the work's not bad."

She stared out the door. The baby was asleep now, sugar tit in his mouth.

"But the Rockies, they're something to see. Nobody for miles around and chilly even in summer. Glittery stones and forests of little trees that are shivery and beautiful. Waterfalls and trestles over steep valleys—what they call *gorges*. I had a flying bird carved out of smoky quartz I was bringing to Mama, but I lost it. You could see the whole world through the wings, just the same only darker."

The boy imagined the coolness drifting out of the deep clefts. That would be good, right now. He wondered if the quartz looked like his eclipse, only without the ache afterward.

Fayella slapped the floor next to his leg. "I've sat right *there* with my baby Harbert, gripping on to him and the doorframe, peering a thousand feet to the treetops and a stream so loud I could hear it over the noise of the wheels.

"Once when we didn't know no better, we climbed on top and rode near the engine, and we went through tunnels. Blow-back and cinders everywhere—the coal smoke would hit the ceiling and spread out. In a second we'd be inside it, choking and crying. Harbert was black as could be. Had ash between his toes, even."

The baby howled as if awakened by the memory.

"You was a real cinder snapper then," Gandy said.

"It sounds"—Pip paused—"pretty thrilling."

She unbuttoned her shirt again and stuffed the baby's head inside. "Well, I don't go up there anymore," she said. "That was it for me."

"Don't ever ride outside when there's tunnels. And don't ride on tank car catwalks," Gandy added. "There's only about twelve inches between you and dropping off. The rods are bad, too. Riding a board across the truss rods? You have to be crazy for that.

"Yes sir," Pip said. "I got no intentions of riding under a car."

After a while they came to a station and had a layover of several hours. Awakened when the train stopped, the drunk carefully maneuvered himself over the brink of the doorway and staggered away.

It was hot in the boxcar, so they slipped underneath and sat in the shadows, and Pip told a long story about the Rebellion and the heroism of soldiers on wings of horse.

"And that's how the king's horse routed the rebels," he concluded. "You know, I always think of it as a big clay-colored stallion." *With pinions the same shade as the sky in spring,* he thought. *The king's horse would have to be something mighty rare.*

"Lord, you can talk a streak." The girl fanned gnats from her face, and they settled on the baby's eyelids.

"He's been high-balling, heading out," Gandy agreed. "Those things don't hardly seem real, what with kings and princes flying around. But that was the way in the old, old days. They had pharaohs and talking fireball bushes and frog rains and such. The world got ordinary before we came along."

They lapsed into silence, drowsy in the warmth. Later when the engine was switched onto a siding, Gandy built a fire in a nearby ditch and put most of the boy's raw sweet potatoes inside.

"I'll grab those fellers if the train starts," he promised, "but I don't think we're going any time soon. Looks to me like they've sent for another engine."

While they waited, Cinders slept with the baby on her breast, and her brother Bobbie wandered over to the station to see if there were any odd jobs he could do. He had offered to go halves on whatever he came up with if somebody would keep an eye on his sister. In a little while he could be seen, wielding a broom.

Digging in his pocket for a piece of chalkstone, Gandy taught Pip some signs, drawing them on the side of the car: "This is a man with a gun. This is a doc or somebody good with sickness and wounds. This is a dog that bites.

"This is where the railroad bulls are mean. That depends on the people, so it changes, sometimes pretty quick, and it's important. Sometimes they kill us. I've seen the bodies of poor stiffs rotting, or nothing left but bones. Seen the wagon come for hoe boys, murdered when they weren't harming nobody, just eating a mulligan stew in the jungle. They call the bulls *special agents*, but they ain't anything special. Bulls can get you arrested for a month or more. Then you have to sweat for free until your sentence is up. Never give them your real name if you get caught, and maybe you can chance it and get away.

"This sign is where there might be a job. This is somebody who acts like a Christian. This one's just nothing—no hope for food or work or a bed there."

"I don't like that one." Studying the symbols, the boy pondered the O that meant nothing. An O was round, like a full belly, like a woman with a baby inside, like the wheel of a train going somewhere, like a plate loaded with food. The start to a drawing of a round infant's face, it was not like Harbert's, thin and smeared with the remains of Pip's Tootsie Roll. *O* meant *Otto* and the round circle of brotherhood, two Tattnals together and understanding each other as it seemed no one else could do.

O was Otto, and Otto was nothing now, nowhere he could find. How had it happened that O had gone wrong? It was sad to think that an O sign could stand for O for no food to eat, O for a well without water, O for no work, O for nowhere to lay his head, O for nothing at all, O for the hole of eternity into which his brother had tripped and fallen. He touched the shell through his bib pocket. *Was* what was left of his brother trapped in there, a wisp of his living self?

Twilight deepened before the other engine appeared, chugging backward, its coal smoke darker than the night already coming on. In the car, Pip lay on his stomach and watched white-globed signal lanterns swinging in the dusk. He was not conscious of being hungry because he had eaten a sweet potato and because he was used to eating less than he needed. Bobbie arrived with a package of arrowroot biscuits for the baby, a licorice stick for his sister, and a broken bushel basket loaded with fruit and vegetables. He had picked them out of the garbage behind a nearby canning business the brakeman had shown him.

"You too," he said, shoving his haul toward Pip, who felt his inclusion as something unexpected. Sudden tears spilled down his cheek, and for a moment he could not say a word.

"This is a good station and train, way better than most," Gandy pronounced. "See Mr. Can o' Heat anywhere in your travels?"

Bobbie shook his head, mouth full of fruit peels, and swallowed. "Saw him right at first, diving into a pool hall across the street, and that was it."

"He's a goner," Gandy judged, "now or later, poor bastard. His innards must be shot to tatters."

"There was a soldier hacked up in the English Rebellion—"

"Hush, now, Pip. Not while I'm about to eat." Cinders yawned, rubbing her face. "When I get home, I'm going to heat me some water on the stove and take the biggest bath you have ever seen."

Nobody answered. Probably nobody present had been well acquainted with bathing, or at least not in a long time. Harbert began to cry, his voice sounding feeble, and his mother handed him an arrowroot biscuit. Instantly the child's mouth closed on it, sucking at a corner. Cinders settled him on her lap, kissing the top of his head.

"Wish I had me a light," Bobbie said, "believe I just ate some wildlife. Either that or these peelings have learned how to dance."

That did not stop anybody from feeling through the basket, eating and tossing the rinds and shells out the door.

"Miss Versie says yellow presses are the best peaches in the state of Georgia," Pip remarked. "That fellow I was talking about before? The book says his head was rammed on a stake like a piece of fruit on a—"

"Stop it!" The girl laughed and handed him a spiral of peel.

"Well, it seemed to me that it was like a peach, and I wondered whether it was an Elberta or maybe an early peach like a May Bell. Or maybe it was a white peach, like the one they call an Indian—"

"Hush!"

When Cinders rapped his knee, he stared at the place in surprise.

"These ole raw vegetables just play havoc with my insides, but I'm so damn hungry I can't help but eat up."

As Gandy spoke, Pip could hear the trainmen shouting and two long notes from the whistle; the car slipped backward and then began to roll forward.

"We're off," he said in surprise.

The train accelerated, their own car jarred and shaken by force, overpowered by the fresh engine that was even now crying out to the hot night that *Southern Serves the South* while the brute thrust of the piston rods mastered the wheels and the rails and the intractable heaviness and stall that belong to Earth.

Clacketing down the tracks, the train finally headed into the last leg of its journey toward Savannah. The world at night poured by the open door, the trees and occasional houses looking as if they were clipped from black paper by a silhouette maker. Above, the heavens were the same dazzle of lights that Pip knew from the Orphanage, blazing as if an immense oil lamp were burning behind miles of blue-black pricked paper. Even a sharecropper, even an orphan could be wealthy when he looked up at the stars, which were willing to glory-roof a paintless shack swarming with mosquitoes and flies.

"The Master Engineer's lighting his glims," Gandy said.

"Sure is pretty," Cinders whispered, holding Harbert so he could see the sky. Pip looked at the baby's face, the glitter of stars in his eyes, and remembered Otto's dead irises with the sun starting to creep up on their surface. It occurred to him that Otto must have been alive only minutes before because an eye would dry out, wouldn't it, in the hot night? Or had the eyes been moistened by dew?

"Sure is," he agreed, but the girl had already gone back into the shadows and was busy packing up her bindle.

"Tomorrow I'll catch a ride to Tybee, and I'll fish until we have us enough for a fry," Bobbie announced.

"Tomorrow," Pip repeated. It had seemed to him that this evening would never end. He did not want it to be over.

Gandy spat.

"I don't want no ocean fish for my supper," he said. "Give me a nice bluegill or bass, fried and the grease drained off on a paper bag and still hot. I like a pan fish. Give me some fish tails, fried crispy—I could eat me a bushel right now, just the tails."

"I don't care what kind of fish, I'll eat it," Bobbie declared. "We got us a big board table under some water oaks by the river. Man, that's something. Peaceful. When Daddy was alive, we'd have a fish fry every Saturday. Invite all our friends and just have a high time. And shrimp—man alive, I can eat the shrimp."

"Seems like human beings have always had it tough in this old world," Gandy mused. "Ain't nothing like a fish fry to perk somebody up. Gets a crowd of people to just *hush*. Wonder what kind of fish it was at the feeding of the five thousand? I'll bet it was some sweet little bluegills. Sure it wasn't crappies."

"You like fish?" Bobbie was asking.

Pip looked around, uncertain whom the boy might be addressing. He had forgotten that Canned Heat was gone, missing out on whatever came next, probably locked up in jail unless the locals did not want to feed him, in which case he was probably lying spread-eagle in a patch of weeds.

"I like fish if I can get it. I used to go fishing with my little brother and my daddy. He'd take us to a bridge on the Ohoopee River. But Otto was too little—"

"You ever eat shrimp?"

"No, I never ate any such thing in all my life." The farm boy made a face, squeezing his eyes shut and sticking out his tongue. He had seen a picture of shrimp and thought that they looked like bugs. He did not eat insects, although sometimes it seemed like maybe he'd better start, they being the chief wildlife available on the farm, which had been picked clean by Mr. Jimmie and the orphans.

"Man alive." Bobbie stared out the door. "They're the best stuff—you can't imagine. I got me a shrimp net back home. You come with us, and I'll get you a mess of shrimp. Boil them up, heads and all, and have a picnic."

"Well, I could try." Pip felt a glow of pleasure, despite being fairly sure he could not stand to put such a downright sea bug in his mouth. "I guess a person can eat most anything," he added to be polite. He felt certain it was not the case. Why, the list of acceptable foods was bound to be pretty short! But he felt glad to be asked. If you did not belong anywhere, it was good to be invited to go somewhere in particular.

The moon rose, her outline the most perfect O Pip could imagine, and at once it seemed to him that the whole universe cried out his brother's name. The moon was Otto's, and the stars dancing in orbit around its O, and the thousands of miles of interplanetary space into which his brother's soul had been flung, seeking the door beyond time. Unless maybe it curled inside a shell in the pocket of his bib overalls. Grazing a finger across the place where the conch lay lodged, Pip wondered whether a ghost might be the same thing as a soul or whether they were different entirely so that one's soul could be flung like a stone from a slingshot across the worlds while the misty limbs of a ghost remained behind like a thumbprint.

"Otto Tattnal, Otto Tattnal, Otto Tattnal...." He chanted in a low voice, his words matching with and lost in the rhythm of the train.

After a while he saw signs of the approaching city: a barely seen group of boys who walked along the track, each carrying a candle lantern carved out of a gourd; then a house with a lamp near a window; then another. Yearning to belong to those boys with their vegetable lights, to one of the houses emitting a pale yellow welcome, he leaned out the door. He caught sight of bulbs dangling from ceilings, their glare harsh. A woman and a man with a suitcase stood in the glow cast from a window, talking so earnestly that it seemed they must be about to part. But most of the residents of outlying areas were keeping farm hours, it seemed, for it was not until they reached the train yards that he saw a few people moving about, though it was too late in the evening for the bustling activity he had imagined. A man strained against a baggage cart overloaded with sacks of mail. He saw a pair of redcaps smoking at the lip of the platform, saw swinging white gleams in the distance, saw a man with a lantern navigating the interlace of steel lines. Well beyond the station, he glimpsed engines and a jointed length that was a long snake of Pullman sleeping cars; just then, the brakes seized the wheels with a sharp smell of hot iron.

A series of chalked bull's heads, fresh and white, stuttered by. Gandy let out a whoop: "Cinder dick! Scatter—"

With a broad leap that must have brought him small-town fame before he left school and home, the young man launched himself from the moving car. A figure took off after him, and Pip heard the crack of a nightstick. Bobbie followed Gandy out, yelling for Cinders to throw the baby. Transfixed, Pip watched as the boy galloped along the train, catching the child handily—the infant must have been used to such tossings because it did not make a peep, only the eyes round in its head suggestive of any alarm—and pulling his sister from the train with a jerk.

"Run for it," Bobbie shouted over his shoulder.

Brother and sister dashed toward an alleyway between two sheds as Pip jumped from the slowing boxcar, sprawling on a patch of crushed oyster shell. Stumbling up, he began to lope awkwardly after the pair, his odd gait made more so by the twist he had given to his ankle in the fall.

He paused, remembering that he had forgotten his bindle of blanket and the leftover sweet potatoes. But when he heard yells, he struggled on. Spying what might be a bolt-hole, he shot into a narrow shaft between outbuildings.

As he broke from the darkness into a moonlit space, he heard a roar—a bull was after him, a nightstick in one hand and a spike in the other. Pip veered away, his eyes streaking along the detective's shirt until he met the long expanse of face with eyes pale and burning like fire in a lantern of ice. A horror of men ignited in him, and he opened his mouth to scream as he had screamed in the morning when the sun boiled from the ground and lit Otto's dead face.

It took a long time for the eyes to stop flickering blue and for the fingers with the spike to meet flesh and bone. It was long enough for the boy to learn dread so that in his nightmares afterward he often met a man with eyes like blue flame in a face like a white rectangle that covers the corpse of a child.

The hand with its quick and summary trial and judgment banged the steel gavel onto Pip's skull, and he dropped onto a path of oyster shell that shone like snow in the moonlight. Then the boy forgot the blaze and the rectangle, forgot the world, forgot his own name. Only one simple shape was in his mind: a boxcar door, opening wide; he was backing until the wall was behind him, and now he was sweeping forward smoothly and flying like a released pigeon from the gap, but because he was not a bird, he plummeted downward into the black spaces of night until there was nothing left in his mind but the steepness and sheerness of fall. His hand, which had groped to touch the pocket of his bib overalls, trembled and lay still.

The bull nosed the ground with his boot and gave the child's body one swift kick. It was hardly worth chasing after kids; the other one though, the one with his skull split, he was a worthy target. With a fingernail the dick dug at his nightstick, making another notch.

6

A battered Pip's in hell with ball and chain
But wakes beside the spires of paradise.

When Pip woke near the Savannah train yards, his hands and cheek cut by oyster shells, the gouge made by the train spike had stopped bleeding. His hair, matted crimson, was stiff and stood like a cockscomb, and the whole right side of his face felt tight. He dragged his knees under him, tucked his head. The world was in thudding eclipse, blacker than he had ever seen it before, with a tinge of red that he at last realized was blood, pooled across his right eye. Because he had never been accustomed to any sort of comfort, he did not feel sorry for his outcast state or expect assistance. Feeling for a lump in his bib pocket (he no longer knew why), he felt reassured by its presence even though a prong of the shell had punched through his overalls and into his chest, which throbbed at the puncture site. He remembered the blue-eyed bull with the burning eyes, but he was no longer afraid. Tottering, he pressed against a shed wall. He recognized that the railroad agent had hurt him badly, for along with the familiar pain that was like a star—one made from a fistful of polished rail spikes—was something new, a dizziness, a spasm in the brain. Still, he knew to move from the spot.

Groping along clapboard or corrugated metal, crawling on dirt and sand and oyster shells when he found nothing to seize hold of, the boy emerged into an area of weeds and scrub where he slept for some hours until the sun was high overhead. It prodded him, urged him to get up and slake his thirst. The craving for water raged at his slowness and helplessness, jerked him to his feet, made him spin around and catch at limber stems and twigs to keep his balance. The star of spikes, like a medieval weapon of war, crashed on his brow.

"Thirsty," he said, the syllables slurred.

Tripping, catching himself, he pushed away from the station, for a time following tracks. Some black children called out from a rear yard, and once Pip thought that he was at the crossroads near the farm until he raised his head and squinted before thrusting doggedly on. It never occurred to him to beg for help. He had the idea that he was going somewhere in particular, although he did not know the location or what place it might be. He was following the star of pain in his head.

"Home?" Once he stopped and repeated the question several times.

How long he tramped, his wrenched ankle aching, he did not know. Later he recalled only paved and unpaved streets, corridors of oak with shadows hanging down—Spanish moss—that made him dream about the Rebellion. Once he seemed to be gliding the length of a vaulted English chamber hung with battle flags. Events were cloudy in his mind, and the question of whether he might be walking into a trap puzzled him. Fragments of violence came to him, and now and then the name *Prince Rupert*, the phrase "wings of horse," or the image of a child crucified against a fence. During this period of what felt like an exceptionally long day, he became convinced that he dwelled in a country of king's men and rebels, and that he had been unhorsed and was trudging home after a skirmish. Had he been injured in the fight? Could he make it back to his family? Delusion spurred him; the furious need to drink and the star kept leading him on.

"Who's this?"

A watering trough materialized before him. He considered, suspecting that it might be—what? a black piece of magic? some sleight of hand? a trick by the enemy? Thirst and heat won out. Plunging his head into the tank, he cooled the star, yet when he raised his face again, it burned worse than ever. He thought about lying down in the trough with his whole body buried, to see if the fiery points would sizzle and sputter out, but in the end he only dipped low and drank, his hands clinging to the sides. The walls were sickly green, and tiny-leaved plants rode the edge of the water. Larval shapes twitched near his eye, and he felt them tickle his throat as they slid downward. He gulped for a long time, throat pumping with desire, before he closed his mouth and rested it there on the surface.

Only as he staggered off, leaning once against a live oak to spit up a froth of green and evil-smelling liquid, did he realize that he was hungry. He yanked up a root from a September garden and chewed it, soil and all, crunching hard and swallowing convulsively.

In Pip's memory afterward, the journey remained stubbornly surreal, its landscape unpeopled, a no-man's-land. Once he encountered a white cow and stopped dead, enchanted by her visionary appearance. She ambled off, teats swinging, but when it occurred to him that milk was close at hand, she had vanished. He never knew whether he was seen as he battled on, head down. Perhaps if passersby did not get a close look at his glazed face, still shiny and slick with blood despite a dunking, the shape might not have looked so different from other unfortunates. He was bowed, sunburned, his overalls filthy: hardly a figure to command notice.

When he tried to pee in the road, he could not, and pain seared him. But that was nothing compared to the smashing in his head. It seemed that he was being repeatedly struck by a mace that wanted to knock him onto his knees, to make him howl in the dirt. Somehow he had taken the wrong path and blundered in ignorance until he stumbled on enemy lines. Now one of the brutal foes dogged his steps, battering at his forehead with a studded ball on a chain. The scraped, raw voice of the soldier complained without pause against him. But Pip would not halt. He could not. If he checked his steps, that was the end. He deliberated, back and forth. He would cease. He would arrange himself honorably, placing his hand over the bib-pocket lump—it had proved to be a shell, a talisman of significance—and he would let the man with the iron sphere bash his pate. But he could not do that, could not arrest his feet. It was a betrayal of something to falter. Endurance was all. He kept shoving himself forward, heels dragging their faint wings of dust. The soldier's voice grated against his skin. He covered his ears, not realizing that the long harangue came from his own throat.

After a time Pip came to the conclusion that he was already dead. He could see a long glitter in the distance. Had he crossed over Jordan? Something, not a trough or a cow or a banner-hung roof, glimmered in front of him. A spasm shook his limbs. Wavering, he peered at the pearly towers of a city, pink and white, with signs he could not read and mosaics whose patterns he could not make out. A blessed silence hung over its pinnacles.

"Otto," he whispered though no longer knew why. It was a comfort, the name that worked the same backwards or forwards, beginning or ending, alpha and omega the very same.

Dizzy, he was axed at the knees and crumpled. He slept and woke, his brow banging with pain. Once he saw a column of flowers tiptoeing around him. Once he gazed up at a tall black obelisk, carrying a block of night and crowned with golden streaks. When he blinked his eyes, there was nothing at all but the sun like a great instrument of war, prickled over with ten-penny nails. After that he lapsed into sleep and did not wake again that day, not even when dusk came and cool air poured from the Savannah River, dividing around roofs and spires.

When he finally cracked open his scorched lids and peered out, Pip saw that the world had changed once more. A kerosene lamp burned on a packing crate. He was lying on a shuck mattress, the canvas cover stained with blood, and next to him was a bowl of glistening paste. The boy dabbed at his forehead, slippery with poultice. The head still pounded, now as if anvil and hammer had been bound and muffled in chamois.

"How do, how do, how do," a voice sang out.

Pip stared at the scuffed boots, the twill work pants with their mended holes and frays, and then rolled sideways until his eyes tracked up a sleeve. The words belonged to a man, and thank God, he had brown eyes like shining glass floats caught in a net of wrinkles above a protuberant, out-of-scale nose that looked as though it were made of wax that had just begun to melt. His eyebrows and ears bristled with hair, and his chin was lost behind a mass of twisty beard. Like a figure from another century, he wore his hair long. It was white except for the rosy part-line that flashed higgledy-piggledy toward the crown.

The boy looked him over more closely than he'd ever examined anyone because the windings of his trek seemed confused, the landscape foreign, and he might have wandered to a spot anywhere, might have been taken in by anybody.

"How you feeling?"

Pip considered, his gaze caught by the fissures at the old man's temples.

"Not bad," he whispered.

"Not bad's not bad, considering. You took quite a blow to your brainpan. Who done it?"

"A bull. Railroad bull."

"Huh. You come all the way from the yards? That's miles and miles off."

Pip's eyelids were sinking down.

"I guess so. I guess that was it."

"See, it ain't good for you to stay asleep too much. I been trying to roust you. Get some food in you. Here, I'll get me a rag and scour your face. You need anything else?"

"No." The answer was barely audible.

Pip could hear water pouring into a basin. When the man came back, some sloshed out and splattered on the boy's arm so that he jumped and the hurt in his head flared.

"Dadblame clumsiness," the old man muttered.

He knelt on the board floor and washed the injured forehead, carefully avoiding the poultice, and rubbed gently at the seared lids and eyelashes, sticky with matter.

"What's your name?"

Stirring, the boy looked around the room as if he might find it daubed onto a board. His eyes looked huge in his staring face. They gave him an air of pleading impossible to ignore.

"Never mind. Don't try to find it. It'll come back. A blow like this and a lot of words scatter. A mind ain't but a sieve, mostly holes."

He stopped speaking for a moment, his gaze on the bolt of wound jagging through the boy's hair.

"My name's Excelsior. Excelsior Tillman. Damn fool kind of a name for a grown woman to give a helpless baby, ain't it? *Excelsior* means wood shavings, or a kind of print type, or 'ever upward.' That's in the Latin language. Nobody much messes with that no more, but when I was a boy, the teachers still taught it if you got the chance to go. Wonderful old stories in the Latin tongue, I tell you. You can call me *Till*."

He sat back on his heels like a child.

"I worked on the trains a while in the highlands. North Georgia, Western North Carolina. Nantahala, Robbinsville, Dillsboro, Brevard, all those places in Carolina. Little old logging lines. I was ashcat—the fireman. Never knew a trainman to hit a boy that way in the coves. Don't think mountain folks would stand for such as that. They'd give a rail bull a drubbing."

Pip's eyes slid onto the shiny brown ones; off again. The wind in his face and the stars in the door came back to him, and he remembered the train and his short, cut-off dream of freedom.

"How'd you make them go?"

His voice sounded rough and strange as if it had rusted during hours of disuse.

"In the mountains, the fireman's earl and duke of the train." Till nodded, wringing out the bloody cloth. "It'd take about four hours to fire a cold engine. I'd start out with wood till she got up to steam. Then I'd bail in coal—about thirty shovelfuls—until the boiler fired. But it was better to start out with a bank. If you pile the live coal at the back of the firebox, it'll just smolder and keep her hot till the next morning."

Pip listened. Often he didn't hear when men were talking, but he liked the timbre of Till's voice, and he liked the brown eyes although he didn't need to look at them any longer now that he knew them, and he liked the tenderness of the hands on his head. His throat felt burned and sore, and for once he did not want to talk.

"We'd use about a ton of coal a day on some runs. Other lines would take up to eight. Freight runs, round trip. That took a lot of fuel. You'd know she was going good when the smoke was right. None of that white smoke. It's got to be black."

The old man's fingers moved delicately in the boy's hair, checking the wound.

"If it wasn't right, I'd just fool with the grate, rake the coals around. It gets so you don't have to think, which is good because some days you'd work sixteen hours on a freight run. That's a lot of shoveling. It's hard on the body, balancing without holding on, working that shovel. Wish I'd kept to it and had me a big pension. But it's a tough job. Scoop the coal, toss it in the fire door, scoop some more. End of the day, you'd have the ashcat's waddle from standing so spraddle-legged, one foot on the tender and the other on the engine. You'd be pure rubber legs next morning. Get up and trip over your feet like in a circus-clown act."

Here he got up and walked off to the stove, and the boy drifted again, his thoughts unmoored.

"Don't you go to sleep on me," Till warned.

Jarred awake, Pip opened his mouth to yell, and the old man put a palm on his forehead and leaned toward him.

"Calm down, son. Here, drink this. It'll ride easy on your belly."

It was hot. It was nothing he had tasted before, and he did not like unfamiliar food. He liked hominy grits, hoecake, johnnycake, lady peas, field peas, crowders, okra, summer squash, sweet potatoes, cucumbers, fried or baked meats, panfish, custard pies, velvet cake, and fruit eaten straight from the branch, still warm from the sun. He was willing to sample desserts he had not tried before, but he had an intense dislike for candy. What he tasted now was like none of the flavors he knew, but it was close to scalding, and he was thirsty and chilled. He could not peg what it was, but it felt like a spark of flame.

"That all you want? How about one more sip? That's just five sips. About right for a hummingbird."

"Thanks."

"It's good broth. Made it myself. Got some eels and lake catfish and onion in there. Eel is strong muscle for a man. It'll cure that limp feeling."

Squeezing his eyes shut, Pip turned on his side.

"You going woozy on me?" The old man patted his shoulder. "You're a decent sort of boy, I can tell. You'll get over this and go on home to your friends. Don't you worry—I got my name to live up to. I'll make you better. It won't take long."

Rubber legs in the morning. That was how he felt, wiggly and weak, as eel-legged as if he had been shoveling coal in the mountains. The air felt chill there, he had heard, probably like dipping your burning head in a trough. He had heard that the mountain air was thicker than steam, the air rife with clouds that snagged on the trees and tumbled into the icy creeks. Perhaps it was like the wraith-like mist rolling off dry ice, a magical substance that could burn the skin with cold.

He shuddered once at the idea of the cool and the heat together and then again, remembering how he had been drinking eel and catfish broth. Nothing wrong with a fried catfish, he thought, although he did not like the slime and the whiskers that could spear right through your hand or the skin that had to be peeled. The Ohoopee with its sand banks and slow currents and herons swirled into his mind.

"You just lay easy," the voice was advising, its syllables arriving from a long way off. Although he seldom obeyed without some trouble, often not even focusing on the words when men spoke to him, this time he did. A pain in his throat was impossible to identify—an illness? a yearning? what? It seemed to Pip that he was sinking into a trough of water, letting the murk soak his clothes. He breathed the greenish liquid in through his nostrils like the last sleep and opened his parched mouth to drink its still silences and its voiceless larval dreams that jittered and sprang.

Just before a stone weighed him down and sank him to the bottom of the tank, he remembered that he still knew almost nothing about the old man, and he struggled up, staring once more at the face that in his weariness seemed a soft-edged rectangle. A mote of fright, insect-small, wriggled through him. He had never been able to judge expressions, and now he looked at Excelsior Tillman with something like despair.

"It's fine," Till told him. "Sleep a bit and I'll wake you in an hour or so, just to make sure you're right. Feed you some more broth. When you get better, you can rest in the sun under the live oaks. There's a breeze from the sea that's just full of health. Salt airs can cure what ails you. I'm never sick. You go on, lie back down."

Pip felt warmth like sunshine from the man's hand, and he recalled the sheen on the river and the pink and white city shining in front of him. It was the prettiest sight he had ever seen, though he didn't know how or what it could *be*. This place was no heaven, eel broth no heavenly food.

"What—"

The new feeling in his head that was like an uncoiling spring seized him, and he gave in. He could see the water tank again. Somebody had lobbed a stone into it, and the ripples were widening and breaking against the walls, above the pale figure glimmering at the bottom.

7

Pip stumbles on a chance for family;
Excelsior and Casimiria,
The woven marriage-bed of Clemmie Shook.

It was almost a week before Pip crawled into the sunshine and saw his visionary city again, glowing under the oaks, with the luster of the river in the background. Then he felt sure that the trough, the moon-white cow, and the chamber hung with banners were real because the miniature town's pink pinnacles were no dream but solid and touchable. The little world of Roseville was the first manmade thing he had seen in his whole life that was meant for nothing but pleasure. He had never known anybody to craft something that he didn't need for the farm or the kitchen. The astonishment of it seeped in.

Till's streets and buildings and signs were marvelous to the boy. Some thirty edifices ranged in size from the Crumbox Cottage to the grand Plaza of Government, topped with a dome of blue-and-white mosaic, its shards of china intricately fitted together. There were gates through which he was small enough to bend down and enter, a Cathedral with Gothic arches pieced from bits of sea-tumbled glass and broken bottles, bungalows with porch rails that were worn slivers of shell, and shops displaying tiny goods behind scavenged glass.

"Pretty little conch you got in that pocket," Excelsior Tillman said, breaking the mild silence that seemed the proper atmosphere of Roseville.

"It's mine."

"Don't you worry, Master Pip. I'd never take what's yours."

"It's not that." He hesitated, unsure what he had meant. "There's just something about it," Pip said slowly. "In a way, it belonged to my brother. I like to think...." He stopped. If anyone could understand how a shell could be imagined as a shelter for Otto's soul, it would be the architect of Roseville. Yet to say it aloud would be to reveal too much—perhaps even to disclose an absurdity in the thought. No, it was better not to speak.

"Oh, it's funny how a little whorl of shell can mean something." Till looked dreamy, his eyes resting on the river. Then the mood slid away, and he began whistling.

Pip lay on a mat and watched the old man mix brackish water from the river with clay, crushed oysters, burnt lime, and sand. Till puttered about the yard, his pants floury white; when he had shells to crush, he'd go off to a big bowl-shaped stone and pound until he had enough to suit him.

"It's nothing but walls of tabby," he confided as if passing on a secret, "with a dab of mountain clay to tincture it pink. Tabby came from Africa. I met a man—his daddy was a field slave—who claims there are castles and harbor walls made out of tabby in Africa. The slaves brought the cunning of how to make it, like they brought peanuts and okra and field peas. Can't feature a world without black-eye peas, can you? This tabby, it's fine stuff. It'll last. There's Georgia tabby that's been here for about two hundred years."

He surveyed the grid of streets with their parks of moss.

"Keeps me out of devilment," he added.

It made sense to Pip, this pint-sized district with its lore and complexity. Till's sense of mission chimed with Pip's tendency to amass facts about a single obsessive interest. Hadn't he been mocked for knowing the railroad schedule by heart back when he was only eight? Couldn't he recite pages and pages of the Rebellion? It gave him a pleasure to do so, the words streaming from his mind—a power emptying out. He wanted more. He wanted to *know,* but there had been nobody to help him find out and not many books. It felt good, having a hoard of knowledge in memory.

The city had a history like that of a real town; pearl-like, it had grown slowly over time, becoming more and more detailed. Its builder could say which of the waist-high structures were built first, and of what materials. He could remember who gave him the enameled passion flowers and crosses set out in the Cathedral garden, the porcelain animals cemented onto the grounds of the Roseville Zoo, and the broken dolls. He had a special affection for the Garden of Lost Dolls, with its arms and legs planted like boles and spreading into fingers and toes, and its cracked heads crowned with shards of pottery.

Till liked to page through an ancient ledger that he'd scrounged at the docks, reading aloud the names of occasional visitors and their comments about Roseville.

"It's a kind of fever that gets me," he confessed. "It just eats at me when I'm busy and can't work or when it rains and the tabby won't set. Even then I can be chipping up busted plates or fiddling with shell patterns. But the best part is working under the trees with the wind coming off the river."

"I know what you mean, I think," the boy said. "Want me to tell you a story about rebels and horses and fighting?"

The breeze lifted the hair from the old man's face, showing him intent and careful as Pip began to recite the saga of his English rebellion. Many years later he was to say that Excelsior Tillman was the first grown man whose features he had understood because they were only one thing: peaceable, akin to the pink kingdom spreading under the sun. And maybe the boy could not have found any refuge better for healing than the four-room house beside the flushed walls of a toy metropolis.

In a moldy box he found some books, and years later he could still recite lines from Herrick's poems. To a girl he might call out, "A sweet disorder in the dress / Kindles in clothes a wantonness." Or he would launch into "His Farewell to Sack" when lifting a glass, or recite to children the little poem, "Upon Jack and Jill." It ended with those memorable lines, which invariably pleased and made its young listeners think better of poetry: "Let poets feed on air or what they will; / Let me feed full till that I fart, says Jill."

At Roseville, Pip read while Till stuck blue bottle glass in concentric rings around a door, churned tabby in a bucket, or painted signs on strips of lathing and set them in place. Poetry was not the boy's first craving, for he wanted to explore history and set the Rebellion in its proper niche, with a *before* and an *after*, but the verses eased some longing in him. It seemed right to pillow himself on earth with the river below and the pastel city around him. A mystery at its heart, he was the growing minotaur in the maze. He often slept, a book sliding down his chest and live oak leaves fluttering down to catch on his overalls.

He was knitting himself together with the kindness of the old man, the fantasy of the town, and the power of poetry. (Long afterward, it struck him as a first encounter with beauty. His bridge-building father might have made arches worth admiring, and perhaps his mother had loved to sew or sing. Who knew? He did not remember. It occurred to him that history might tell him these things if he could only gather enough detail.) He could travel nowhere, could hardly stand without a spring unwinding in his head, revolving toward dizziness. Till made no mention of departure and managed to stock the larder with what he caught from the river or received in trade from nearby families.

And the injured boy was not his only charitable concern. Before Pip was able to venture into Roseville on his own or poke about the house and find a box of speckled books, he stumbled onto another evidence of the old man's generosity. It did not happen immediately. Not until he grew strong enough to venture into the next room on his own did he discover what had made the murmuring and laughter he'd heard from time to time in his dreams.

Curious, he made his way to the door and fumbled with the glass knob: gloom and an odor of lily of the valley mixed with urine met him. In what appeared to be a parlor furnished with a daybed, several chairs, and a mat woven from sea grass, he spied an immense heap of newspaper. He thought to take it and read, but as he approached, fingers on the wall to steady himself, the bed sheets stirred as if an animal had made a nest inside and was now awakening.

"Hey!"

The boy looked about, putting his free hand to his forehead.

A rill of laughter, surprising, girlish, spilled into the room.

With a crumpling of news, a topknot appeared, composed of multiple braids twisted together. Pip stared as a black eye appeared above the litter, and he reached to rest a palm on the lump of shell, safe in his pocket. In another moment an entire face rose out of the mass and grinned at him.

"Surprised you, didn't I?" It was an old woman. She chortled, showing a dark tooth. "Eh, Pip? That's your name, ain't it? Pip?"

He nodded.

"Funny sort of a name. You got the pip, Pip? You ain't much bigger than a pip, are you?" She tittered at her own jokes but stopped abruptly when he did not join in.

Two or three dark shapes slipped from her lap, making him start back and clutch at the air.

"Nothing to frighten you, nothing but babies." She groped for the dogs and hauled them in. "The mother's dead, yes, she is, poor little bitch, and I'm raising these bird dogs for Mr. Tillman to sell." The babies squealed as she shoved them into the gap between cushion and chair. "Velvety pups, they are, with more skin than flesh. Very nice animals. If you like, come and pet them."

Pip leaned against the wall and slid to a sitting position. He noticed that the puppies had doodled a line of puddles near the matting.

"Feeling poorly, are you? Well, you can play with them another time." As the old woman shifted in her seat, a rapid succession of squeaks punctuated this assurance.

"I have some lemon drops somewhere, which I will offer you. If only I can find them." She pawed about, eliciting more high-pitched shrills and turning up a saucepan, some handkerchiefs, and an antique beaded reticule that when she opened it contained only equally ancient lint.

"I don't eat candy. You keep it." The boy eyed the rubbish pile in the chair, wondering whether there was more to the decayed lady than an upper torso and arms and a head. He could not make out more in the shadows. "Are you Mrs. Tillman?"

The old woman laughed, again surprising him with a sweet and bell-like tone.

"Bless his heart, the young ignorance!" She grabbed one of the pups and rubbed its flat nose against her own similarly buttonish one. "Am I *Mrs. Tillman*? What a tickle to my fancy! To be the mistress of Roseville and its streets and byways. What a wonder, what a monstrous queenship *that* would be."

Here she burst into merriment once more. Instead of wiping her streaming eyes on one of the many handkerchiefs lying in wadded balls beside her, she rubbed them on a puppy, which stuck out its tongue in interest.

"No, my dear, I am certainly not Mrs. Tillman. And I do not believe there ever was one such or ever will be. Unless some limber girl comes along to foozle Excelsior Tillman in his elder years. Which would not be the first time such a thing has befuddled a man." Her face pinched up, the mouth caving inward. "Do you think it possible?" She lifted the smallest of the litter to her eye level, shaking it slightly. "Well?"

"I don't know," Pip offered, unsure whether he was meant to answer. He would not have been astonished in that moment had the pup proffered its own juvenile opinion instead of thrusting out a tongue in hope of salt tears.

"It is a worry, a terrible worry." Though the little dog wriggled and dropped onto the chair, she paid no heed but began to open and shut her bag with much snapping of the clasp. "I never unharnessed such an idea as that before in my life, but now it seems likely and is bolting away with me like a wild mule. I shall have to take the creature up with Mr. Tillman this very day. This very hour. Oh, dear,

dear, what a squabble that would be for us, depending on him as we do. And those half-naked children keep coming over to play in Roseville, nothing but pickaninnies or white trash, and sure to grow to be lithe young sylphs and maybe allure the fellow. He won't be the first one to make such a dreadful mistake! Old men are fools; everyone knows that. They are fools," she repeated with an anxious tone. "Fools, fools, fools. He'll regret it ever so much. It will be the ruination of him and me and us. When do you think it will happen? Such a peril! This terrible marriage!"

"Well, ma'am," Pip replied, recollecting what he knew of genteel manners from his three books, "please, ma'am. Upon consideration, I do not believe it will happen at all. And I have never seen any children here." He was puzzled, uncertain whether this woman who was not Mrs. Tillman could be quite sane and serious. Or was she having him on, fooling him in some new way?

"How prettily the boy speaks! I wonder if he has been to school," she said, leaning on an elbow to watch the pups roll in her lap. "People used to chat so pleasantly, but now it is rudeness and nonsense." After a minute of silence, she added, "You have done me a great service. I thank you, as it is a relief to my mind, what you say. A very—a very tremendous relief. When doddering old fools of men can be so unreliable."

"I'm sure Mr. Tillman is reliable. Who—what is your name, ma'am?"

The question launched another gale of trills. When she had dried her eyes on another puppy, crumpled the newsprint a bit in sitting up straighter, and peered once more into the derelict reticule as if to find out the answer to his question, she spoke.

"I am Casimiria Pulaski Fogg. I am the great-great-great-great-great-great-great—something like that, ever-so-many greats—granddaughter of Count Casimir Pulaski, the Polish lover of freedom, commissioned in the Revolutionary Army and slain in the siege of Savannah. Not precisely legitimate, this line, you understand. But very close to it. Count Casimir was much admired in Savannah. You have heard of Casimir Pulaski, my great-great-great-etcetera grandfather?"

Pip nodded.

"Good. The child *has* been at school," she informed the puppies. Graciously, showing her dark fang, she smiled upon the boy and said, "They still teach Georgia history, it seems, and we are not forgotten. Although I was properly brought up, I condescend to my present surroundings. I have no pride, no unsuitable pomp. You may call me *Miss Casimiria.* There are those who call me *Princess* Casimiria. *Countess* is another of my titles. But I do not require these. My parents lost everything after the War of Northern Aggression, and a simple *Miss Casimiria* is acceptable."

Feeling faint, Pip groped for a castoff handbill, folded accordion-style, which he had seen lying on the mat. After a moment he began to fan himself.

At this juncture a door to the outside jerked open, and two silhouettes stood against the brightness. The old woman lifted a hand to shield her eyes. "Clemmie—is it Clemmie? And who's that with you? Bill?"

"Yes, ma'am, Miss Cassie, Countess," a voice drawled.

"Where have you all been to?" she demanded.

"Been to Savannah. Sold Clemmie's weaving at the stores. Didn't do too bad. Then we stayed with my cousin at Tybee, had us a good time."

"Hah. Better not be having too swell a time."

"He's fine," the one that must be Clemmie said. Coming farther into the room, she caught a glimpse of Pip, seated on the floor.

"Well, how are you?" she cried out. "Stronger, I hope."

"Some. Yes, ma'am," he replied, looking from her to Bill. They were a handsome couple, Clemmie in a white dress, Bill in work pants and a homemade shirt, and both of them with black eyes and hair sawed off awkwardly, the young woman with a purple flower tucked behind one ear. Bill was sallow and dark; Clemmie, red-cheeked.

"I guess you don't recollect us coming in to gawp at you," Bill said, squatting down. "But we did. What a sight. Never saw such a mess as that."

"He's looking better now," Clemmie declared. She kneeled next to Pip and inspected him with interest.

Miss Casimiria let out a hoot.

"That head is as colored as a rainbow, red and blue and yellow. Why, with gauntlets and a Malacca cane mace, he could drum up a parade," she told the puppies.

"Countess," Bill cautioned.

"Yes sir, he could." She rapped on the arm of the chair for emphasis.

Excelsior Tillman came in through the other room, lugging a bushel basket.

"Old fool," Casimiria muttered.

"Is she angry?" the boy asked in an undertone. "She thinks he's going to marry some girl—the Princess, I mean."

Clemmie glanced at the old woman and gave a quick shake of the head. "No, it's just her fancy—most things are—she's always gallivanting after something."

"I don't know where you got these," the old man said to Bill, "because it's too late in the year for crowders."

"They ain't much. Buggy. Dry on the vine."

Catching sight of Pip, Till smiled at him.

"Now look at you. On your own. You've met the Countess, hey? And Clemmie and Bill Sojourner, they're my tenants. Really, they're more like young cousins. Live in a three-room house close by the water."

The boy made no response. He was used to strange alliances.

"You like crowders? Bill picked them up somewheres."

"I like any kind of field peas."

"That Clemmie, I knew her Mama from when I was a fireman in the mountains. She's a Carolina girl."

"I reckon," Clemmie put in.

"She's a weaver. She does pretty work."

"Nothing but four-harness weaving," Clemmie corrected, shaking her head. "Old-fangled stuff."

"She makes some mighty nice cloth that way, stripes and plaid and houndstooth," Till added. "How about we just squat down and shell these crowders and cook them up? I got a heel of pork and a hot pepper to throw in. I just relish pepper and onion with crowders." He looked about the room. "Countess, Miss Casimiria, could you bestow a page of the paper on us? To catch the hulls?"

Before long they were talking at once, laughing, shelling crowders that were, indeed, old and simple to shell, the hulls dry and light and flyaway. That was the first time Pip saw Till's makeshift family all together, and he felt content to witness, to hear a riot of squeaking whenever the Countess adjusted herself in the chair, to look at the tendrils escaped from Clemmie's hairpins, to listen as Bill told about fishing at Tybee. He remembered the brother and sister on the train and how the boy had said he would go fishing at the beach, and he wondered if they made it home and had a fish fry and whether the girl was sorry that Pip hadn't escaped the bulls and gone with them. With a flicker of unease, he remembered the *crack!* as the nightstick met bone—Gandy's head, perhaps. Pip looked around the circle and was glad to be in a house that he could call his, at least for a while. He could picture the Countess as a grandmother and Mr. Tillman as a grandfather and Clemmie and Bill as elder siblings. He could not imagine any of them as parents, could not imagine a mother other than Mommer standing by the pantry as the glass jars smashed on the floor.

The sea grass mat was a fine place to lay his head down; until his dizziness passed, he did not want to think about what was next, where he might go, what he might do. He could not ride the rails with a light head. That much was sure.

Gandy had told him a story about a young man who caught a freight in the Rockies. He'd been camping by himself, dozing near the tracks; when a warning whistle blew, he woke and darted to the train.

A couple of hobos in the doorway tried to haul him inside after he started screaming, thrashing his leg, and Gandy had glimpsed the tail end of a big rattler sticking out by his boot. It squirmed higher into the straight-leg pants as the train rocked, clambering the grade and onto a trestle. It seemed as though the fellow wanted to jump, but he was dangling and could not get off any longer—already the trestle was high above the ground. Meanwhile, the rattler would not shake free, even when the boy kicked upward and banged his leg against the car. Gandy had seen his eyes, wild, showing the whites in fear, and it was as if he could not listen to the men who were calling for him to take hold of their hands, that they'd kill the snake. When the train was laboring halfway across the gorge and Gandy could see the black sticks of the trestle between the swinging legs, the kid let go and sailed away toward the firs and the shimmying aspens and the granite rocks, his arms spread like kite struts, the tip of the tail still hanging from his pants.

Someone at the door had just groped for and seized hold of his hand, and when the boy panicked and plunged from the train as it lurched, the man was catapulted outward. The others heard the yell and saw his body strike the earth and bounce.

Hopping trains was a better way to travel than most, but you had to be prepared. You had to be strong. You could not go hoboing with a head that might get swimmy and lure you over some fatal edge.

Pip watched as Clemmie scrubbed the floor where the puppies had wet. Just now she had exclaimed over the puppy mess—"Oh, Princess!" she had said—and fetched a bucket of soapy water and rags.

This was a place worth staying in, he decided. Both of the old people were lunatics and might be fetched and locked away in the loony bin at Milledgeville any day now, but there was no harm in them or Bill and Clemmie. It seemed to him that Georgia and probably the whole country had its share of the squirrelly, and maybe this part no more than most. From experience and the examples of the

Countess and Excelsior Tillman, he concluded that the U. S. of A. was, in general, a land of looners and that perhaps madness was essential. His own feelings seemed peculiarly mixed so that at one moment he felt distrustful and at the next surprised by a surge of something like affection for the old man—not that he would have named it such. Perhaps in a nuthouse population like this, one had to be off kilter to get along. Perhaps everyone on the face of the planet was crazy, in one mode or another. He remembered the burning blue eyes of the men at The White Camellia Orphanage, remembered Otto's head with its barbed crown.

It was not the lesson that most people would have drawn from the actions of the old man who had borne him home in his arms and cared for him, though the boy was a stranger, damaged, bloody, unclean, and poor. But it was the lesson Pip Tattnal took from events, and one can hardly blame him for that.

8

In which Pip Tattnal stays in Savannah—
With what he learns, and how he gets along.

"Mr. Tillman, your grandson is what I can only call strange—"

Till put up his hand.

"Pip is a good boy. Yes, he is a little unusual, but we're all made different." He paused, and then chose not to correct the woman. *Grandson* would do. There had been a little trouble enrolling him, a boy without a birth certificate—many births still went unrecorded out in the rural districts—who claimed to have attended no school, though he spoke well enough and could read and write and talk about a few events in English history in detail. A lack of consistent schooling was true enough, for the orphans had been kept home to work more days than not.

"I shall condescend to go and talk to this—this hireling of the state of Georgia," the Countess Casimiria had announced. Till and Clemmie had looked at each other, startled. The old woman had hardly been off her perch in the best room in years, save to attend church or sit in the sun by Roseville. "I shall go as *Princess*, mind you. That is the more impressive of my titles. My Sunday title."

"And I'll be your sis when we get to the school," Clemmie had told Pip. "We're all brothers and sisters, I reckon. She don't sound so friendly though. What does she look like?"

But the big dun-colored face of the teacher remained a blur to Pip. He knew that she could never manage the middle button of her blouse so that her speckled skin showed through the gape at mid-back, along with the formidable horse-harness that gripped and held motionless her—and here what popped into his head was childishly mean—her seriously gone aspraddle dugs. His fingers itched to pull at her blouse, fasten the round button. Yet he would not have touched her flesh for the world. In the child's portion of his mind, she was a four-thousand-year-old walking and talking mummy.

"I don't know," he had told Clemmie, "because I don't look at her."

The meeting "didn't go all that well," as Excelsior Tillman said later, out in the dirt yard, turning his face to survey the ranks of windows. The ones that had let light into the boy's classroom were marked by a flurry of paper snowflakes that defied the winter-blooming camellias in front of the school.

Pip was not listening to this judgment, being busy telling the Countess Casimiria that he did not believe one whit of what she had said in his classroom, and that he could not abide her flat-out storybook lies.

Miss Cassie was not one to accept reprimand.

"You weren't even listening!" The royal head wobbled with the force of her accusation.

"I've got a radio in my skull," he told her. "I can listen to more than one station at a time."

"Oh, s'durn high and mighty," she hollered, flecks of froth appearing on her lips.

But the clash might have been worse. For it was not that the boy's teacher had rolled victorious from the encounter with the boy and his Savannah entourage. She had been direct enough at the start but was quickly derailed.

"Men-tal-ly de-fec-tive," Mrs. Ogrens enunciated to Till, who looked puzzled. "He is difficult in all ways, and he hasn't the least idea how to play with the other little fellows in the class. He is not bad at English and History, but he makes up the longest, wildest stories. All of which is very peculiar. He is unlike any child I have ever taught."

In the months Pip had spent with him, the old man had never doubted his intelligence. Clemmie had told Pip that he was about the smartest boy she had ever met, and even Casimiria, when consulted, uncrimped her mouth and acknowledged that he was as "sharp as a haystack needle."

So Mrs. Ogrens had settled on the wrong tack with Pip's friends.

"I can't seem to get a handle on him," she added, sounding uneasy.

At this, the boy seemed to wake up for an instant.

"I'm not a pot," he murmured.

"Exactly so! He's not a pot!" the Princess exclaimed.

"Or a pan," Clemmie added.

"Not a rice pot, not a lady's rouge pot, not a crab pot, not a scent pot, not a pot for shrimp or eels," Till said with glee, leaning back in the schoolroom chair until the wood creaked in retort.

The teacher had been unprepared for a visit from Excelsior Tillman, Clemmie, and especially the Princess, who had entered the room clinging onto the girl's arm and riding a wave of odors. Mrs. Ogrens had recoiled, noting the competing smells of cloves and urine and a bridal scent of orange blossom. Perhaps that three-pronged assault had confused her.

For if she had begun with an account of the boy's radical inattention to her homilies, his lack of eye contact, his ability to daydream about events enormously more interesting than her own words, his furious reading of history books under the desk, his brand new obsession with Asia, his grandiose and often comical word choice, his utter inability to remember abstract terms, the ridiculous faces he sometimes made to emphasize a point, his monologues, his veering changes of subject, his too-loud voice, his refusal to eat anything but what was on his personal list of approved foods, his separation from the other children, his lousy fine or gross motor skills—if she had begun with any one of a hundred complaints, Till would have smiled. Clemmie would have hooted in pleasure. The Princess would have cackled and wiped her eyes, using the hankie embroidered with the letter *P* that she had thrust deep in her reticule before departing the environs of Roseville. Hadn't they all roared at

Pip's odd ways, or at times been annoyed by his talk about battles and warriors?

But to impugn his brains! These were a source of pleasure to the old man, who would often say to the Countess, "Well! He's surefire smart," followed by some disclaimer: "even if he's got no more common sense than a pail of grits."

"I assure you," Mr. Tillman said, shifting in the wooden school chair, "the boy has a first-rate head. It's grade-A coal and burns hot. You could fire and drive a locomotive on it."

He turned aside. "Princess Countess! Clemmie! Do you hear what the woman is going on about?"

Clemmie jerked her head to look at him, her face serious.

"Teachers," the Princess Casimiria said. There seemed to be the barest hint of a deckle edge of scorn to her voice. "One would like to think them fetched up from the best sort, wouldn't one? One would like to feel that they had a hold of sympathy and taste. So as not to despoil the treasure of childhood. When I was a girl, I had the most marvelous tutor—he was as well favored as Midsummer Day is long. Well, any day's not really so long, is it? He was as handsome as three months of Sundays—"

"Can we please—?" Mrs. Ogrens turned her glance slowly from one to another. An unpleasant sensation took hold, as if her head were being slowly filled by lint.

The Princess began to weep. "We had a sweet little pool inside a hedge of boxwood, and he would go and bathe there, and my sisters and I would peep at him through a hole in the greenery. Just a stripling he was. He was pale with eyes like train coal and lips as red as the rose by the greenhouse door. Now I 'spect he must have known we were watching him because he was always smiling."

"She's a sensitive soul, the Princess," Till explained. "She came from greatness and wealth, she did. But she's come down far in the world."

"Princess," Mrs. Ogrens said faintly.

"We're here to talk about our boy, Countess—Princess, I mean." Clemmie patted the old woman on the crook of a shoulder blade. "About Pip."

"Princess," Casimiria said. "We need our best titles for the big occasions. It's just that I'd forgotten my tutor for such a long time—Horace, his name was, I believe. Yes, Horace. Unless it might have been Horatio. Or perhaps Hamlet." She patted her eyes with a bolus of lint. "Once that boy was my moon and stars. He died, you know. He died of the flu. Was it the Bolivian influenza that spring? The Patagonian flu? Some little ague-like thing from somewhere. He got to keep young and fine forever, never got to fall out of love or grow wrinkled and forget what he was saying in the middle of a... that's how much luck he had, no more! They washed him, and we were made to help and bring the soap and basins. In the parlor he was, all laid out naked. Skin like cream. The maids dressed him in his best suit. I wonder if he looked a little bit like this boy? Maybe that's why I remembered it?"

"And you loved him, didn't you?" Clemmie was smiling, her eyes on a pair of December camellias outside the window. The petals were snow against the shining towers of leaves.

"Oh, he was a dear fellow. He had the best head for calculus and poetry I've ever known. Hamlet, he was."

"I didn't know you knew—whatever it was—the calculus," Clemmie said.

"I never learned. There were other things we found more interesting. But he taught me poetry. Every word that fell from his lips was a poem. He showed me that my body was a poem, every curl and cranny." The last words were high-pitched, and the Princess's eyes glistened.

Mrs. Ogrens had slumped slightly. Her mouth was only a little ajar, but it made her look silly.

"This boy, Lady Princess Casimiria," Till reminded.

The boy in question was staring into the distance, seemingly engrossed in his thoughts, although his mind had not entirely let go of the conversation. He had made an enormous discovery that week; after much struggle with his English reader, he had finally understood completely and finally what was meant by a metaphor. Until then, he had always laughed when people made such comparisons. The apple of someone's eye or a girl who was a rose: how absurd! But then he remembered the gaze of the men at the orphanage: not *like* ice but ice itself, so cold it burned.

The idea that two things could be unalike yet oddly the same had transformed all things for him. The Princess was a wrinkled-up prune! The river was an eel sliding on grease! Clemmie was a flower by the water's edge! Even the past and its memories were changed, and for the first time he had really understood the knife he had seen in the sky on the morning of Otto's death as the union of two things: *cloud* and *blade*. One frail and one steel, the two had met and fused in a forge of dawn. That was a kind of magic. He was veering between thoughts of word sorcery and a faint attention to his friends and his recent reading about Japan. This last topic was sweeping into dominance, seizing his interest more vigorously than anything else.

"Pip—"

He looked up, his glance settling on the collar of the old man's white shirt.

"What you thinking, boy?"

"Did you know—did you know that from 1192 Anno Domini to 1868 Anno Domini, the shoguns were overlords to the samurai, and that they ruled the emperor of Japan even though the emperor was the descendant of the sun goddess and worshipped with incense—"

"These tales! You see what I mean," Mrs. Ogrens began, heaving her bustline into the air in a way that caused Till's eyebrows to lift.

"Excuse me, ma'am, but I see no dadgum thing of the kind," he replied.

"—and he was considered so sacred and wonderful that the ladies of the court could not raise their eyes in his holy presence—"

"You would have fit right in, son." Mr. Tillman slapped his leg in amusement.

"—and so in his bamboo palace in the City of Peace and Tranquility, which is what we call Kyoto—"

"Stop. It. Pip." Clemmie leaned into his face, and he quit talking and went back to dreaming and staring out the window.

"You see," pursued Mrs. Ogrens.

"Yes, ma'am. Please, if you can, tell me the concept—"

"No, Mr. Tillman—"

"Yes'm," he repeated. "I was not quite finished if you don't mind. Now, ma'am. Tell me the concept and history of *Bushido* among the samurai of Japan, and say as how's it different from the feudalism and chivalry notions of Western Europe. Tell me the three peasant crops of feudal Japan, and why they were possible because of the weather and the lay of the land. Who went and built the Great Wall of China, and why'd he bother with such a confounded business? How'd it happen that the Great Ch'in Emperor, who despised that wise old fellow, Confucius, was followed by emperors in the Han dynasty who jumped up and started a school to teach the Confucian classics? Paint me a word picture of the sort of gaudy death that rejoiced the hearts of nomads, larking about the Mongolian Grasslands in the Middle Ages. Tell me all about how the Indomitable Emperor, Genghis Khan, put together armies out of those wild rollicking bands of boys. Tell me how, just a bare hundred years after Mohammed whisked off to Medina, Moslems fought the T'ang emperor for control of China's routes to the west—and all that ruckus only a few years before the Arabs sacked Christian shrines in Spain. How come we ain't all Moslems today? Say how Charles Martel, the Hammer, and his Frankish axmen put a dandy stop to their hullabaloo at the Battle of Tours. Can you do it? These are things Pip can tell and does tell. All the time," he added. "He's been a regular education to me."

"But those are stories," Mrs. Ogrens protested.

"My dear miss," Mr. Tillman began, leaning toward the teacher. (It was his unalterable policy always to treat the opposite sex as youthful maidens.) "If you will think over your classes for the last few years—the no doubt small number you've taught—you'll recollect that you don't see other children who can answer questions like that or tell such *stories*. They shouldn't really be called *stories*, I reckon. Educated people go and call them *history*. Maybe this boy will grow up and make a teacher at the colleges. And then you and me can be learned something new out of his books."

At this point, Pip began paying closer attention. Mrs. Ogrens looked flummoxed. Mr. Tillman stood up.

"It was interesting, having this chance to talk," he said. Oddly, he looked every inch a Tattnal, eyes planted firmly on the middle distance and resolute not to listen to another word. "Good day, ma'am."

The boy was working on a metaphor. It seemed to him that Mrs. Ogrens was softening and spreading as if she might drip off the sides of the desk, leaving only stiff undergarments, skirt and blouse, and a pair of stout shoes behind. She emitted a noise, lodged halfway between a quack and a snort.

"Come along, son."

For once Pip was listening, and he came right along.

So school was where he could not fit, it seemed. Till simply let him be, as did Clemmie, and Bill was often away working. Casimiria often liked to take a jab at him, seemingly out of high spirits. Or perhaps it was just the royalty in her, unable to avoid taking a poke at her lessers.

And school was "a long row to hoe," as the old man acknowledged.

At the end of that year, there was a ceremony with a podium and flags and guests. Mrs. Ogrens cautioned Pip repeatedly not to interfere with the visitors, for he had, she claimed, humiliated her by talking with a speaker during the presentation at the last assembly. A retired sea captain had come to tell the upper grades about his travels in the Far East, and Pip had embarrassed himself and his classmates, or so Mrs. Ogrens told him. She asserted that the boy had known what he was doing but had done it anyway.

"I don't feel bad. I don't feel wrong. I didn't do anything."

He had tried to explain himself, but the teacher would not listen and punished him by making him go sit in the tiny school library for an hour, an exclusion he enjoyed, lying under a table to read where it was dim and quiet and smelled pleasantly musty. Slowly he forgot how Mrs. Ogrens had wronged him. He had felt interested in what the man had to say, so keenly concerned that he had followed the words closely and only jumped up when he could no longer contain his curiosity. Wasn't that what school was for? He still did not know the meaning of the teacher's phrase, "the terrible thing you did," though he felt obscurely unhappy and unable to divine the wellsprings of his misery.

In the small clapboard gym, Mrs. Ogrens installed him at the far end of the rows allotted to the class where she did not have to look at him. Once out of eyeshot, Pip removed *An Introduction to the Ancient and Noble Philosophy and Art of Bushido* from his pocket and began reading.

He imagined himself as possessed of secret nobility. He was a master of jujitsu and fencing, archery and swordplay. His arms inscribed powerful shapes that were characters meant for those who could read the language of the air. He pored over the words of Confucius, learning the rules for right living. His politeness was incomparable, tea ceremonies famous, hair and eyes shining, form perfect.

But a shame came upon him; his leader, a squat and brutal fellow encased in a glittering girdle of armor, accused him of treason. During a ceremony in his teahouse, cherished for its stepping stones of jade and cloud and its lantern of rubbed red coral, the chieftain had found a scurrilous death threat under his cup. Many suspected that the man himself had planted the message. This new hero was too popular with the peasants and his fellow samurai for the chieftain to like him. The boy flung back his head and denied the charge, showing no sign of the terror and anger in his heart. Despite his innocence, he was ready to plunge the long knife into his own belly and rip open his bowels. Such shame could not be endured without remedy of *hara-kiri*! Others sprang to his rescue, revealing the chieftain to be guilty of skullduggery. Gifts of armor and jewels were heaped before the young warrior. Happiness surged beneath his breastplate, but his face remained austere: the gold-leafed brow of a Bodhisattva.

That was a good metaphor, Pip judged, and he paused to savor the thought.

"Among flowers the cherry is queen, among men the samurai is lord, among samurai Pip is emperor," the men shouted. Their trained samurai faces were masks of repose, but their hearts burned with ardor, sending up fume of incense and sparkles of fire.

The chieftain was led from the teahouse to jeers and recriminations. He was too cowardly for *seppuku*.

"That's okay," Pip told the crowd. "I do not want to see bowels spill from his shiny girdle. That would make me *sick*." Everyone knew the young lord was just being merciful to a scuttling chicken: a poltroon.

"You must rule us," cried the other samurai.

"And never," he told them, bowing low, "will I bring shame upon my followers and their noblewomen or their descendants."

"I shall kill him, the slithering slug," hissed a samurai. With his surprising hazel eyes and intense stare, he might have been the young man's brother.

"The merciful Buddha stay your blade," Pip cautioned. "Rudeness, a fat belly, and dishonor are his punishment. Cut off some protuberance, an arm or leg or some other, and call it a day."

A crowd of peasants trudged up, bearing baskets of rice as a tribute. He waved his hand and sent them home, still laden.

"Noble and wise," the peasants sang.

The ideal of the samurai shone in his thoughts as he let the men hoist—rethinking, Pip blotted out that picture. Surely a samurai would not let himself be bandied about like a schoolboy hero along the stones of jade and cloud! Instead, he bowed low, and then stood straight as a stem of bamboo, lifting one hand in blessing.

"Honor be upon us," he began.

A word penetrated Pip's dream. Someone was calling his name. He got to his feet. They called again. Children were being urged to the front of the auditorium. It seemed to him that he was, indeed, worthy of summons. Gifts were being presented before the chosen filed back to their seats, their manner excited. Clearly, they were not samurai. Pip would not profane his cheeks by showing feelings, a weakness which seemed as absurd and uncontrolled as if he took off his clothes and revealed naked buttocks. But there was something worthy in him, something bright and gold-leafed. It was deserving of notice, had been waiting years for reward. Putting the book in his pocket, he walked forward; the class murmured, and the sound of grateful peasants trembled against his back. The voice of the old chieftain could be heard. *Pah!* He kept on walking, all the way to the podium.

"I'm sorry, dear," the principal exclaimed. "There's nothing for you here. You'll have to sit down."

The boy eyed her chest, encased in a striped jacket, and touched the *Bushido* in his pocket. With a face as smooth as a stepping stone of jade, he floated to his class.

"You *idiot!*" Mrs. Ogrens leaned forward. Pip was not certain but thought her tone sounded exasperated. Perhaps angry. "That was for *Trip Battle.* Why would anyone be calling you?"

Trip Battle. Pip Tattnal. It all made sense now.

He looked at the teacher's thighs, encased in poplin. Black dishonor poured on his head—the pollen shaken from a rotten lotus, the disapproval of an obsidian Buddha. He was only a peasant, bringing dung for tribute, his heart sluggish and mired in humiliation.

Better to be in the Japan of a thousand years ago than here. His face stilled, calm as a camellia blossom. He let his eyes fix on a point in the air.

The peasants had tumbled pell-mell to the teahouse, their screams blunted by fog and the absorbent valley marshes. The old chieftain had stabbed the handsome young My Lord Pip, who lay bleeding on the cloud stones, the cries of peasants fluttering around his head in the shape of luna moths. How the poor samurai ached! The wound had broken open the chambers of his heart. Unhoused, blood without ceremony drenched the stars of moss between stepping stones.

In the background, snow twirled downward, the gingko trees shed their fans, and thousands of tallow chinaberries bounced on the beautifully striated leaves. Cicadas and katydids shrieked at the same hour. Tobacco bloomed in rice fields. A silkworm bit down on a cotton flower. All the tea in China and Japan grew as sweet as sugar cane. The hazel-eyed samurai closed on the old chieftain, hacking with brute strokes of the sword and the long knife.

Pip bent his face, not wanting to see the ugliness of the dead man, whose name he could no longer remember. *Fat Girdle? Souse Meat? Lard Slab?* Words were failing him, and black flies crawled across his vision. Was this, then, death? It was as sour and repulsive as the old bully's face. He wanted to slay its image, but when he reached for a sword his arm faltered, and his unscabbarded soul slid into the middle distance and he died.

Only through a child's dream of *Bushido* did he make it through that school day. In the afternoon he walked home along the river, and when he stopped to skip stones on the water, he failed, the stones falling with a plop to the muddy bottom.

He wanted to flee; he had the impulse to head for the train line and vanish. But a prior longing called him back to Roseville and the shack near the river, and he decided to stay. What desire kept him from going, he did not question.

"You're well shut of that dadgum female," Till told him, unfolding the card of final grades. "She wasn't up to you in the brains department, and you didn't know how to treat her. Don't guess I would either. She sure as shooting didn't know what to do with you, did she? Not one earthly idea. No more than a bare-butt monkey would know what to do with a peacock."

The boy let out a weak smile.

"You'll do all right. It's better to read and know things than to get along with idlers without a thought in their heads or with a female battleship like that one." Till rested a hand on his shoulder.

Pip felt a sudden desire to weep, though the reason was not clear to him. He wanted to go back to the days, almost a year ago now, when he flopped on the mattress and let a stranger tend to him as though he were tiny, unable to sit up without aid. He wanted to quit thinking about school and his classmates and getting along. He just wanted to be.

"Hey, look here." The old man cocked his head, angling for a glance.

Their eyes met, the child's gaze sliding across the brown eyes and away toward the river.

"Get on down to the water. It's summer and you're on the loose. Free as a doodlebug puttering in the dirt. Go fish and loll about and have you a high time. Forget about this harpy. Next year you'll get a new teacher, smart and sweet and pretty. I promise. You're going to do just fine."

Till watched the boy lope off before he turned to his bucket of tabby.

"I sure hope that's right," he said, rolling a ball of the stuff between his palms.

He could hear Pip calling for Clemmie to come out and play as if she were a girl and not a young woman with a husband and an infant in her belly. The old man wondered if they were all twelve years old to him, each one satisfactory insofar as they met his needs and desires—to romp, to be fed, to talk to somebody who would listen and not break in to interrupt the gush of thought. *That baby better watch out! Why, in the boy's mind, the poor little creature probably would be newborn going on twelve....*

"Pip, Pip," he mused. "You're a blessed wonder."

9

Pip risks another turn of the school year —
The wheel of months — a new inhabitant.

Belva Collins was Pip's teacher the next year, and she was everything that Till had prophesied. They all turned out to see her near Christmas, though they had not been summoned. Clemmie was as round and tight as a maypop, but she insisted on coming along. She did not like to be left at home, not when Bill was away with the CCC, saving his time off for a visit when the baby would be born. The three were waiting on the low wall in front of the school when the children spilled down the double stairs and onto the pebbled concrete walk.

"My teeth are all shook up." The Countess took a large mirror out of a pocket in her coat and examined herself. Lozenges of reflected light swept across the dirt yard before the school where a hired man was sweeping up a few live oak leaves with a broom.

"That's a rattling ride, all right." Till said, glad to rest. It was hard work to get all of them to school.

"Let's go on in." When nobody stirred, Clemmie pushed herself onto her feet. "I need me a drink." She pressed one hand to her belly.

The old man got up to hoist Casimiria onto her feet.

"Well, here we go, Miss Countess Cassie," he said.

"Where'd you put my car?" She looked as though she had been crying, but it was not that. "My dratted chariot. Oh, I'm just so old," she said fretfully, blotting her eyes on the soft flap of her reticule.

"Didn't you see me park it and come running, Princess? Look yon. Over there behind those weed trees. See? Little flash of red? Nobody'll bother it there." He spoke consolingly as if she were gripped by the loss of the precious vehicle.

Casimiria wavered as they approached the steps, and the other two took her arms and lifted her up, one at a time. At the top she looked back and let out a cry.

"All those to be got down again."

"Pip and me, we'll make a chair with our arms and tote you out in style," Till promised.

"Style? What style?" She was agitated, clutching at the door.

In the office they were given directions that the three began repeating and arguing over until a pigeon-breasted lady—in a shirtwaist with what Clemmie claimed "must be thousands" of tucks—pushed her chair back and led them to Pip's classroom.

"Here you go." The woman opened the door slightly and fluttered her hand at it, at once indicating that they should go in and shaking off her responsibility to them. Staring at the fingers, the Countess leaned forward so that it seemed she would topple.

They made no move to enter but watched her vanish back down the hall, their faces still. They were listening to the tapping of her heels and to the voice from inside the room.

"—and Tecumseh came to see the Red Sticks in 1811, and the Spaniards at Pensacola up and gave them guns. So that was the start of the Creek War. The Red Sticks went along the Alabama River and just plain old sacked and burned Fort Mims. They massacred most everybody in it. Then they ran amok all over that country—"

Excelsior winked at Clemmie, who had started to laugh.

"Pip, it's time to stop. Because it seems that I have guests."

To the surprise of the visitors, the story ceased.

"Beats all," Till whispered. "Beats all."

"Come on in, whoever's there." Belva Collins's voice was light, pleasing to the three paused at the door.

"I forgot you were coming." Pip sounded a little disappointed to Till, who knew that the boy never liked to be interrupted in his steady flow of talk, not when it was tales from history. And sometimes it was just about as hard to stop him as to halt the flow of time itself.

The teacher made him introduce each of them in turn. Pip made a grand flourish of presentation with each name as though he were a cavalier announcing a fresh and noble arrival to a queen. Casimiria enjoyed this ceremony immensely, bowing until the bunch of artificial heliotrope and roses on her hat trembled.

"Aren't you nice to come here to meet me," Miss Belva said, pouring each of them a glass of water from a pitcher on her desk but serving Clemmie first. "Especially you, Mrs. Shook. You must be worn out."

Pip wondered what she meant by "Mrs. Shook" for a moment; then the voices blurred and lapped at the edge of his consciousness. He was still thinking about the Red Sticks, but he smiled as he watched them chat, not because he was remembering the bad meeting of the year past and comparing it to this—when he put something aside, he put it aside completely—but because he felt suddenly content. Another boy might have been ashamed of the Countess or the retired trainman or even of the big-bellied girl, but the thought never occurred to him. The room brightened as if the sun had suddenly fallen a great deal closer to the earth, and the figures became indistinct in the light. Years later, he could remember almost nothing of that half hour except the Red Sticks, pounding along the riverbank, and how the teacher had touched him as if anointing him for a task.

Miss Belva stood up and rested a hand on the crown of his head. He could feel her fingers in his hair and the warmth of her palm. It woke him up, made him pay attention.

"He's a good boy," she said. "He's learned a good deal of grammar and arithmetic and done a lot of writing, though he has dreadful penmanship."

"He grips his pencil like a knife and grinds it into the paper." The Princess sounded gleeful, darting him a look to dare him into argument.

"Well," Miss Belva replied, "I try to get him to relax his hand and hold a pencil loosely."

"He's a house afire over history." Till raised his chin, looking her straight in the eye.

Miss Belva's hand drew back toward her face, sinking through her shoulder-length waves of hair. "I can't teach him anything he doesn't know about history. We've been studying some English history—he likes the old stories about battles with Viking marauders and chiefs and bards in the hall. I guess he has told you. We're very proud of him. Sometimes I let him climb up in the window seat and read behind the curtain because he's so fast with all his work, and he doesn't like the noise of the class. He reads the encyclopedia or a history book. I wouldn't dream of doing more than guide him there. He has been learning about Indian wars lately. You probably know that too."

"We surely have been dragged by the forelock up and down the Tallapoosa with the Creeks." Casimiria let out a remarkable cackle, a "regular egg-layer" as Till would have said had they been at home.

"I liked that story about Logan and those Ohio River Indians," Clemmie said. "Sad. The soldiers murdered his family. So he went rummaging the countryside—"

"You mean rampaging," Pip interjected, his attention lured by the subject. "Or maybe ravaging."

"That's a good tale," Till agreed. "That and how it fired up Lord Dunmore's War. And how old Thomas Jefferson hankered after what Logan said so much that he put it in a book. I'd never even heard of such. I like it when he says that part about Logan always feeding the white man. And his blood—what's that piece, Pip?"

"There runs not a drop of my blood in the veins of any living creature."

"Yes, that's fine, ain't it? Sounds so grand and dressed up, like an Indian in a storybook. I like the bit about turning away—"

"He will not turn on his heel to save his life," Pip quoted. "Who is there to mourn for Logan? Not one." Although Miss Belva smiled at him, Pip felt a pang, saying the words. Wasn't he another sort of Logan? Death had come and cut down his people.

"They killed his sister, and the men gouged her baby out of the womb and impaled"—he liked that word, *impaled*—it on a pole."

"Oh," Clemmie said, her voice faint. "I didn't know that part."

"The sense of a goose," the Princess exclaimed. She made a great show of digging in her reticule for a small fan, which she handed to the girl.

Miss Belva refilled Clemmie's glass with water. "Yes, he's a wonder on history." She glanced at Pip, watching him go dreamy and distant. "But sometimes he talks about a time when he rode the rails and how he might do some of that again. He needs to stay here, don't you think?"

"Well, he's welcome." Till shifted in the too-small child's chair, making it creak from the strain. "We've got the heart to keep him. But he's a freeborn boy. He'll up and do what he does."

"I reckon he'll keep with us," Cassie put in.

"Maybe he'll linger right on," Till added. "Or maybe that whistle will call him away if it's his shining time—I'm an old fireman, and that's what we called it when a locomotive is ready to head out. Sometimes I see him looking off when the trains are sounding so mournful at night, and I don't know what'll come. He's no ordinary child."

The Countess was sitting in a bright patch, her eyes closed, imagining the uncanny paleness of her tutor as he rose from the bathing pool, water sluicing from his back and thighs. As if lost but glowing years were drawing near, she felt heat resting against her skin, and Hamlet slowly turned his head until he met her secret gaze.

"Oh!" Her eyes were clenched shut.

A penny for the old lady's thoughts. The idea came to Pip, and he shrugged. *Two pennies for her eyes. That's what they used to put on the lids of the dead to weigh them down. And a coin in the mouth to pay Charon.* Like a girl in a fairy story he had read, from whose lips gold was scattered. That was a better coin on the tongue than one whose weight sagged the dead flesh. The ferryman would have her fee soon. She would be taking that ride ahead of the rest, the strange old

Princess-Countess with her reticule of lint—always heavy with some quaint item fished up out of the past. Out of some sea of lost time. She was almost gone, flashed away into the pages of a history book. Only he did not believe that one would ever record her unless he wrote it himself. Which was a funny imagining—him, with his ploughboy hands.

"A penny for your thoughts," Miss Belva said, and he looked at her, startled.

While he was dreaming, the afternoon light had become a pale gold, and as he looked across to Clemmie and Till and the Countess, they appeared costly and warm. A surge of feeling prickled his skin, and he reached a hand toward his chest. His throat ached, and he drew his breath in slowly.

"I feel—happy," he said in surprise. A breeze from the open window pushed at his hair and set the curtains to belling outward into the room.

That school year was simple in its plan, satisfying a desire for order in Pip. Monday through Friday rolled by, just the same. Then came a day when he could make a little money, laboring at a little country store. The walk, the work, the walk back: then there was visiting with the others, even with Bill when he was at home. Sunday came last, and that was remarkable because of the chariot. In the morning they walked to church, and he and Till would take turns pushing the old lady. Her car was nothing more than a faded red wheelbarrow, softened by a blanket and a purple cushion. The boy loved to set it jouncing on the dirt road while the Countess screeched bloody murder and gripped the sides.

"Offspring of Satan! Child of the powers of the air! Imp! Changeling! Block of wood on the devil's fire!"

Her imprecations, broken by the rough ride, only made him laugh the harder, until he slowed and finally lowered the handles and gave himself over to whoops of laughter.

"You hack like a demon! There's nothing natural about it! Whoever heard such a false and inhuman howl? Powers and principalities, help!" she hollered, waving her reticule in the air. "Clementine! Excelsior!" Eventually Till and Clemmie would catch up, and the old man would commence pushing in sedate fashion, paying no attention to her outcries.

"Bill, she enjoys every bit of it," the girl told her husband when he first glimpsed the strange scene, but it did not keep him from running after the barrow and catching hold of the handles, or from giving Pip a clout on the ear.

Her Royal Highness insisted on the vehicle's being stashed in a hiding place well away from church. It took two of them to grapple with her and set her feet on the ground without toppling the wheelbarrow or accidentally hiking her skirts so that her skinny calves and shanks were visible to the world. This dismount, too, was risible to the boy and a notable pleasure of his week. It was a good thing, for otherwise he might have refused to go to church and incurred Till's disapproval. Because he did not much like hearing somebody else's monologue, and he refused to sing, spending the entire time drawing at furious speed in a cheap unlined tablet. He covered each sheet with battle scenes: Indians and settlers under a rainbow of arrows; Beowulf attacking the monster Grendel, about whom he had read at school; English cavaliers tangling with Puritans; Arthurian knights jousting, viewed by cone-hatted ladies; or crusaders battling to rescue the Holy Sepulchre. He paused only when the round silver tray packed with minute glasses of grape juice was offered, but that happened rarely.

"The eye of the bee," he would intone as he hefted and passed it on. On his second visit to the church, the Princess had pointed out that the server looked like an insect's eye, and he always remembered the comparison.

He did not like grape juice, not the taste and not the faint smell.

"He's no Baptist, is he? For all that he was dunked in the Ohoopee." The old lady had said that to Till, her mouth screwed up at one corner and stained purple.

"He's a good boy."

"He ought to go join up with the wine-bibbers." Her voice was sharp, her long claws digging into the meat of Pip's shoulder.

He did not care. Whatever happened, he kept on drawing as though his survival depended on seeing through a peephole into history and a scene that then had to be rendered on paper. His figures were crude, his armies mere stick figures, but there was a curious vigor to the pictures, along with a lot of detail describing anything not human—weapons or animals or structures. After the call for repentant sinners to come forward after the final hymn, he would finish and tuck the sheaf under his arm. The pastor, Reverend Sojourner, was patient with him. Every Sunday he would ask to see what Pip had made this week, and they would stand at the door after everyone else had left while the boy explained his latest creations.

"You love history, do you?" the pastor had asked in a puzzled way when he first saw one of these drawings. "I heard that from Excelsior. God is in charge of human time, you know. The fulcrum of time is Christ on the cross."

Pip had nodded, eager to get on to the explanation, which over the months became one of the high points and rituals of his week. It was joyful, the walk there, the drawing, the talk, the trip home.

"It's all right," Reverend Sojourner had told Till. "Just let him come and do as he likes for now. Get him to illustrate some scenes from the Bible." Soon the pastor's study was covered with scenes of Roman soldiers and crucifixion, Israelite slaves before the pyramids, and the battles of Judah and Israel.

They were part of the rhythm of Pip's week. Few events marred the seamlessness of his days. The unscheduled time of vacations disturbed him, so he divided those days neatly between odd jobs and visits to the library. Notable days—birthdays, Christmas, Easter—he found enjoyable enough, but he had no patience for long celebrations, not even those in his own honor. The dinner to celebrate his thirteenth birthday, at which he received a new set of clothes, was bolted in the same manner as all his other meals. Perhaps the most disturbing and memorable day of that school year was the one, close to his own birth date, when Clemmie went into labor.

It upset all his usual calculations.

First she had felt too unwell to come to dinner, even though she ate with the three friends every night when Bill was not in town. This lapse disturbed Pip; he had gradually become used to her heaviness and no longer thought about it as a source of difficulty. After eating, he went down to the shack, but when she answered the door, she did not want to come outside. It was already dark, and the stars were sliding on the river, and Pip wanted to talk. So she came out "just for a minute," and they stood watching the smears of light on the surface while Pip told her about the battle of Chief Joseph in White Bird Canyon and how he led his people over the Bitterroot Mountains.

"Get away from me!" Clemmie pushed at him, and he stumbled backward, hearing a splatter of liquid on the ground. She squatted, one knee on the ground, and hoisted her skirts.

"What?" Surprised, he stared as a wash of fluid poured across the earth: once, again, and a third time it gushed and then pulsed more slowly and at last subsided.

"My waters, you ninny! Didn't you ever see a cow or a horse give birth?"

"That's not what I meant—I've never heard you talk so," he began.

She was breathing heavily, still squatting. "You help me get up off the mud right this instant, Pip. Run up to the house to let Till know. Then fetch who he says to fetch. Tell him not to worry about a message for Bill because he'll be here tomorrow in the afternoon. That's soon enough."

Her slip and skirt clung to her backside, and he saw blood on the toe of her shoe when he helped her inside and turned up the lamp by the door. The girl leaned on the bedstead and let out a quavering moan.

"Clemmie, are you all right?" He remembered how Mommer had died from a baby. People said it was modern times now, and things were better. He hoped it was so, but they had not done his mother any good. An edge of apprehension arrested him in his tracks.

"Go on! Or else you get to see a big-bellied woman with no clothes on." She shoved at him again. "Hurry! I don't feel so good."

At that, he slipped out and loped to Till's door, and before long he was racing down the road, his heart thumping. He stopped at the seventh house, a good distance away and set back in trees, and woke Mrs. Ruby Looner from a nap. Although he did not remember her in the least, she appeared to know him. He squinted at her, examining the narrow wire-bound glasses and the cloudy eyes, the unkempt curls hanging onto her neck, and the nose that looked sharp enough to poke into a good deal of other people's business. No. He did not remember her at all.

"I'll just go take a peek and see how Miss Clemmie is doing," she said, rummaging through a cabinet for her supplies. "See if she needs more than I can give, or whether we'll do just fine together."

After tossing a calico from its nest in stacks of cloth, she sifted through them, remarking only that "cats are a very clean animal." Despite this, she would not let the creature jump back up, crying "No, no, Tinible!" Pretending that nothing had happened to assault her dignity, the cat stared down the boy, her round eyes looking perpetually startled under long white eyebrows.

To Pip, the supplies seemed to be only big squares of cotton, with a waterproof liner stitched to one side. She filled a sack with them and pushed it into his arms, then began piling more into another. Tinible stalked away, tail in air.

"And I'll need my gauze and iodine." She counted off items on her fingers, and then clapped her hands. "Everything else is in my bag, so let's vamoose—the cats can take care of themselves while I'm gone."

The two of them headed down the lane, Mrs. Looner carrying a lantern and chatting volubly. He, on the other hand, felt stunned by the rapidity of events and by this new acquaintance.

"I haven't delivered more than two, maybe three babies since Mr. Looner died. I used to be the main one for babies around these parts for women who wouldn't have a man doctor about. There's not many left that want me—the doctors rule the roost. But once I was famous with the ladies, up and down the river. See these fingers?" She held up her hand, the thumb and little finger touching and the three remaining bunched together. "These fingers have been inside a judge's wife. And didn't she squall!

"I just had the best time, going about to deliver my babies and coming home to my sweet man. He'd bring me breakfast in bed after I was out all night. Sometimes I'd come in late, and there he'd be, waiting up with a pitcher of tea. And then Mr. Looner died and I just lost heart. Didn't get out of the house or eat or comb my hair. Him and me did every blessed thing together." She swung the lantern forward so that light flooded the treetops for an instant.

"The fire babies are popping out, quick as a wink. Just getting born. See up there? Just crowning and poking out their bright heads. Mr. Looner and me liked to promenade down the road and look at the stars."

Pip wondered if the two had ever delivered babies together. He was remembering Logan's sister, and he was thinking about the long groan he had heard as he left the shack by the water. The memory made him feel strange so that he wanted to throw down the cloths and race off through the darkness until he came to Clemmie's window and could peep inside.

"Was he a doctoring man?"

"Bless you, no; he worked in a hardware store. He was a slim small fellow his whole life, and he would just monkey up those ladders to the top and fetch down some tacks or screws of just the right size. Wink, and there he'd be, up on the ceiling almost. Blink, and he'd be down. It was the finest sort of a store, with drawers of every size and everything all filed away nice and orderly. He was the best employee Mr. Mason ever had, and nobody else knew all the contents of those little sliding drawers. 'To every thing there is a proper place and a season and a purpose,' he would say. *Ecclesiastes*, with a little Looner addition. He was a well-spoken man. And well looking, just as dapper and bright and dark-eyed as a chickadee."

Pip kept imagining Logan's sister's child impaled on a stick, and he slapped the side of his head to shake out the ill picture.

"Why—"

He fell into silence, unsure what it was he wanted to ask.

"Oh, he died of his heart. It just give out on him. He was always having trouble with it pit-pattering too fast." She sighed and walked a little more quickly. "Is that as smart a clip as you can travel?"

He lengthened his stride and matched her easily.

"I keep thinking about Chief Logan—"

"And who would that be?"

"Logan. Thomas Jefferson wrote about Chief Logan; he was famous."

"Are you talking about some kind of Indian?" Mrs. Looner cocked her head and scrutinized him, raising the lantern.

"Yes, he was a Creek."

"A creek? I have no earthly idea—whatever do you mean?"

"The name of a tribe—see, I was thinking about his sister because the soldiers came and butchered her and chopped the baby out of her belly and speared it and set it up for a warning."

Mrs. Looner's lips parted, and she came to a full stop, drawing her head back. "Well if that's not the most purely barbaric thing I ever heard! Stuck on a stick like a candy apple! A warning for what? And this was done by American soldiers? When did all this outrage happen? I never read about any such event in the papers."

"Yes, ma'am. At least they would be Americans in a few years because it was only 1774 when they—"

"That is just disgusting. And President Jefferson wrote about this man?"

"Yes—"

"Why are we at a standstill here? Let's get moving. We're almost there, I expect. You know, that tale really lowers Mr. Jefferson in my eyes. Virginia was always a trouble to the South, getting us into boiling-hot water and so forth. Belly-flopping into war before anybody else was ready. Hogging the presidential office when we had perfectly good men right here in Georgia. Thought they were the high-water mark of civilized people. Spreading such a tale! But Jefferson was smart, and maybe he knew the best. Bless your heart, Pastor Sojourner told me that you were just a bug for history and knew all kind of queer things about battles. But I never heard such barbarism in all my life!"

"The Indians did some pretty awful things," Pip said. "Some of them had the most ingenious tortures! Miss Belva says she expects they were people of great imagination because she'd never known how—"

"I believe you'd better not mention this misfortunate baby on a stick to Miss Clemmie." Miss Looner's tone was severe.

"She knows all about it already—"

"Oh, for sweet pity's sake! If that's not ridiculous, I don't know what is. Look, that's the place isn't it?"

"That's Till's light shining, but in a minute you'll—"

"Now, Master Pip, you and I will have to part company because I will not have a fellow with me in that bedroom. A woman's hinderparts are sacred. Or they are with me, anyway. And I will not be scandalized by the presence of a man. Not unless I have to make way for the doctor.

"But you come and visit me sometime at my house, and we'll have some iced tea and cookies, and you can tell all about these Indians because that certainly sounds curious. I never met an Indian or knew anything about them much. You just give me that bag, and I'll march down to the house by myself since I can see that they've left a lit lamp outside to mark the door. Very considerate, I must say."

She did not wait for him to respond but made a shooing motion with her hand as if he were a chicken.

"Now you all get on to bed, you and Mr. Till and Miss Princess Casimiria or whatever she calls herself. This ruckus could be all night and on into tomorrow, so you just go have yourself a nap, and when you wake up there might be a squalling newborn, or there might be some female shouts." With that, she bid him goodnight and left him gaping at the shack and the on-running river with its stars.

He meant to tell her that midwives were important back in medieval times, but she had run away with the conversation and left him lagging.

In the morning Pip woke and did not remember about the baby until he looked from the window and saw Excelsior standing in the city limits of Roseville, looking toward the river. He must have dragged the Countess out in her chair because she was seated nearby, facing the shack.

"Morning," Till called to him as he came outside, a cup of milk in his hand.

"You ever hear Apache war whoops?" Casimiria bunched up her mouth and nodded toward the water.

He could hear the cries now, loud and regular.

"Bloodcurdling is what that is. The pangs of Great-grandmother Eve being visited on her daughters." She scratched her nose with a long fingernail. "Of course if I had that old woman Looner tending on me, I'd be screeching just as loud and free."

"She ain't that old. Not yet." Till grinned. "She just out-talks you, Princess."

"Hah. She's got the gift of jibber-jabber, all right."

"It's quiet. Listen!" Pip could hear nothing but a mockingbird in a distant pine and the slap and splash of the river.

"Don't you worry until there's something to worry about," Till murmured.

But Pip was anxious, a piece of him tight and coiled. It felt so tense that he thought he might break inwardly. When a train sang out in the distance, he was surprised to find that he longed to go racing toward the tracks and leap onto a car and never come back.

"Clemmie." The name in his mouth surprised him—he hardly knew why he had spoken.

The three of them watched as Mrs. Looner came out with a blotched apron tied over her dress and hung some stained cloths on the clothesline.

"Come on—we're taking in visitors!" She was waving them forward.

They stood unmoving until she flapped her apron and shouted, "It's all right. Everything's fine."

"You run on," Till said. "I'll totter down with the Princess."

The boy looked away, wanting to go and yet wanting to stay, not wanting to see. But then the spring inside him came loose and he flew across the yard to the door and pulled it open by the flimsy tin handle. He passed through the tiny parlor and paused at the entrance to the bedroom. And there he saw a sight that has seemed sweet to men from the beginning of the world: the mother lying pale and near stillness with the newborn child on her arm.

"It's a girl, Pip," Clemmie told him. Her lips looked chapped and bitten, but she smiled at him. "I wanted a girl. I wanted whatever I'd get, but I wanted a girl most. You want to hold her? You'd be the first after me and Mrs. Looner."

He stared at the rose-colored face with its tiny features and wild, up-ended hair. The child's immense irises were fixed, perhaps on him. The boy felt unsure, having always been more secure with events that were written down than with the happenings right under his nose. And the stained cloths on the line had made him feel that he was entering a zone forbidden to his sex.

"I might—"

Mrs. Looner picked up the baby and plunked it in his arms. "There you go." She yawned. "That's a good-looking specimen of a child if I ever saw one. And I have seen a right many." She bundled some more cloths into a basket and carried them out of the room.

The boy looked over the infant. There were minute yellow polka dots on her nose, and a crust of blood in one ear. The eyes gleamed, round and dark. He could not remember when he had last seen a child so new. He put a finger against the rosy fist, and it grasped at him. The arm wavered, tugging his finger. After a minute he laid his cheek against hers and smelled the sweetness of her skin. Lifting his head, he gazed into her eyes. Her feet tapped against his arm, pedaling inside the outing blanket.

"You're alive," he told her. "All this time I forgot you would be real."

The morning sunshine swept across the room, touching the newborn so that she blinked and screwed up her face. He felt something in him go out to her, a feeling that widened in the light. The last of whatever had been cramped and coiled in him was unwinding and falling apart. Oh, this was—what? He had approached the crux of something, though he did not know what it was. He felt quite certain for a minute that something indefinable was close to him, almost on his tongue, some coin of meaning—something about life and how to spend it. Did the baby have some news for him from the world before birth? He felt strongly that he was about to remember something that he had once known and then forgotten. The sun shifted and slid across the room.

Yet he could not pin down the indefinable sense of news and answer even though he floated in its midst. He felt certain that the infant saw him completely with her wide eyes, perhaps that she saw him more clearly than anyone ever had, perhaps more than anyone ever would again. There was no mortal word that would not have shattered from the weight of what he was feeling—as if everything he was and everything he might be was at once seen and embraced and praised by the little creature.

"What do you say?" Clemmie was watching him, still smiling.

He glanced down at her and shook his head. He was not sure he could speak, and could hardly bear the idea that this feeling would wriggle away, out of reach. Then he would be drifting again, lured by every cry of a train, not quite linked to anyone, even to these people who had taken him in and cared for him.

"I don't know."

The baby's grasp tightened on his finger.

114

He lifted the newborn close to his face and whispered, "Where do you come from? Where are you going?"

He nodded as if acknowledging a claim on him before he raised her up toward the sunlight and said, "Welcome to Roseville."

10

Pip talks philosophy and history,
A smidge absurd, with Casimiria,
And in his pride lets go of happiness.

"When will you leave?"

Pip shifted the baby in his arms.

"Maybe next April."

Clemmie swung the lantern, making rings of light wobble, and snared the shining eyes of ground spiders. Searching for them was a favorite idle pursuit of hers in the summer and early fall evenings. Since Bill was gone, she often knocked at the door and invited Pip to join the hunt. She loved the jewel eyes that glittered under the oaks and pecan trees.

All afternoon Clemmie and Pip had been picking up fallen nuts from the dirt until their fingers were stained from the outer hulls and their backs were tired. The day before, he had scrambled up the trees and repaired crude ladders—slats screwed to the trunk—before shaking the branches with a long forked stick. It could be a dangerous job, but the nutmeats fetched a decent price in town. Today's labor was safer. The pair of harvesters tossed the nuts into bushel baskets. Almost all of the outer husks still remained on the tree like stiff flowers, but Pip had knocked down a branch studded with nuts. It would be the Countess Casimiria's green-nailed job to pry off the remaining hulls. Last, they would rake the yard with gallberry brooms until a sea of sandy waves lapped the island of Roseville.

Pip did not mind the work: he now thought that the only reason he had not left Mr. Tillman's house was Clemmie. The warmth he felt for Till and occasionally the Countess came only intermittently, and in between he subsided into a state where he lived half in a dream world, seldom paying any keen attention to those around him. He would be fourteen in January of the next year, and he had grown a great deal since arriving in Savannah. The measuring lines on the side of the Countess Casimiria's door marked 5'3½", 5'6", 5'7½", and 5'8."

Late in the evenings Till sent him to guard Clemmie and sleep on a pallet in the parlor. He stayed there for her protection almost every night because Bill was rarely home, still working for the CCC. Until he fell asleep, he thought about nothing but Clemmie in the next chamber, undressing next to the loom. Once he had seen her naked, seated on the edge of the bed with a pan of water close by; he had been seized and held in the doorway by rampant curiosity. With a rag she had scrubbed her face and neck, splashed water onto her hair, and soaped herself so that her pale skin gleamed in the dim room. Seeing her hair scrolled on her head, her hips wide, with the dark fretwork between her legs, he remembered what Bill had said, that his wife had the shape of a fiddle. And he remembered Herrick in the speckled book under the bed, how in a dream the clergyman-poet had turned plant and had covered a girl with randy tendrils before awakening to find himself "more like a stock" than a vine. Stepping into a tin tub, Clemmie had sluiced rinse water from the basin down her breasts and belly. Perhaps she saw him; he could not say, as he had not met her eyes.

Since then he had dreamed of her incessantly.

Being a Tattnal who had not been trained up and civilized by a mother, he knew no proper modesty about the changes in his body and promptly told the Countess and Till about his maturation, the wisp of new hair, the way his member surged "like a mighty mountain" when he woke in the morning. At this revelation the Countess cackled, but Till just looked at him with a faint smile and told him that he was becoming a man. Something, however, kept him from telling Clemmie. Decades after, he would laugh about the erratic manners of what he called his "barbarian youth," but he never mocked his passion for Clemmie, which had not diminished when she became pregnant by Bill or when she gave birth or nursed the child in front of him. Even though he had no intentions of creeping into her bed at night, he daydreamed endlessly about running his hands over her body.

In this he did feel guilty and disloyal to Bill, whom he continued to admire. Yet his imaginings made him feel oddly close to the man who had embraced and mastered and fertilized the woman he longed to touch. Bill was the fiddler and Clemmie his instrument, but Pip was the artist and dreamer of a thousand fantasy nights. Perhaps this gap in his usual moral rigidity was as much due to the memory of old Gilead as to his desires.

He knew a lot about the couple because Clemmie could not read, and it was left to him to render Bill's letters out loud. For some months he carried one in the pocket to his jacket:

My darlin Clemmie,

The camp is just gettin emptier and emptier. A lot of the CCC boys were sent home last week, and I don't know how much longer therell be work for me. Theres a lot of empty beds. I tell you, I sure am tired of planting this ol ugly kudzu creeper. Its just about the most dull thing they give us to do. How can they call us Roosevelt's Tree Army when what we're planting is Japan kudzu? I'd rather girdle trees and chop. Anyway, Im sure sorry to be plantin so durn much of it. I told my foreman I wanted to go back to stone work because I beleve I could make me a livin when times are better from walls and bridge abutments. Now theres a job worth the doin.

I miss you very much and when I get home next we will have us a frolic for the week and make the Countess and the Page Boy wait on us.

Your lovin husband Bill

When a letter came saying that Clemmie should join her husband during the coming summer because he had found a place for her and the baby with a family, Pip was dismayed. He faltered in reading the lines, and he thought about lying. But what he felt to be right pressed on him so hard that he yielded up the words.

Bill's request was what had made him abruptly say that he too would be leaving. He looked at the baby in his arms, realizing that he might never see her again. He scrutinized the face, the fine eyelashes and the lids that looked moist and slightly shiny, the upturned nose, the cheeks and lips of a deep coral, the skin with its faint sheen.

"Here," he said suddenly, holding out Lanie.

Clemmie put down the lantern and gathered the child, who twisted her head and yawned, settling back into sleep.

"What will they do without us?" she asked, looking toward Till's house and the low roofs of Roseville.

It was not something Pip had considered. The two would just go on being themselves, he expected, Casimiria as the Countess-Princess residing in the stuffed chair that emitted a peculiar fug composed of the odors from dried flowers, unwashed royalty, cloves, dog pee, scented powders, and mothballs. Excelsior Tillman would keep on building the fabulous city, Roseville, matching its progress to a dream in his head.

"Where will you go?" she continued.

"California, I expect." He meant to be nonchalant, but he had never learned to control his own face, any more than he could read the moods of others. He was always grandiose in his expressions— his shoulders sagged, and his voice held all the weariness that a thirteen-year-old could muster.

She begged him to stay. When he shook his head repeatedly, she reached for the lantern.

"Don't you want to look for more spiders?" His voice quivered.

"I'm too sad. I'm going in."

For a long time Pip stood there in the dark, gazing over the Savannah River though he saw nothing, not a boat slipping by, not a smear of light on the softly moving waters. Somehow he had churned up everything so that now it seemed he had to go. He had not meant to depart, the boy told himself, but had planned to stay and help Clemmie and Till with the Countess and the chores and the pink toy city until he became a man.

He had imagined that Bill might die in the course of things and that he could marry the widow and be the father to baby Lanie. Yet he liked his neighbors; it was not that he wished any sorrow on them. He liked the way that Clemmie's husband was always in high spirits when he came home, the way he'd race whooping from the river to Till's door, the way he called Pip *squire* or *knight* or *page* to go with Casimiria's titles. But in his dreams, Bill had to fade away. He had pictured himself reading the news, consoling Clemmie for the death, showing his loyalty—he felt himself to be utterly loyal—by caring for the child.

After the proper time of mourning had passed (he was not sure what that length would be, but he thought at least a month), he would kiss her under the moon, beside the onward-flowing Savannah, and he would put his hand inside the top of her dress and feel her breasts and press his mighty mountain against her until she clutched him and swooned. Then he would ask her to be his wife, and she would say "yes." They would marry; in his imaginings the ceremony always took place immediately. Till and the Countess Casimiria would be witnesses. A preacher would be called, and he would wed them in the streets of Roseville beside the Cathedral, and Pip would hold Lanie as mother and child looked adoringly into his face. Then the Countess would take the baby back to her chair with its exquisite funk—this never failed to put the child into a slight stupor. And he would lead Clemmie back to her bed where he would slowly peel away her clothing until she shone in the dark room. The rest of his fantasy was not unknown territory to Pip, as he had seen a number of couples, white and black, making sexual hay in the fields and woods near the orphanage. He knew a good bit of what could be done with his mighty mountain. What he knew was enough to go on, for a start.

But now he understood that nothing like that would happen, for Clemmie belonged to Bill and Bill to her, and he had no part in their plans. It was another loss, with no word of comfort from anyone. He shoved a hand in his pants pocket and brushed his fingers along the lip of the conch plucked from Otto's grave. How had Otto's passing and his grief been acknowledged? A few hours of unrest at the Orphanage, a wedge of pie, a grave marked by this shell. A jag where calcium had been crimped and laid down stingily by the little gastropod caught on his skin, but it could not hurt the scar tissue on his fingertip. It had bled too many times to ever bleed again. He no longer thought that Otto's soul dwelled in the little horn, but the echo of that idea lingered.

Whenever a blow was struck to Pip's young life, he thought of Otto: Otto was always the original wound, the first he could remember with great clarity. The sharpness of his memory of the event came about because he pressed it deep into himself by reviewing its features again and again until the least flake of fire from the dawn, the least gleam of an insect's back, the least eyelash fallen onto Otto's cheek stood out, each element separate in its fateful place.

The morning after his talk with Clemmie, Pip woke up determined to finish out the year and go back to the rails. As soon as he received his eighth-grade diploma, he would be gone. By then, he would be fourteen, a man, or close enough.

"Don't you think you better stick here a while?" Till asked.

Pip's eyes were on the road winding through a grove of live oaks hung with moss.

"No sir," he said, "I told Miss Clemmie I would send her a postal card from California."

"There's no hurry in that, is there?"

"I promised."

"There's a plenty of years ahead of you. Wait till you're eighteen or nineteen. It's not far off."

"It's far to me."

"Well, we'll be missing you, but I guess an old man oughtn't to try and teach a spry young mule to outgrow stubborn ways," Till said, and he went back to grinding oyster shells.

It took a while for the words to sink in, and even after they did, the boy turned them about in his mind, testing one way and another as he trudged through the moss-hung tunnel toward school.

"Fortitude," he pronounced. "It ain't stubbornness."

Telling the Countess was a bit trickier.

"You don't want to be westering," she told him, straightening on her throne. "It's still wild out that way. That's so far from Europe, it's practically to China. Why would you want to go on a harebrained jaunt like that? You don't have the gold fever, do you?"

She dug around in the cushions and unearthed a decomposing photograph album, the black pages gone soft and half the pictures slipped free of the glued corner mounts.

"Here; you see here," she ordered. "Wait just a minute. See this?"

She held a large brownish photograph on heavy card stock.

"See that little squirt in galluses and rubber pants? That's my Uncle Cas. Don't he look the Gold Rush idiot with his pick and shovel and tin pan? Thought he'd make a fortune, didn't he? So cocksure of himself. Took a ship from Charleston in 1848 and never came home again. Thought he had a lone good idea, but when he got to California, here came Chinee, Aussie swagmen, islanders from the Marquesas, fellows from England and France and Germany and Spain and Holland, trotting in behind him. Gold-fired fools, with one idea lusting in their heads."

"Did he get rich?"

"I believe he did, but not from gold." She paused, staring intently at the photograph as if to fix the memory of him, and raised one trembling finger. "It was the moving picture business."

Pip made an anguished face, and the old lady jumped.

"What's that conniption look for?"

"Movies weren't even *invented* then, Miss Casimiria. In the encyclopedia at school, it says that Thomas Edison's peep-show Kinetoscope went on display in New York City in 1894." Rolling his eyes, he groaned freely and with some verve. "In 1895 Louis and

August Lumiere achieved screen projection in France; Robert Paul, in England; Thomas Armat, Francis Jenkins, Woodville Latham, and various others in America."

Restlessly stirring the potpourri that was her chair, the Countess frowned.

"So you see," pursued the boy, "he couldn't possibly have been in the movies because *he would be too durn old*." This last he said in a shout so that the Countess bounced in her seat, releasing a complex, pungent odor.

"He would have been even older by the time the nickelodeons opened up. The first theatre was the Electric Theatre in Los Angeles, owned by Thomas Tally. The second was Castle Theatre in New Castle, Pennsylvania, begun by Harry Warner and his brothers. The third—"

"Enough of your freakish recitations! You just don't know my family. The descendants of Casimir Pulaski—Count Casimir Pulaski—are invariably handsome, and they keep their fine forms long after others fade away. They don't grizzle and droop. There is a touch of the vampire about them, I'd say. In jest." She grimaced to signal a joke. "My Uncle Cas traveled to Chicago and Philadelphia to make his first movies, and I believe he once took a ship to France at the behest of Adoph Zukor. He was in a movie with the great Sarah Bernhardt. And *Birth of the Nation*. I'm quite sure he had a number of roles in that one."

"Did you ever see him?"

"Yes, all the time when I was a little girl. My mother would take me to the theatre and point him out to me. 'There's Uncle Cas,' she'd say. 'Isn't he beautiful? The hair on that man, the eyes!' Of course, they made him up for the movies; we all knew that."

"But you"—and here Pip's voice flew into a shriek—"*were a little girl before the movies came out!*"

"Look at you—just a lad and such a historian," the Countess countered. "It's very provoking. You and your pranks of memory. They're outlandish! All right, Master Pippin, so I wasn't a little girl.

So it was about twenty-five years ago. So what? I saw him in all those movies just the same, and my mother was alive to point him out. Can I help it if we Pulaski family members maintain our vigor? Other people would like to be movie stars in their seventies and eighties, I tell you—they just don't have the freshness and shine for it. They don't have the blood of Casimir Pulaski firing their veins, that's the trouble."

Fishing in the crack between the seat cushion and the arm of the chair, she retrieved a crumb-strewn discolored mirror with filigree frame. As she peered into it, Pip caught a flash of wrinkles and dark eyes in the glass.

"How old *are* you?" he asked.

"That's not a polite question to ask of a lady, and I am a lady. However, I will say that some years back when the First Baptist Church gave an award to the eldest person in the congregation, they found me to be a not inappropriate recipient. Three of us claimed to be over a hundred, but I was honored above the rest."

"That doesn't make any sense," Pip complained, considering the story of Uncle Cas, the movies, and what he knew of the Countess.

"Dear boy, so often it seems that life is not reasonable. How did I get to be so dreadfully old? We are grass, our lives fleeting, our golden morning lasting no longer than the yellow flower head of the dandelion that runs to seed and which some passing child plucks and blows upon, scattering all its silver threads." The Countess paused, her arm trailing gracefully along her shrunken breasts. "Go on, get us the Herrick and read a bit of poetry, will you? And what was it you were going to do out west?"

"I'm going to work. I'll move around with the seasons. A man told me that the farmers need people to harvest cotton and wheat and apples."

"Well," she said, her eyes drifting toward the next room where the Herrick moldered, "gather ye rosebuds while ye may, I suppose. The peasantry must pick, and the Countess, too, when times are bad."

Come early June when Pip was to abandon his friends, Clemmie and the baby were still living in the shack near the water. Bill was to come for them in a few days, and they would head to the mountains. Till made a grand outing of the boy's departure. He borrowed a horse and wagon from a man who lived down the road in exchange for a big tabby jardiniere. The planter looked like an immense crown, and the maker abused it for ugliness, saying that he would not have such a monstrosity in his own yard. But the fellow with the horse was pleased. He and his sons helped carry the Countess's throne into the yard and load it onto the wagon bed.

"Faugh!" one of the sons exclaimed, "something dead in that chair," and the father shushed him. He was clearly an ex-farmer, his pants hitched up high and the hems cropped well over his brogans.

While Clemmie stayed in the bed where she could watch the baby and keep the Countess from toppling off her perch if they came to a sudden halt (now and then they did, moving aside for a car), Till and Pip rode on the seat. Along the way they paused to eat a picnic of ham biscuits, washed down with sweet tea. The ex-fireman knew exactly where they were going—a crossing not far beyond a water tower where the trains stopped and there would be no yard bulls to threaten a boy bound for the West. A handcar seesawed past while they sat in the shadow of pines to talk. Pip found it hard to conceive that the moment when he was going away had almost arrived.

"It was a pretty ride out here. If you want, I'll carry you back home again," the old man told him.

Pip jerked his head. "No."

"In case we don't meet again in this world, I want you to know that we enjoyed having you with us," Till said. "And I also want you to be sure that you're welcome to come back any time. We ain't got much, but I guess having little makes it that much easier to share."

Clemmie lifted her chin, tears in her eyes.

"Why don't you tarry?" she whispered. "Wait and see Bill. Why don't you stay on and help Mr. Till and Miss Casimiria? They'll sure miss you."

The baby's eyes were black marbles; mouth ajar, she looked from face to face.

The Countess snored in her plush cushions.

As he thanked Excelsior Tillman, Pip was not sure what he felt— less than he should, he suspected, though he knew a loss could be felt more deeply as time went on. A certain dislocation set in, and his hands seemed to do their work of tying and shouldering the sack without direction from him. Despite the picnic, his belly felt like an empty cave in which something flickers wildly in a remote corner. He could see the far-off smudge that meant the train with his name on it was approaching, and he jumped from the wagon. *Rubber legs*, he thought, remembering the old man's long-ago talk of shoveling coal. Clambering after him, Till stood with a hand on the horse's head as the distant whoop of the whistle made her feet shuffle and her ears prick up.

Clemmie leaped with the baby in her arms, stumbling a little as she landed so that Pip reached out to steady her, and she flung an arm around his neck. He breathed fast, could smell the sweetness that was nothing but Clemmie and a trace of the bar of soap she kept on the windowsill.

"Come down to the track?" he asked her, and she smiled.

As they hurried across the field, the train sang out a staccato warning song to some heedless creature on the tracks, and Pip could see the black spoor of smoke on the sky. In his very flesh he could feel the pistons pounding forward, jarring the earth with their thrust. His heart seemed to be hammering with them, his pulse jumping as the train poured its length forward, clattering along the line, and suddenly he longed to be on the road—not alone, he realized, but with Clemmie, the throb of the engine propelling them forward, the thrump of the train drumming against their bones. His mind lit up and flamed with a dream of clean straw and Clemmie glowing in the dusk of a boxcar, with the baby nested in hay while the powerful engine thrummed the rails and battered the dark and cleaved the air, striking forward with its coupled cars in all its thundery glory as the steam whistle shrilled. Oh, he was a boy, and his desires were as plain and simple as the cartoon picture of a train shooting into a tunnel: to lunge in the rocking boxcar gloom against her white thighs, to force his mighty engine inside her secret recesses, to penetrate with splintering sparks, bolt forward, drive home with all his unspilled cargo—

Stillness had come over the world; the train had been checked in its flight and was taking on water.

"Come with me," Pip whispered, the idea so new and bright and large in his mind that he never thought to hold back the words, any more than he could think to keep the orb of sun from cresting the horizon at dawn. He had grown another inch in the past month. He bent down and kissed her on the mouth, and under his hand he felt a flutter at her throat.

Clemmie laughed and then kissed back, pressing against him until the baby squalled and she drew away.

"Come with me." The words seemed potent and magical, like what he had imagined back in the Emanuel Primitive Baptist Church as Preacher Bell described the peal at the world's end when souls would be threshed from their husks. Would it be so different from the two long whistles that meant the brakes had been released and the train was moving?

A black thunderhead sprang from the chimney. And at once Pip understood that this was what he had been meaning for years: *Come with me.* Had he known all along that the three of them would be standing by the train, that he would draw Clemmie by the sheer force of his own wish, and that they would swarm, laughing, into the shadows of an empty boxcar? They would be a family, flying across the flatlands, feeling the earth swell under their heels and break from the plains in mountain surges. It was not anything to do with Bill; it was about *Pip.* In the light of his rapture of need, her earlier bonds looked wrong and weak, would crumble to dust and drift across abandoned farms like ghosts exposed to the dawn.

He could see the double-headed engines now, black boulders crowning a rockslide barely held to the groove of track as it eased to round the curve—then the train was upon him, the rumble quickening and the whistle crying the crossing signal of two long notes, a short, and another long that seemed to pluck at his skin, alerting every inch of his body. The lead engine shot past, the engineer and fireman towering above him, sparks from the wheels zinging onto his pants legs like beetles of fire, but he did not stop staring at Clemmie, who was laughing again but not shaking her head. For once in his life, he was locked onto a woman's eyes, her pupils widening to take him in. He grabbed her hand and began to race alongside the train, the baby shrieking in bursts like a small steam whistle. When he leaped for the boxcar, Pip made it easily, but their hands uncoupled, and he shouted at Clemmie to hurry.

She did start after him, lifting Lanie as if she would throw the child into his arms.

Then, calling "goodbye, Pip, goodbye," she stood stock still. She shouted something else he could not hear and waved vigorously. He swung outward, one hand in the air. The landscape widened, and Clemmie shrank; he could see the fields and the road with the wagon and the horse, Till steadfast by its head but not waving, and on the wagon a purple blot that was the Countess. Near the scratch lines of the tracks Clemmie was so dwindled that he could not tell where the baby left off and she began. When the color of her skin and dress flattened and blurred into the color of dirt and fields and she was lost utterly, he still did not turn his head away. Only the shift and swerve of the tracks could make him do that. Soon there was nothing to be seen of wagon or throne or the farm through which he had passed, toting a baby in his arms.

Now he felt what it was he had grasped for an instant. This midday grief was like steel at his throat, cold and hard. It was not a daybreak sorrow; no one was dead. He realized that he was not breathing, and so he leaned from the clattering car and drank at the wind. He could feel his hurt spread out, westering, feel it pour across the seas of grass and dash itself against the flanks of mountains. Pain surged across the continent, past the divide, and sopped the whole world with itself. As he suffered its outflow, he did not remember the girl at all. He was not thinking of the line of her brow or the curve of her back bent in the tin tub.

Loneness bore down. He was the bird that crosses the watery face of the sea and finds neither branch nor rock on which to rest. He recalled neither Clemmie, walking over the spring rows with Lanie in her arms, nor the Countess, sprawled and snoring on pillows, nor Excelsior Tillman, seating himself on the wagon box. He did not consider Clemmie's husband, Bill, or the wrong he had almost done to someone who had been kind to him. He could think only of himself, bereft, absolutely alone except for the conch in his pocket and nothing of Otto trapped in its whorl. He gripped the shell until his palm bled.

It was simple, all about him, from beginning to end.

No one contradicted him in this thought, for the car was barren as a deserted stable. Like a golden manger a single bale of straw, warmed by a shaft of sun from the open door where Clemmie might have alit with the baby. He kneeled down on the boxcar floor that appeared to be alive because of the throbbing like a heart underneath but was not. He leaned forward, and he cried for a long time.

11

In which the heart of an Opal is glimpsed,
All glittery with veins of fairy fire.

Maypops were growing along the line, but Pip did not notice. He was hunched close to the tracks in a spatter of pebbles and the stink of coal smoke. The boxcars jerking and squealing at the curve might have been meant for an evil destination, their steel rails the slick road to hell.

He was leaning toward the cars, his hand not yet out to brush the metal, almost as if he might collapse under the driving wheels. A girl came by, and he registered her presence without looking, knowing which one of his current pack she was by the color of hair and the white oval of face at the corner of his vision. He smelled her skin, the peculiar mixture of filth and tar and sweet powder that identified her more clearly and which he liked. In an olfactory way, he was well suited for a life on the tramp. He did not listen, though she was speaking, pressing against his arm, wanting something he did not recognize because he was not paying attention; his mind had gone junketing elsewhere. Restlessness had flared up in him the night before, and he was giving in to the urge. It was already a pattern with him, the weariness with the people or the work or the place and then the desire to shove off to a better world.

She shook him by the shoulder, lifting a hand toward his face, laughing.

"What is it?" After a moment, he turned his head to see.

"It's a passionflower, Pip." She knew his name though he could not recall hers.

Between her fingers was a single blossom, twirling like a lady's parasol—all furbelow and fringe.

He stared as if he had never seen such a wonder before. The girl brushed against his arm as he took the offering, and a curly tendril caught around his thumb. The bloom was startling in the purity of its petals, the richness of purple corona filaments, the strange shapes of the stigma. The saturated colors satisfied him, pleased him, but there was more.

Lost in the trickling words of the migrant, beneath the clash and rumble of the train, he heard another voice and other words like the tune of a distant stream.

The oval resolved into another face, that of a woman kneeling on the ground, her hand pointing to a passionflower. He remembered a white dress, slender arms, and an odor of violets from a white box stamped with purple and gold. Light and warmth washed over him. He shut his eyes and recalled the raked sand of the yard and the broken maypops on the vine with green and yellow seeds shining in a glue of sap. He was wearing a single boot, much too big. That was to smash the fruit, to hear its loud retort. Otto was lolling against his mother. He too wore a white dress, and Pip smelled the truth of him, the little boy's stamp of sweet earthiness and urine. The memory was a single rightness, plaited together from the look of his mother and the scents and the rise and fall of her voice explaining what the passionflower meant.

And Otto was there next to him, barely more than a toddler but palpable and warm, absolutely his blood and his brother—the mother wrapped her arms around the two of them and made no difference between them so three were not separate but one, the beginning and the end of security and joy. It was everything that he had been wanting for a long time, and so he stood with the stem bruised between his fingers and his eyes tightly closed until the last sense of their presence drained away into the earth, until the train with its bruit and body heat and peppering stones was gone, even its last hint of notes swallowed by distance.

When he opened his eyes, the clods of coal by the rail bed looked unfamiliar, clinkers rained from the moon. The girl was far away, trudging along the line. He touched the rivulets of tears and rubbed away the telltale marks.

"Tracks." His own voice and word startled him.

In the lull after the memory departed, it came to him that this was all, that there was an utter randomness at the foundations of the world, and that only a few stray moments of beauty and intensity shone in a cold and ever-widening space. In its precincts could be found the murk of cruelty and evil and the cold boredom of pre-dawn mornings squatting in frozen scrub next to steel and sleepers. All he could hope for was enough stars to illumine a way.

He vowed that he would live in the abandonment of that night; he would not let the shadows win, would not let them devour him as they had eaten Otto. His hand went to the conch. An old man had drilled a hole near the lip of the shell in exchange for cigarettes, and it was now a crude pendant, threaded on a doubled-up line of string.

"Light," he whispered. He would collect, slowly and laboriously, a sufficient radiance. He remembered the pink walls of Roseville, Clemmie with a woven rainbow around her shoulders, the old man's voice saying "Look here, son" as if he belonged.

It would have to do.

It would be enough to go on. Perhaps even one restored memory of happiness could be enough: could make him strive to piece together a life.

The flower dropped from his fingers.

"Hey," he shouted to the girl, "wait—wait a minute." She halted, one hand on her hip, and he began to gallop awkwardly, his arms high and stiff against his sides.

He had not really looked at her before, not in the eyes, and was surprised when he did. Because she was not a girl. Pip was a boy by the numbers, but she was close to thirty.

"You're married?" He touched the hoop of gold on her left hand, and she twisted off the ring and slid it onto her other hand.

"He died," she told him. "He died on the road. I buried him under an apple tree. It was more than a year ago."

Pip thought maybe she was teasing about the apple tree; most of the dead ended up in pauper's ground. He said nothing. But he followed Opal to the grain belt, and in the evening after a day's harvesting while a group talked around the bonfire, she came and sat by his side.

Taller than she if not older, he found the boldness to put his hand on her wrist. It was golden in the light, not the color of a sheaf of wheat but a lamp-lit paleness that belonged indoors. He could feel her pulse ticking, hear a cricket chirping in the stubble.

In an instant of turmoil he remembered the slice of peach pie and the parson with the tree of yellow presses singing out, "How you like them peaches, Miss Versie?" A rebellious anger at the preacher surged up and spread even to the fruit that he had never really shared—he had eaten a slice of Mr. Jimmie's pie but had not tasted it. Even just after licking the plate, he could not remember one mouthful that had tasted of peach. It was as lost as his old happiness; it was as denied as respite from pain. Where was the peace and rest that he had glimpsed at the bottom of the rickety-sided well? Wasn't his world a landscape like a furnace of burning darkness, without one tendril of the hope that comes to all? Well, then, he would be damned; he would taste pleasures that might be a reason to live. There was nothing but *now* for him anymore, no goal or dream of the future, and no guide but his own desires.

"Hey, kid—your name's Pip, ain't it?" The little man was talking to him, a fellow he had seen rocking from side to side as he walked in the fields. His legs were stretched out in front of him, bowed and wrapped in rags.

The boy turned as in a dream, the veins and nerves in his body all alight.

"Me and my friend Joe, we met a lady down South—you're from that way, ain't you?"

"Course he is. He talks like it, don't he?" The friend's voice creaked like an unoiled gate, all corroded metal.

The bandy-legged man cuffed his companion.

"Anyway, see, there's this lady who helps the 'bos. People hump themselves hundreds of miles out of the way to get her feed. There's marks that say a nice Christian lady is close by, right on a boundary stone by the tracks. She gives a hot meal to anybody who'll spread the word that she's looking for little brother Pip to come home."

The boy was still holding Opal's hand, and he looked into the fire as if for an answer.

"That's never me."

"She's a fine woman," Joe gasped out.

"I ain't forgotten that meal or what we owe that lady. She's about the best one we've met."

"That's right," Joe said.

"You know what she told me? She said that she prays every night for her brother to come home, and she feels words going out on the rails like night trains."

"Huh." Joe leaned back, staring at his friend. "Ain't *that* a glory road."

The mesh of Pip's nerves tingled. He spared only a moment to think of this woman and her prayers, crisscrossing America at right angles, multiplying her wish until it had flown a quarter of a million miles of rail through swamps and mountains and plains, tangling with the spider webs of city train yards and resting at sidings. That pure petition hummed in the line, blessing the metal—the way the rails sometimes sang like a struck tuning fork when a train was on the way. In Oregon and New Mexico and Maine, her wish was trilling in the steel. He saw the truth of it because his whole being had become a kind of continent flashing a single piece of news on its lines of nerve and blood.

"She says that every night after she prays, she knows in her marrow that he's going to come home. She says the Lord God heard her plea."

"Maybe it's you," Opal whispered, but she clung to his hand as if to keep him.

"It's not me," Pip murmured. "Nobody ever heard my pleas, nobody but you."

"Joe, I believe that woman. I ain't never met somebody so set on what she wants."

Joe attempted to answer, shuddered, and reached a hand up to his throat.

"It's not me," the boy said with firmness. "I don't have any brothers or sisters. I don't have anybody in the world that would be looking for me."

"And you the first 'bo we ever met named *Pip*." The short fellow leaned forward and rubbed his legs. "Damn floaters never get a pinch of luck. Would've give me some hope in things to find him. You sure that ain't you? Around fourteen years old—"

"Maybe we *did* find him, and he won't say. Ever think of that? More fool him." After this speech, Joe spat into the fire and lay down, fingers curled protectively around his throat. He was long and narrow, a curious-looking friend for the little man with the shrunken legs and heavy torso.

"You feeling all right, Joe? Say, Joe—"

The voices around the fire slid away. All Pip's thoughts were gathered and reaped: there was nothing in his mind but Opal and the pallor of her wrist with the little blue vein flicking across—he tightened his grip and claimed her for his own. A surprising power burns in the demands of a boy who has seen and known too much.

Her dead husband under the apple tree made no protest. Already he was nothing but bones, shreds of cloth, hair glued to a skull. The blackness of the universe, with which Pip was already acquainted, made no comment. The earth trembled slightly under his feet as a train swooped forward, ten miles off.

For days he had been sleepwalking along the wooden ties, feeling detached and ghostly. Suddenly the world slipped into place and was again genuine, and the connection between him and Opal glittered in the air like the lace of a quarter-million miles of steel track, the paired rails racing side by side over into valleys once jammed with men dreaming gold as they gouged a pickaxe into the hip of earth. Lines shot across the continent, gripping down and holding North America in her place on the shifting seas.

"Come on," he said, "let's go for a walk."

Strange that Opal, being his elder, did not guide him that evening in the wheat. He was the one to lure her out of the firelight to a place near the camp where the grass rippled in the prairie wind, the blades so green and narrow and soft that they seemed to curl against the ground. Pip led her to a crooked elbow in the creek as cottonwood leaves pattered in the prairie wind. As if it were a thing he had done a thousand times before, he husked away her clothes and stood naked and bold, his manhood standing like a mighty mountain...

"Lie down with me," he said, the rapid flick of her pulse tapping out a message against his hand.

Along the creek the cottonwoods spilled their seed into the air. The tufts caught on the long ribbony grass or flew toward the full moon as he buried himself to the hilt, slaying his virginity in short, sharp strokes. When he raised himself to look at her, a mist swept across her breasts and sailed into the air.

"Like troops of prairie fairies," Opal said. She kissed her lover's neck.

Grain hulls were in the hair that he heaped with a crown of cottonwood silk. The extent of him, heel to pate, wanted to split open; a slick trail of semen shone on her inner thigh. She smiled at Pip in a way that Gandy had told him migrants smile, her eyes unchanging and serious. He peered at her in the moonlight. Was she the first woman he had truly seen since Clemmie's hand loosened in his and the train jerked him west? In that instant, he felt it to be so.

"You're—really beautiful," he told her. It wasn't exactly what he meant, but it would serve.

"You," she whispered, sliding her hand across his chest, which was tougher than any boy's body had the right to be, locking in a heart that seemed to be jumping out of a thousand boxcars at once.

"What's the shell?" She held it on her palm.

"That's Otto's." He gave no other explanation, pulling the cord over his head and dropping it in the grass.

He was not much of a child; he had almost forgotten how to play.

"Again," he demanded, pinning her to the earth. Streamers of seed clung to her arms like wings.

Although few men could have broken his grasp, Opal wriggled and laughed and raced splashing into the creek, and he followed. Cottonwood seed clung to her damp back. In the whirling air he groped for her as in a maelstrom, and she seemed entirely cloud before she plunged under the water and let the seed slide away on the current. Her pale side flashed like the gleaming scales of a fish as she fled from him, diving into the fishing hole.

"Opal, stay with me," he cried.

She surfaced, her hair clinging to her neck, face smooth and shining and quizzical, and for an instant he remembered Otto shouting as the face of a river otter peered at them from the Ohoopee. That night Pip's sperm floated like milt on the water with the silks of the cottonwoods; the next day they were both scraped and sore from the stones in the stream.

In the evenings through the harvest, they lay together under the trees, although Opal sometimes fought against it.

"You're too young," she told him.

"I've been like a man since I was a little boy," he replied. "They never let me be."

"It's wrong, our sleeping together." She would look at him with an expression he could not master.

"But it would be as wrong to be apart," he would say, pushing the hair behind her ears so he could see her face better. He had learned to look into her eyes, and when he stared at them he could see little flecks glinting in the irises so that it made him think of her name and the stones that changed color. It gave him a sensation of falling—an idea that he might tumble inside the dark pupil of her eyes and be lost. He was not unwilling.

"I've broken my marriage vows," she told him.

"You can't make promises to a corpse." He rested one hand on the small of her back, lightly pressing her against him. Yet he was not altogether sure that he had not made some of those promises himself.

"The dead are at peace," he added. Of that, also, he was not sure.

"I don't know," she said, resting her forehead against his chest.

"I do know. The whole planet has sinned against us. Everything was taken from me, even my brother."

"I thought you said that you didn't have any brothers or sisters." She lifted her face to look at him.

"I had Otto. He was my brother, but he died."

"What happened?"

"It was a long time ago. But I haven't forgotten. He was all I had left."

"That's so sad," she told him, a hand on his cheek.

He swept a hand over his face as if to throw away any tears.

"We should seize hold of any happiness. We earned it by suffering. That's what I believe." He kissed her and forgot about all else.

In those days of harvest, he never asked himself whether he loved her, any more than he had questioned himself about Clemmie. It did occur to him once that she had replaced Clemmie for him, and that what he wished—for her husband to vanish utterly—had come to pass in Opal. That she was deserving of love, he never considered. Nor did he wonder if the two of them had been drawn together by the dead they carried always with them.

The day when the harvest ended, they raced for the cars with the others, and Pip leaped easily onto a rung and scrambled upward. He saw her slip and almost fall—saw her catch hold again and be pulled inside another boxcar, saw it with his own eyes. Yet when the train made its next stop and he climbed down from the platform and looked inside, there was a different woman with reddish hair sitting

138

in the shadows, not so pretty as Opal. He searched to the rear of the train, car by car. A couple of fellows said they had seen a girl jump from a boxcar and then slowly walk toward the migrant camp. He mounted to the deck and looked out toward the now-vanished bend in the stream.

"What does it mean?"

No one answered. He reached his hand up to the two loops around his neck, the one with the shell and the one she had fastened there, a silver chain with a tiny pendant—an opal stone in a metal hoop. Cracked into two pieces, the gem shone with eerie colors, small patches of green and pink glinting as he turned it in the light.

Whether Pip was feeling sadness for lost nights tangled in Opal's arms or for something more, he didn't know. As they pulled away, an inertia held him from throwing himself from the train; he was already caught by its pulse and movement, its life that seemed more potent that his. In its grip, he and his troubles did not seem to matter.

But in time he felt the loss as deeply as he had felt anything since the day he left the Orphanage. Now as the train pushed east, a thousand warm lines of linkage between them were snapped and rent. How deep a tear that was, how long it would take to heal, he did not ask. For days, he thought to turn back; then the moment passed, and it seemed there would be no use, no Opal waiting for him anywhere. Perhaps he could never have measured what he felt. A callus that thickened on the wound kept him from feeling more in the weeks afterward.

Perhaps he should have returned on the next train west, should have called her name up and down the banks of that creek. He pilfered a volume of mythology from a small-town library not long afterward, and now and then when she visited him as a ghost of memory, he fancied that she was a sylph of the air or a nymph of a stream and that her husband must have really been the guardian spirit of an apple tree. He might have found her hiding in a great hush of cottonwood seed or swimming, silvery sided, in the pool below the bend. Perhaps she would have materialized when the moon rose in the branches of the western trees.

Sometimes Pip felt sure that he should have gone on searching and calling her name until he found her, even if it took years. He had seasons enough to throw away a few—what was he rich in except youth? And the story of Opal had the resonance of a fairy tale in which mere children tilt and suffer and marry.

"Why didn't I go back?"

For a long time it was the first thing he thought when he woke in the morning—preceded by a vague sense that he had lost something precious and needed to find it. He picked up the habit of scanning crowds, searching for hair of a certain color. At night he dreamed of glimpsing her at a station and following on and on through the harvests until he became an old man and could do nothing but lie down and die in the world's wood. Sometimes she came to him then, and they walked through blossoming trees, all wound about with passionflower vines. Sometimes he dreamed that they picked fruit, filling their baskets but utterly alone, without any other migrants to be seen.

Yet the train had gone on singing in his blood, carrying him from the prairie, and by the time he once again reached the camp, fifteen and tight with desire, he found that no one had seen her at the harvest. Despite their many nights together, he knew no other name to ask for than Opal.

A couple of floaters recognized him from the year before, called him by name; he couldn't remember theirs, though he knew one by his stunted legs. The other one he recalled when he spoke in a low and grating voice as if his throat had been injured.

"Thought maybe you'd go on home to that missus I told you was looking for her boy Pip."

"Her brother," the tall one croaked.

"Yeah, you got it right. Her brother."

"I remember now—but I told you—I don't have anybody. I'm alone." He was looking past them, searching through the crowd by the bonfire.

"Where's your lady?"

"I lost her—she didn't get on the train when the camp broke up. I thought she did at first, but it was somebody else. You seen her?"

"Last year? How can you lose a dame? That don't make sense—"

"'Less you want to lose her, maybe." The rough voice broke in.

Pip lifted his glance to their faces for the first time. They seemed to reproach him. Something about the eyes seemed to condemn or mock. He raised his hand to shield his own, remembering how he had seen guilt shining out of the eyes of men. Well, he was older now, a man or close enough. Maybe it was time.

"Why didn't you go back?" The short one leaned his weight to one side and then another as if his legs hurt.

Pip was not listening. He wondered briefly whether the short man could be a dwarf. He had read about how the ancient dwarves had mined through the earth to expose crystals and seams of gold, making gorgeous hallways under the ground. Like old Gilead, they were famous for their torrents of beard. Later on their numbers must have dwindled. Then they served at the European courts, dressed in motley and bells; as fools, they were allowed to say the words that the king needed to hear but no one else was hardy enough to say.

"Are you—"

He could not decide: was it okay to ask or not? Then he remembered Till cautioning him not to make personal remarks that might insult the Countess and so held quiet.

"Why'd you leg it? Why not go back?" The fellow with the raspy voice offered him a torn piece of flatbread, and Pip took it, holding the scrap between his hands without eating.

"I don't know."

He could feel the sorrow of the loss pouring through his chest, filling him with emptiness. It seemed all wrong to him because to lose something should make a person feel diminished. But grief was not like that. It kept flowing until he ached with its bigness.

"I wasn't thinking. I wasn't thinking about her, I mean. I was just moving on. It's hard to stop sometimes—"

"I'd get off for a girl," the dwarf—if he were a dwarf—said, kicking a leg out to one side and shaking it. "Hoo, doggie. That'd get my rocks off. That'd make me *jump*."

"Jump right on her," his friend agreed, letting out the creak of a laugh.

Pip looked across the wheat, barely hearing the low hissing sound as the wind swept through it.

"I don't know," he said. "At first, it was like she wasn't real anymore. She'd fallen out of my life. It seemed that my life was about me. It wasn't about other people. I was alone. So when we got separated, I didn't try to do anything."

The whispering of the wheat died away and then began once more.

"At first I wasn't thinking about her, not really, though I felt something. I felt sorry, but I couldn't do anything. At night I missed her the most. Later on I felt bad. And the badness just got bigger and bigger until it was all I could think about."

"You one crazy 'bo," the dwarf said. "That was a bird worth keeping. I see lots, and I know. All soft and warm and full of jelly. Sweet jellyroll. You done lost something precious when you lost a good woman. Ain't that so, Joe?"

"That sweet thing might be dead now," Joe croaked mournfully. "She might be nothing but bones, no man to protect her on the rails."

"Uh-huh," the dwarf agreed. "And him so busy feeling bad about his own self that he's hardly even thinking about her."

"Wait a minute—"

Joe cut off Pip's protest with a rusty groan. "That's just wrong. Wrong, man. She was your piece. A juicy little bird like that—fox gonna nab her."

The dwarf was laughing at his friend, stumbling and clutching his arm. "You sound like a corroded old pump handle, sawing up and down. Screeking away."

"I feel like an old pump handle. Oughta flail on this misbegotten punk. Give him the lockjaw." Joe fell into a spasm of coughing, and the dwarf thumped him between the shoulder blades and waited until the hacking slowed before he resumed talking.

"Nah, he's just a road kid. Don't even know what he missed. More fool him." The dwarf shrugged. "Where was your lady from, anyway? Maybe she went back home."

Pip shook his head. He did not know.

"Don't know where she's from? What's her name?"

"Opal."

"That's all? Just Opal?" The dwarf whistled. "This punk didn't know nothing except the little flower between her legs. That's one snatch you'll never see again, kid. Ain't it so, Joe?"

With a gasp like the breaking open of an iron door, Joe let it be known that he agreed.

"Come on! Ain't you got no more respect than that? Ain't a woman more than a rag for greasing a tool?" The dwarf plucked the flatbread out of Pip's hands.

After a final croak of displeasure from Joe, the two walked off.

In the days to come, this conversation played itself over and over in the boy's mind. He felt separate from the Pip who had spoken. Yet he brooded on those words, and they made him uneasy. Soon he would leave the camp, he decided, though memory and desire made him want to stay. He had known Opal much better than it had seemed to the two men, he was sure. But he had not known her well enough. In the court of his thoughts he was tried and judged lacking because he should have known more. He should have asked her more about what she thought and felt. It was part of a history he had failed to read and master.

He knew the Asian travels of Marco Polo better than Opal's; he could point on a map to where the Assyrian kings had built their palaces on the east bank of the Tigris at Nineveh, but he did not know where Opal had been born. The words from library books picked up in his travels across the continent came back to him like reproofs, for an uncanny memory for quotes and dates and complex accounts of battles and civilizations had been of no avail with another human being worthy of knowing.

The ones that he now called *the Dwarf* and *the Throat* were right; he had lost something precious, and it would never return. The message on the shack wall that began with the name *Opal* scratched in four-inch high letters would probably never be read. And she probably would not want him anymore—he who had cared to learn so little about her.

He remembered Opal lying on the cottonwood leaves, her hair outspread like the flames from a sun.

"You're not like anybody else, Pip," she had said, drawing him close. "I like the way you are. I feel like I've gone exploring and found a new country where they do things different from all the world. Like I've gone beyond me and all I knew. It's so strange. And I love it, this other place. I love it."

What had he said to her? Had he even once said that he loved her? He feared not—had he taken hold of love and not even known it? If so, he had let it drift away like cottonwood seed, to take root somewhere else.

"This is heaven," she had said, lying in his arms.

"Yes," he had answered, his eyes shut.

She had leaned on one elbow and tickled his neck with a wisp of cottonwood down. "What would you have for a heaven on earth? If you could pick your own from the whole world?"

"I'd have you. And I'd keep a bit of prairie and the pool by the bend in the stream. I'd add a grove of trees and stars and a little pink town called Roseville. That would be my earthly heaven."

He had opened his eyes and seen her smile, waveringly at first but truly so that even her eyes seemed happy and without a migrant's sorrow.

"I'd have you, too," she had said. "I knew this was heaven."

That second summer at the camp, standing in the wheat as it rustled and bowed under the wind, Pip came to believe in one simple idea: he could have been happy with Opal. He waded into the high stems and flowers a mile beyond camp, and he shouted her name, listening to it pour in waves across the untended prairie sea. Tears were on his face before he knew that he had wept.

He pictured the two of them living in a hut on the edge of the whispering grass with an infant as bright and shiny as a moon, new minted. The baby was the beginning and the end—the purpose—of all things. For his sake they were bound together as one flesh. They named him Otto, and at night he slept against their backs, curled like a burden but light.

"Do you hear me, Opal?" He called into the wind. "His name is Otto!"

12

The road to Thera crosses railroad tracks
Near silver wands of eucalyptus trees.

Now and again Pip lit and lodged like a seed caught in the seam of work trousers. But like the beggar lice that hooked onto cloth, he never stayed for good. It appeared that it might be long before he once more resolved to keep to one set of people, one scene. Restlessness flowed through him, bending and bowing him to its will, as fluid as the wind that sweeps a field of wheat. When he did linger for a time, the pause seemed to be for no thought-out reason but because of some dim apprehension of kinship with a site or a person. He was groping for a change that would help; it was as simple as that, he told himself.

Once there was a refuge where he lived for months, and in his mind afterward it was unclear what had drawn him or why he put down the first tentative roots of his being. It was migrant housing, the remains of grandeur built by a fellow who had emigrated from New England seventy years before and was now buried out back with his two wives and several of his children. Although imposing, the mansion had never worn a coat of paint, and the wood had gone dry and silvery. An unusually large Gothic structure with board-and-batten siding and steeply pitched gables adorned by fly rafters, it appealed to the boy in its strangeness and beauty—for despite the fire that had gutted portions of the manse and mutilated the western gable, it was still lovely.

A man in the hop fields had offered him a place in his room in exchange for help with expenses, and Pip agreed. After all, he had no place to spend the night. And perhaps he was homesick for an accent more akin to his own; Swain and his wife were Tennesseans from the eastern mountains who had sold everything and fled to where work was plentiful, looking for a city of gold in the West, and now their nails were broken and stained green from picking hops. The house where they camped was visible for a long way across the valley floor, partly because the ground was flat and partly because the building was marked by an island of eucalyptus trees.

"That's it," Swain said as they emerged from a field of hop poles. "It's getting dark, but you can make it out. See that canvas at the top—see where it's slanting down for a roof? It's all coated and waterproof. That's our room. Plenty of fresh air is what there is. Very healthsome."

Pip did not respond.

"Ain't a bedbug in the whole place, either. Nothing worse than creatures swarming over you in the night. We had us a bad time with bugs the last spot we stayed—got ripped right to pieces."

"I've been eaten up a time or two," Pip volunteered.

"Well, they say it's these euc trees keeping the vermin tribes down. Clears your head. They've got a power of smell."

While Pip was often slow to pay attention to his surroundings so that to him one camp was much the same as another, he was taken with the arched windows and the grandiose size of the place.

"There's a raft of fellows holed up inside," the man told him. "If the old place hadn't burned, we'd be bunking in the fields, I reckon. But the boss got him a pretty new house."

Ancient army tents and makeshift canvas shelters clustered at the front and sides. The scene pricked at Pip's interest in history and faraway lands, though he was not sure why.

Swain led the way through the tent village, warning him against feces and mounds of garbage.

"There's a backhouse," he added. "No reason for this filth. And a kitchen and hearths outside with all the wood you want. That euc makes the brightest kind of a fire."

Pip cocked his head, taking in the peaked front door, the glistening gray boards of the house, the burned gable, and the immense crowns of the eucalyptus trees towering above. A shimmering noise of leaves swelled and crested: Swain's jerry-rigged canvas top snapped in the breeze, and one of the nearby tents collapsed and began rippling in the grass, struggling to unpin itself and somersault away. A pair of dirty-faced boys crawled out from the heaving tent and began wrestling with the heavy cloth.

"Tents get wind-throwed. But we've got a better deal, what with the trees and the walls that break the breeze. Smell something? That's euc. Some people can't abide it."

But the boy had an instant liking for the pungent odor. The stink, the tent village, and the great house conjured—he smiled as it came to him—a medieval town with a collection of tiny cottages clustering like fleas around a cathedral. He imagined the lanes and houses inhabited by a bawdy and disreputable collection of the poor, craftspeople, and merchants who washed even less than he did and wore potent perfumes and chewed pungent seeds if they could afford them. Maybe it was not so different from a trainload of floaters, squatting in boxcars.

"Did you know that these pointed doors come from the Middle Ages?"

He did not wait for a response. His pent-up knowledge swept forth, freed by the old-fashioned quality of the place.

"The only schools and libraries were in big churches and monasteries. The architects made the churches look like Roman basilicas, only they made them in the shape of a cross. The peasants didn't know anything much except from what they picked out from the sculptures over the doors. And they stank of animals and sweat. In castles the servants put rushes on the floor to keep it clean, but they sure could have used euc leaves—"

"You're a scholar, ain't you? That won't come in so handy in the fields, but we won't be cooped here for always," Swain mused.

Pip didn't hear, engrossed in his own words.

"Only the priests knew what was happening. Monks ran the world—or maybe they stayed in the library and read if they were smart. It was just bandits and black plague buboes and giant foraging rats outside their walls. But they knew Latin and English."

"The giant rats," Swain repeated. He took off his hat and ran a hand through his hair.

"Not the rats. The monks. They knew how to read," Pip said. "They wrote in Latin. And they argued about when the end of the world would come. They said that devils were always sneaking out of hell to tempt men and grab their souls. What they didn't understand, they made up a story to explain and called it a miracle—"

"I thought you looked quiet."

The migrant laughed, and Pip was startled to see that his eyes were a vivid blue. The boy's hand jerked toward his cheekbone as if to ward off a blow. But it did not matter. He had learned on the road that the color of eyes was not the key. Those old medieval priests were right. A man was full of devilment. He did not see it in Swain's face. Yet he did not trust his own appraisal because he had been wrong too many times. But he could leave easily enough if the face that was tanned and friendly and the long rangy body proved to be an enemy.

He touched the low paneling in the hall, attracted to its ornate carving. As they passed doorways, he caught glimpses of crowded rooms and children shouting in play. It was gloomy inside, and only the chance spark of a cigarette or the glimmer of a candle showed him the angle of a face, a figure collapsed into sleep, two men playing at cards and sharing a bottle of beer. The staircase wound up past the second floor where he heard a woman groaning and a male voice lifted above her noise. *Maybe a baby on the way*, Pip speculated, *or maybe her old man beats her.* Over time he had learned to pay more attention to the people around him since it could be costly not to do so.

At the third floor they had to stoop to enter a hall roofed with a strip of canvas. A man was sleeping in the narrow way. Faugh! Pip hated the sickly sweet waves that poured off a drunk.

"That's Jere," his guide noted. "He used to be a big man, back in Missouri. But he was a cheat and a swindler, and he couldn't hold on to his wife and children and his job. He went into land speculation and lost everything. Sometimes he talks about it before he passes out. Wants us to forgive him. Irisanne's forgiven Will Jere seven or eight times already."

The canvas roof bellied, whipped up and down in gusts of wind, and gave out a loud *crack!* as they stood up in the gutted room. In half-darkness Pip could see flares of black on sprigged wallpaper. The only lamp was a teardrop of flame that guttered in a tin pan.

"Swain, you're so late—"

He heard the woman's voice before he could make her out, a dark shape beside a cot.

"We made us some extra money. Did some work for the boss."

She rose and came toward him, and he fumbled for her in the gloom. She laid her head on his shoulder.

"I was worried," she whispered.

They embraced briefly, but Swain pushed her away and told her about the room's new inmate and how it would make things better for them all.

"It'll help with the money. And he'll get some home cooking. He's a Georgia boy, and he's a scholar, Irisanne. He knows things. It'll be fine."

By the glow from the grease lamp, Pip had thought the woman lovely. But when she came nearer, he thought that she looked weary and older than he had imagined.

"What's he going to sleep on?"

"I've got my own blanket," he explained. "I'll just make a pallet on the floor. I won't be a bother."

"The babies are asleep, Swain. They were worn out and couldn't bide till their daddy got home." She looked toward the cot.

"That's all right. It's looking up, Irisanne. Extra money and someone to help pay for the grocer's bill and kerosene for the lantern. It's not bad."

"No," she murmured.

Turning to Pip, she eased out a smile. Again she looked younger. "I've got a brother at home who's right about your age," she said. "It'll be nice to have a boy around for a while. There's some cross-vine tea in the kettle under the towel—it's the last from my sack of leaves—and there's beans and rice in a pot. I've got it wrapped up in our blanket, so it's still warm."

After his meal Pip lay on his bedroll, staring up at the hammocky ceiling and the gaps where it did not reach the walls. He could see a cloudless sky. Where the branches of the eucalyptus could not blot them out, the stars bristled with short, sharp points. He could hear the couple breathing deeply as if drinking at a well of sleep. They had made love in the squeaking cot, Irisanne protesting that the new boarder would hear. Pip had let out a few snores to let them know he was not listening. To be a few yards from lovers was old hat to him now. And he really was only half-listening, his attention snared by the clatter from the eucalyptus leaves. He could not think when he'd ever met such a talkative bunch of trees. Longleaf pines? *Magnolias*, he thought. If only the wind blew without stopping through the magnolia leaves, they might make such a sound. But somehow he thought they would be slower, more methodical, with less of a shimmy about the dance between wind and leaf.

After a while one of the little girls began crying in her sleep, and Irisanne woke and got up. He could see her sitting on the floor by the cot, her hand swooping along the child's spine. The rushing of the wind through the branches grew louder, made him feel uneasy. When her daughter tossed restlessly in the cot, the mother began to sing an old tune:

Silvering's on the Jordan stream,
Silvering's on the feet that pass,
And bright silvering's on the tree.

It's lessening that time imparts;
Hours of sorrow fall upon us,
And sad and sere are all our hearts —

To Pip it felt eerie and comfortless, the melody even more mournful than the verses. He got up and slipped down the stairs. Outside the house, he could still make out the words, the notes mixing with the noise from the leaves.

Swain had called the trees a windbreak, but they were more like a confined, immensely high forest than anything so domestic and useful. He walked on the aromatic debris, looking up at the chinks of moon through the canopy and pausing to touch the boles. He had never seen anything like the grove of eucalyptus with the moonlight showering down. The older trees had few lower branches, and the trunks were tall and tapering but straight like masts for a clipper ship. Where the saplings were crowded, they spired up, narrow and tall. Some of the mature trunks looked as if they had been sheathed in tattered wallpaper that shed in ribbons and flakes, but underneath the smooth naked skin was as smooth and fair as the inner thigh of a girl—one with hair so pale and metallic that she might be an elf or a fairy. He touched a tree like mottled silver marble. The wind fell away, and the mosaic of leaves above him grew still: blue, light green, gray-green, and jade.

In the stillness he could hear Irisanne's voice: *A silver trail is flung to earth, / To let us climb beyond the moon...*

Never had he seen such a mystic corner of the world. If he had seen koalas leaping from tree to tree with infants clinging to their mothers' fragrant fur, he could not have felt the world to be more wondrous.

"This must be what's meant by a *glade*." He stood in a circle of moonlight, his feet on the uneven litter, and gazed up. Through young round leaves, blue or silvery white with a faint greenish tinge, he glimpsed green and pink patches on brown bark. In a moment he saw that some leaves were short and almost oval while others were shaped like the outlines of green chili peppers, with a reddish central vein and stem. There was no end to the tints of silver and blue and green. Clusters of new silver resembled exotic flowers in the darker leaves.

"Birds of paradise." That was the only name for jungle blossoms that he knew, and it seemed right.

On the forest floor he found a bumpy flower bud, seed heads marked with a five-petaled star, and a broken spray of glaucous buds quite unlike the first he'd found. His hand brushed against tiny blossoms, white and starry.

"Like puff briars." He remembered the pink flowers that grew along the rails near The White Camellia Orphanage.

The rattling started up again, the wind flowing down the valley and shaking the crowns of the trees. He crouched down on the waves of bright litter and watched the branches comb at the wind. What was it they reminded him of? *A disk harrow made of silver, cutting at the air.* And wasn't that outlandish? Miss Collins would have liked it; he wanted to tell her. Now he was not sure whether the few scattered notes that he heard belonged to the song or to crickets and wind in the leaves. The sights and sound and even the odor of the copse gave him a pleasure that was like nothing else that he could recall.

I wish Excelsior Tillman could see this, he thought. *I'd sure like to show him.*

He could picture the old man sitting down beside him with a thump. "Can you feature it? Pretty as a basket of busted crockery, ain't it? Sweet as a teacup. It's as good as a peep through heaven's back gate—did you ever see something so flat-out wondrous fair, Pip?"

"Nothing except Roseville with the moon up, Till," he said aloud. He had an obscure sense that he needed to ask the old man for forgiveness, but the dream figure he had conjured asked for none and made him welcome.

"The world can't be as poor and mean as you think, son, not with this sort of thing waiting and ready for anybody who comes along. You had a nice ride out here, didn't you? I reckon you could carry yourself home again. You're welcome any time."

He was almost convinced that Till had spoken right beside him. Tears in his eyes made the scene into a smear of silver.

"I'm a fool."

The current flowing through the trees went on, ceaselessly stirring the twigs and boughs and neither agreeing nor disagreeing with his judgment.

"Someday I'm going to see you again," Pip promised. "It's not such a big world as all that."

Pausing at the edge of the eucalyptus grove, he looked into the distance. Near the fields some men were laughing around a bonfire. The big farm was like many others, but he liked the house, even with the walls that were scorched and blackened, and he liked the silver wood that talked so loudly when it caught the breeze. He had a good feeling about Swain and Irisanne that reminded him of living above the Savannah River with Till. There was work enough in the fields for six weeks, maybe, and the boss had asked Pip and Swain whether they were handy with a hammer and saw. Outbuildings needed to be repaired and built. He would stay for a while.

Soon his days fell into a familiar fluctuation. While picking, he let his mind drift into the past, and he went roving through the American wilderness or the courts of English kings or queens or racing across the Aztec Empire with a message in his hand. Pip also had a more curious historical undertaking. He spent hours imagining the history of Thera, a world parallel to his own, with much that reflected the history of Earth in a distorted mirror: there was no violence, no hatred in its chronicles. He was the true ruler of that kingdom, but he had tumbled through a rift in the universe into a lesser realm. The Therans now called him *The King Who Was and Will Be Again* and prayed for his return. That message had come to him in a dream, and at moments he forgot that it was not true.

He spent hours lavishing detail on his creation. He might take an afternoon to design one of the fantasy temples of Thiani, the elaborate clusters of rooftop pinnacles symbolizing the Limayah Mountains. A multitude of six-sided shrines represented the six points of the Theran compass. Six perimeter walls were each pierced by many doors, one of which was a gateway to another of the Seven Worlds: to Herat, Heart, Rathe, Erath, Thare, or Earth.

The little girls sometimes trailed after him, eavesdropping on his make-believe as he talked out loud. He did not mind this; although he seldom looked at them, he felt that the older one was attentive and interested. Never too concerned with names, he took nearly a month to learn that she was named *Cora* and the younger one *Nancy*.

At night after supper, Cora would often question him about Thera as if she had been thinking about the kingdom during the day—as if it had become real to her.

"Where do you get through?" she asked one evening while Irisanne rocked Nancy in her arms. The younger girl was only two years old, a spindly-legged baby so impulsive and prone to seize whatever caught her attention that the mother was constantly leaving her work to chase after her.

Pip was daydreaming and did not hear. Cora repeated the question, drawing closer.

"Get through what?"

"Where do you get through to *Thera*?" She looked down on him, fists on her hips. He tilted his head and gazed back. Her hair was dirty, her cheeks sunburned, her faded blue-and-white gingham dress let down to the full extent of its once-generous hem.

"From here," she added.

"If I knew, I'd probably be gone, wouldn't I?" He had never had a sense for the ages and maturity of children, and he now spoke to her as if to an equal. "Then I wouldn't have to work so hard."

"You'd be king," she pointed out. "I'd as lief be queen as pick."

"Yeah, kinging around can be a good job—in Thera, anyway. I wouldn't want to be a king on this planet."

"Why not?"

"Chances are they'd chop my head off. Either the courtiers would or else the peasants. That's us, you know. We're the peasants here. King in one world, peasant in another." But he spoke slowly, still thinking about her first question. "Okay, listen. If you go where someone you know—somebody who's your blood kin—has suffered and died, you'll find a door close by. And if you feel over it carefully, you'll find a latch, and you can lift it and go in. It's as simple as that."

Cora seemed to be considering this. She squatted down beside him and was silent for a time.

"Do you know where one is?"

"A door?" Pip rolled over on his side, his eyes on the scabs and bruises on the little girl's legs. "Well, I guess I might. I don't know why I didn't think of it before, but I know a spot like that, a long way off. And there are some latches and doors already there. But the door to Thera is invisible. You pat the air for its edges and find it, see, and feel for the handle. And when you discover it, you can go in. It's not easy to find. You might know one was near and never touch it. Feels good to know it's there though. Waiting."

Cora picked at a scab on her knee, working it loose bit by bit until a pink lozenge of fresh skin was revealed. She turned the scab in her fingers, feeling its rough surface, and then broke it into bits.

Without speaking, she got up and went to her cot and curled up on the dirty canvas.

Over the weeks, Pip became accustomed to having a warm meal and a few home comforts. Irisanne boiled his spare clothes in the communal wash pot that steamed over a blaze of eucalyptus. In turn he helped with money and labor and chopping wood; he and Swain reset the tarp and added supports so that they could stand in most of the room.

He whittled a crude, kachina-like doll for each of the girls. Cora's wore a crown, and silver leaves were bound around the waist with red string. "Her name is Countess-Princess Casimiria Pulaski," he told Cora, who called her *Princess Cassie*. He had never been clever with his hands, and these toys cost him more effort than they would have another boy more dexterous than he. But the dolls pleased the children and their mother.

"I was nervish when you came, but it's been fine," Irisanne told him. "Seems like every new thing goes wrong. Just about every single one. Yet there's naught to be done. Just go up the trail rejoicing as best you can."

Go up the trail rejoicing. Pip thought about that; it seemed quite different from his own philosophy of trying to find the change that would help. He did not want to rejoice when everything went wrong. He would not yield that way.

"We had big dreams when we come gallivanting out here," Swain added, clapping a hand over his wife's.

"It's not been so very bad," she whispered.

"Sing us a song, Irisanne." Her husband was proud of her nasal mountain singing, and sometimes it seemed to the boy that the melodies kept them all going. She almost always began and ended with the silvery song as Pip called it, and he often slipped out to wander through the eucalyptus boles and try to recapture that first surprise he had felt on the path through the trees.

Now the memory of another time when Irisanne had been singing came back to him as if it had a particular word to say to him.

"Maybe the way to Thera's yon," Cora had said one evening, pointing to a bright patch of foliage.

"Maybe," Pip had answered.

Swain had been carrying Nancy over his shoulder. Her legs were drawn up under her gown, and sweaty curls were stuck to her cheek.

Irisanne had begun singing, and some of the other migrants who were walking in the dusk toward the tent village and the house under the eucalyptus trees had taken up and begun humming the tune until the twilight pulsed with the rise and fall of notes—some gospel song about a garden that he had barely remembered from Sundays with Pastor Bell. What a strange feeling had come to him, being in that river of sound flowing through the hop poles and the truck patches, knowing that all around him were people as tired as he, ready for a meal and a laugh and a sleep. It was the biggest crowd of people he had ever felt a part of: it had seemed as if he were curiously bound up with them and they with him, the pieces of Irisanne's song shared out among them and returning, a larger and wider thing than before.

In the fields he dreamed up Thera as he worked, in the evenings he ate his meal with Irisanne and Swain and the girls, and at night he lay back to read or to stare at the stars and the rattling silver and blue of leaves. The life felt right to him, no matter the work. His time in the burned Gothic house seemed one of those passages too good to last forever.

Then one afternoon while little Nancy played on a blanket at the edge of a field, she was stung by a bee. The death was abrupt and unseen. Although she had been stung once before, her arm turning swollen and painful, Swain and Irisanne had not known to be afraid.

It was no surprise to find bees in the field or near the house. They loved the eucalyptus flowers and made a dark crystalline honey that tasted of herbs and menthol. Sometimes it was mixed with a milder honey for sale. People said it was good for coughs and colds and sore muscles.

But Nancy was stung; she died. The sequence was hard to get through Pip's mind. One hour she was there by the edge of a field, napping or playing with sticks and her doll, and the next she was dead. Cora had stopped digging in the dirt and then started to shriek when she saw the swollen neck and face. Irisanne had taken off running with Swain after her. The woman's scream had gone up in a swoop.

The little body was wrapped in a blanket and carried home. The migrants gathered at the edge of the field and watched Swain with the bundle in his arms and his wife leaning on him, weeping. Word came from the boss that the two would be paid for the whole day but that the others should return to work. There was a crop to get in, and it was close to dusk already.

Pip went over to Cora, who had been left standing by the rows. She had shouted "No!" when Swain had called her to come. The boy could see her brushing the air with her fingers, delicately feeling a way.

"What're you doing?"

"Nancy's dead," she told him, with a slight question in her voice.

"Yeah. She's dead." He knelt down and looked at her. "You all right?"

She nodded, not stopping her search.

"So what're you doing?" he repeated.

Keeping one hand up as if to mark her place, she stared at him. There was a rip in her spare dress. The hem had raveled and hung longer in the back than in the front. She started to speak when a train sang out an arrival somewhere in the distance, and she paused until the sorrowful note had ceased to echo.

"Looking for the door, of course." Cora frowned. Even Pip, so poor at reading faces, could see that she thought him mighty stupid.

"What?"

"The door to Thera," she shouted, almost growling in frustration.

The door to Thera. What could he say? Right then he did not feel much of anything. He was sorry, but it was a remote sensation—a postponed fact that would be felt later.

"Maybe it's not the right time of day. Maybe it'll open in the morning or the evening. Every entrance is different. Some gates never get unlatched because they're high over our heads…"

As his voice trailed away, Cora lifted her chin.

"I'll find it. I'm going to. If it ain't here, maybe in the silver woods. Nancy likes them. And she'd like a silver door."

"You mean the eucalyptus trees," he said in a low voice. Even now, he could not help but talk about his secret world, though he felt troubled. "I've thought that too. I've thought that a road to Thera might be there. The moonlight might show it, looking all silvery."

Someone was calling Cora's name. Pip looked off toward the house; he could see Swain up top, his head and shoulders showing above the burned edge of the wall.

"Look, there's your pap." That was what the little girl called him: *Pap*. He guessed it was a mountain way. "You best skin off and help him. The door to Thera won't shut once it's ajar. You can find it another day. Sometimes you have to bring a ladder and climb up. You'll have plenty of chances to find it. Right now they need you. Go on."

The little girl's mouth went crooked, and she glared at him without speaking. All at once she turned and raced off, and Pip watched as the blot of her dress blurred into the darkness.

That night he slept in the glade, rolled in his blanket. He did not want to be in the same room with Irisanne and Swain. It was their sorrow, not his. The mother had been calm when he arrived, but as other women came to help wash the child, Irisanne had begun to shout with grief. He could not bear the noise. Even in the eucalyptus trees he could hear the uproar of her sobs.

It came to him that he had not found the change that would help him, that he felt ensnared and trammeled. He had run away from death and sorrow at The White Camellia Orphanage, and now here they were again. He pictured the toddler laid out in her faded pink dress with a bead on a string around her neck. She was hardly past babyhood. Through the gaps between the trunks he could see a brilliant sunset, burning like a smithy's fire. A long slender sword of blaze and cloud lay in its midst. It reminded him of something, but he felt tense and angry and twitched his head to drive away the thought.

The box provided by the county was unseasoned boards. Swain had asked for something better, but there was nothing else.

"It'll shrink and wrench and go all slantdicular. It'll let in the rain," he had protested.

"Beggars are not choosers," the officer had replied.

The words bothered Pip more than they did Swain and his wife. At the funeral, he kept thinking about them. *Beggars are not choosers.*

160

None of them were beggars, he decided, and all of them had chosen to venture their lives.

Even now, Swain and Irisanne were choosing to make something out of those boards fit for a beggar. Swain had caulked the cracks and painted the boards white. Sprays of eucalyptus lined the box, and a twig with white buds was in the dead child's hand. Irisanne had made a wreath of flowers that was pinned to the freshly washed hair.

Seven of the women from the tent camp had come to the pauper's field, along with Will Jere and a man who had once been a traveling minister but who now just traveled. Cora tugged at Pip's hand, and he followed.

"That's where they're going to put her," she explained, pointing to the gouge in the ground.

"Yes." He glanced around, hoping that Swain would come and take the child from him.

"Mam says I'll see her again. When I go to heaven. You don't have to find a door. You just go."

"That's what they say."

"I'd like to," she said, "but only if I can play with Nancy. Though she wasn't all that peart a player, really. Not yet."

"I guess you'll get there sooner or later. Personally I'd rather wait a spell."

"And I'm going to find Thera before you," she added.

"No," he said. He could not stop himself.

Pip was glad when Swain came up and told the child to stand by her mother. The bereaved man wore a black armband on his sleeve. Though his eyes looked bruised underneath, he didn't appear so different from what he had been before Nancy's death. Irisanne looked wild. The boy had never noticed how gaunt the woman was, but now that she had wept and gone without sleep, she seemed to have become emaciated. The black under her eyes emphasized their brightness.

For a few minutes Swain just stood there, looking over the county cemetery and off toward the scrub and train tracks beyond. Then he turned and took hold of Irisanne's arm.

"Our baby was born without a roof, out on the prairie, and now she's gone and died without one. She's always been on the road. But not now. We'll get carried off by the crops, and she'll have to bide." He did not seem to be speaking to anyone in particular.

"I might go on; naught else remained to do," Pip quoted.

"What's that?"

"From a poem. 'Childe Roland to the Dark Tower Came.'"

"I might go on," Swain repeated, slowly rubbing his dry, seamed hands together.

As they assembled by the pit, the ragtag mourners murmured, all but Irisanne, who gripped Cora by the shoulders. Though the mother was no more than twenty-five, Pip noticed threads of iron in her hair.

While the women from the tent camp sang a hymn, their voices rousing, determined to praise the never-bare rooms and cupboards of heaven and to lighten the gravity of falling clods, Pip wandered away, heading toward the truck supplied by the boss. He was not so bad as bosses went. The loan of a vehicle had allowed the mother and father to ride inside the cab, away from the others. The remainder of the mourners had told stories and laughed in the truck bed; it was pleasant to feel the wind in their hair and be riding to somewhere that did not mean a job. Will Jere was drunk but had not yet reached the point of asking for forgiveness. Cora had crawled about the floor, clambering over legs, teased and praised by the women. Now and then they had remembered the purpose of their outing and hushed, turning their heads to look at Irisanne through the glass.

He could hear the former preacher's voice until it was drowned out by the noise of sobs, the women crying for themselves as much as for the dead child. In the near distance, a train bored through the perfect afternoon. The thought came to Pip that he had nothing to retrieve from Swain and Irisanne's room—not unless he counted the stars as seen through the silver of the eucalyptus trees. There was nothing else he wanted to take along. His second-best pants and shirt were there, worn thin. He could get himself new rags. Well, there was a blanket, but Cora could use the extra warmth. Without a bedfellow it would be colder in the child's cot at night. He reached up to touch the place where his stake was pinned inside the lining of his jacket, all but a few coins in a pocket.

"Hey—"

Mr. Jere staggered up to the truck bed and searched until he found a bottle. Strange the way he carried a coat even when it was warm, Pip thought. Perhaps it was because he was sick and cold, or perhaps it was just to hold his moonshine. He must have been a big, good-looking man once, but now his hair was long and greasy, and his features looked ravaged—the skin seeming a little too large for the face and blue-black under the eyes' pouches.

He wiped his mouth. "Drink? Farewell drink? You got that going-away look," Jere told him.

"No, I don't have a look. I quit having a look a long time ago."

"Yeah. Right. You got a face like a Mohawk. Don't show no pain." Will Jere leaned forward and breathed out an odor like fermented apples.

Pip stepped away. "Faugh. You're foul—get off."

"I smell like guilt. You smell like guilt, too. Stink to high heaven." The drunk laughed until tears came into his eyes.

"You are one crazy man." Pip was listening for the train, his head cocked.

"Not as crazy as you. What I done was wrong, and I've been sorry every day since. Every damn morning when I wake up. But here you go, skipping away from these people who were good to you. From that sweet Miss Irisanne. Now in their time of trouble—"

"You sound like a dadgum preacher."

Mr. Jere swigged from the bottle.

"Maybe I am a dadgum preacher. I preach the Church of the Bitter End and the news of your guilt, boy, and of your dirty-dog running away—"

"Hush up!" Pip jerked his sleeve from the other's green-nailed grasp. The evil-smelling fellow had passed some taint to him, and he felt it drifting inside. He remembered the dark crimson of Countess Casimiria's medicine, spooned into a glass. The dollop of drug sent up streamers and bled into the water until the liquid was entirely tinted with red. What was this evil that the drunk had passed to him?

Nothing. Not evil, Pip thought, *except that standing near death felt evil. And Will Jere would be pushing up weeds from the bone orchard soon.*

"Nothing," he muttered, turning his back on the man.

"Is that what you believe, buddy?" Jere slipped, sprawling onto the grass of the paupers' field. He pushed himself up and staggered back onto his feet. "Leg it, boy! Run off to Joppa and be swallowed by a whale—"

The train whistled the notes for a crossing, and Pip started away from the truck.

Someone, a child or a woman, called his name.

He saw the train clearly now, pounding the tracks with a coal-black plume streaming behind. The lonesome freedom of the rails appealed to him as never before, its ache a milder and sweeter form of grief than any he saw here. He knew that Cora would miss him, knew that the three would feel let down and betrayed in the midst of their sufferings. They had let him into their private lives, but he had never promised to go where they would go, had he? And he would not stay, neither in the well of their collected tears, nor with them on the road. How had he lowered himself so far into their lives before he knew it?

But he would climb out, and he would leap onto a side-door Pullman as if flinging himself into another world. The doorway between them would seal itself shut. He would never again hear Irisanne singing her "silvering" song while he walked through the eucalyptus trees. He would never work alongside Swain, the older man silent but companionable. There was emptiness in him that found no echo to their pain, though it was not *nothing* that he felt. He did not know what swirled inside him; he could not quit thinking about that sensation, whatever it was.

He pictured the little girl streaking after him, her dress flying with the wind. They would have to chase her and pin her by the hand. He did not like the image of them forcing her to stay. It seemed strange to him that he had depended on Excelsior Tillman for longer than he had known this family, and yet he had departed Savannah and left him with relative ease while these people had set hooks into his skin in a short time. It never occurred to Pip that perhaps he had changed since then, and that perhaps he would not abandon the old man so readily now.

The name came again, sharp and high-pitched as a bird's cry.

"Remember the Church of the Bitter End," Will Jere was bellowing.

He let the struggle to know his own mind sail away like the dark boiling exhaust tumbling into loose skeins and then invisibility. Quickening his steps, he swerved away from the dirt lane and broke into a lope, following a string of barbed wire toward the rails.

13

In which Pip seeks a refuge far away
And finds that hard adventure's everywhere.

Pip was restless until he went east with the berry harvest. Hours north of New York City, he found a farm where he had been content the year before. He was still unhappy with himself, memories of Swain and Irisanne and Cora coming to him at unexpected moments and making him uneasy. But he could forget what bothered him in a fresh setting, or so he thought. Nothing could be retrieved from the past, he was certain, but it was possible to feel consoled—to be as content as a woodchuck in the sun. On the green slopes near the lake, he did not need to struggle to find a reason to live but could just *be*, feeling the coolness of an end-of-summer wind on his face. The green of hills was restful, and in the mornings there was a mist in the valleys. In Georgia the grass would have been burned clean of color by now. The pale soil over Otto's grave would still blaze and hurt a watcher's eye. Fall would feel more distant than a rumor.

And he did not mind the work. He enjoyed picking currants because you could sit down and let your mind idle while you stripped bushes drooping with clusters of fruit. Twelve cents for each tray of eight heaped baskets. It was not like raspberries where you had to mind what was ripening and stoop along the rows, searching in the briars for the day's berries and leaving others that were not quite ready.

At night he slept in an unpainted shack on the slope above the farmer's fieldstone house, with a well-kept pickup and automobile parked in a white shed, and on the lawn a tidy Blessed Virgin backed by what looked to be an enormous shell. He imagined her head haloed and battered by echoes of the sea. The farmer told him that they wrapped the lady every winter as if she were a bulb sprout in need of shelter from the snow. Each spring, they untied and broke open the pod of burlap, stiff from many freezings. He pictured the figure, roped, buried by storms, icy to the touch, and her shell packed with crystal.

"She's an idol?" he had asked.

Mr. Fairbairn had let out a whoop of surprise. "She's the blessed mother of God, boy." He had waved his hand in the air as if feeling for an answer. "Idols are for Belial and Beelzebub and such. It's gold bulls that are made so they bellow when you put a fire underneath, and it's Ashtart poles. Ain't you got a religion?"

Pip had touched the drapery that floated on each side of the lady in a manner unknown to gravity but impressive to behold. "I was baptized in the Canoochee."

"Never heard of that. What kind of a church is it? It ain't Catholic."

"It's a river. The Canoochee River. Near Lexsy. It's where the Primitive Baptist Church baptizes people. Down there with the catfish and the warmouth. Sometimes there's a fish fry afterward."

"A fish fry at a christening. Never heard of such doings." Mr. Fairbairn had patted the virgin on her head. "That's a wild place you got down there. Rattlesnakes, giant lizards, blackamores, vigilantes in bed sheets charging around the countryside. And the priests dunk you, do they? Anybody ever get gobbled by an alligator while they was just trying to get baptized?"

The boy had grinned. He was used to Yankee questions, and they did not make him mad as they had once. "Now and then," he had said. "It only happens once in a very great while. And it's just preachers. No priests." He had liked the grandiose sound of the phrase when he spoke: *once in a very great while.*

Although he had remembered what Pastor Bell had to say about priests, he knew to keep his lips sealed and not let the word *abomination* escape from his mouth. This year Mr. Fairbairn looked glad to see him and remembered his name, though Pip, ever weak with labels, had had to check the nameplate on the rural mailbox. He was glad to be there, and he had come prepared with long johns rolled up inside a heavy wool blanket.

The first time he had spent a summer night in the New York countryside, the boy had shivered and pitched from side to side until daylight. One of the other fellows had advised, "Hook you some fertilizer bags out the barn," and after that Pip had been warm, though well-perfumed by morning. This year he was ready.

And he remained content for some time, despite the fact that one night a floater moaned, lunged to his feet, and slashed several of the men about the face. The outbreak came with no warning unless the single word the man had spoken by the campfire meant something.

"Arden," he had said and lapsed back into silence.

"What's Arden?"

"A girl."

"Yeah, a dame. With legs."

Nothing in the fellow's face had said *yes* or *no*.

"Arden," Pip had repeated. "I know an Arden. It's a forest where people are free, and money doesn't mean anything."

"What? There's no such—"

"In a play. By Shakespeare," he had added.

"Oh, in a *play*," a voice had said, mockingly.

"Shakespeare was a great man."

"Like a god."

"Ah, he's not all he's cracked up to be."

"You ever read him, smart guy?"

"Nah, I never did."

Five of them had been sitting around the fire. A Swiss emigrant was warming some bread and melting a wedge of cheese in a cracked iron pan rescued from the farm dump. Afterward, it was the slippery surface of the cheese, beaded with oils, and the flames that lingered in Pip's memory. The splendid bonfire before the shack was clearer in his mind than the features of the other pickers.

He was focused entirely on the burning logs, the infinitely small crackles and patters like needles sifting onto a path in piney woods—

sometimes musical, like a handful of pins tingling onto a hardwood floor. An abrupt sigh of exhaled moisture, an occasional rising *whoosh* like a Chinese firework about to shoot off into a fountain of sparks, a retort just as a flurry of bark shingles burst from a log and landed on the stones below with a protracted tinkle, a snap like a breaking twig followed by a sudden puff of orange sparks: these sated his desire for the strange and complex. Bark softened and whitened like a fungus in the flames. The skin over his cheekbones felt tight with warmth.

Pip leaned closer, the sight before him seeming like the most important thing in the world; this was what he had wanted, a lull in his life where a fire or a book or a patch of lake was the only news. Behind the big log, blue and gold-red flames fluttered helplessly, their tattered banners blown upward. When he blinked, they became spirits at frenzied exercise, flinging sparks. He stared into a crescent gap in the wood where he saw a pumpkin-colored light and a row of dancing gold spears. Curiously, the heat-split surface of the inner log looked manmade, a stacked wall of irregular firebricks. When someone stood up to prod the blaze, it leaped and multiplied and turned almost entirely golden, magically up-showering thousands of sparkles and threads of frail lightning at the stars.

An old man set a mug of tea down on a stone near the flames.

"So peaceful," he said.

The floater groaned and plunged toward the boy tending a wedge of cheese. His arms flashed in the light, clawing the air.

"Jacknife! He's got—"

"Catch 'em—"

"I'm cut—"

When Pip tackled him, scuffling on the hot stones, the round-shouldered man swept a blade across the deterring hand before exploding forward, hurling himself into the scrub and forest where he crashed like a bear and vanished, nameless except for the moniker, *Dutch Pete*, and never to be found.

Later, Pip was almost glad that the attacker had burst free.

"Just out of the blue," a kid from the Dakotas complained, tentatively pressing the gauze by his ear.

The farm wife was busy staunching blood and taping injuries while Mr. Fairbairn and his nearest neighbor poked about in the bushes, half-heartedly looking for the guilty party and rousting only chickens from the scrub.

"He must have been some kind of a crazy man," she ventured, surveying her handiwork. She was a second wife, several decades younger than her husband and built more sturdily than the one whom Pip had seen in a gilt-framed photograph, looking diminished and ghost-like even in life. When he saw the new Mrs. Fairbairn's arms and legs, thick but as white as porcelain, he remembered the eucalyptus trees and how under the ribbons of bark lay the surprise of the pale bole. Fascinated, he had peeled away the tatters in order to touch its smoothness.

As she washed his bloody hand under the tap, he stared at the curve of her shoulder until she blushed.

"Why did he do it?" she whispered.

Pip bent his head, watching as she wrapped each finger in gauze and tape. He could feel her breath on his palm.

"Maybe it made him feel free. Maybe he had to tear his way out. Maybe he was trying to find what would help—"

Her lips tightened, and she gave a little shake of the head.

"I don't know," he added. "Maybe there was a fever on him that made him want to hurt us. I fight sometimes but not like that. I even like to scrap for the fun of it, but you can't stop madness. You can't fix it, I guess." Still, he had a kind of fellow feeling for the attacker, homeless and a wanderer like himself. Somewhere along the rails Pip had lost the sense that his own acts were justified. He had made mistakes. He had done wrong.

"His eyes were red, red," the old man offered, "like a devil. That ain't no good."

Pip nodded, turning his hand so that the girl could wind the bandage more easily. His fingers, thick with tape, brushed against the thin white blouse. "Maybe he was breaking his fetters. Maybe he went tearing off into the woods and turned into a bear: maybe he's combing the bushes for all the berries and currants he wants and looking for a cave."

"In that forest of Arden," the Swiss boy broke in.

"Maybe."

Mrs. Fairbairn smiled as she cut more gauze with a pair of nail scissors.

"But he must have been a bad man," she murmured.

For much of his young life, Pip had been rigid about what was right. And this event could not be called anything less than an evil. Yet he was trying to make out what had caused Dutch Pete to go wrong, fly out at the fellows. For once, he felt that he understood. Although he had gotten in a few hard punches of his own, the Georgia boy knew what it was to feel maddened, unable to gnaw out of a trap. Twice he'd been robbed and locked in a boxcar, left wondering if anyone would set him free before he starved or was broiled by noonday heat. The first time it happened he had been mastered by the flare of anger and fear and beaten on the metal until his arms were sore, screamed till he was hoarse, and kicked with scavenged boots until his feet were bruised.

But he did not feel cornered at the currant fields. He liked the coolness and peacefulness and the views of the rolling hills with the chill glint of a lake. It was mostly calm there even if you never knew what kind of looner might be sleeping in the next cot, ready to fire half-cocked.

Looking around, he took in the young wife's white-painted kitchen, its free-standing cabinets, the canisters of grain, the work tables, a pitcher of flowers, the pot of tea warm under a towel, a side of fat-streaked beef dripping into the sink, a shining mountain of berries in a metal tub, a powdered disk of dough. The room had a prosperous feel as if the people who lived there could afford more than twelve cents a tray for picked currants.

"Pleasant," Pip muttered.

Maybe that's what had made the man go berserk, he speculated, earning pennies and crouching by a campfire to eat trash while this wife, barely grown to a woman, roasted beef which she then served on an ironstone platter, gleaming and perfectly clean. From a doorway he had seen an immaculate cloth on the dining table, silver and crystal spread across it, and place settings of flow blue china like yet-unbroken pieces of Excelsior Tillman's Roseville.

Or maybe that wasn't it, not in the least.

She broke into his thoughts. "Just one more finger and I'll be done. You're so quiet. Does it hurt?" She seemed to caress his palm with her own.

"No. I was just doubting that I can know anything about what's in Dutch Pete."

She let go of his hand quite suddenly. "I hope you—can still pick."

He flexed his fingers and nodded. He had been dismissed.

Pip wandered down to the lake and squatted by the pebbly rim, looking for fragments of the past. The shore had been inhabited by settlers for 150 years, and it was interesting to see what washed up. Nubs of pale orange bricks, porous and light like pumice. Relics of flow blue and transfer ware, the remains of a lost realm: what would be left of Mrs. Fairbairn's china service in a century or two. Ceramic chips. Bolts and nails so rusty that they had been warped from their true form and resembled the petrified corpses of once-living creatures. Scrubbed lake glass.

His thoughts passed over to Thera. Perhaps one of the six entrances to that other kingdom stood under the lake, and pieces of Theran houses and pottery washed onto shore, lapping from world to world. Perhaps a Theran village was right there, beneath the waves.

No. He had abandoned its roads, and he would not think about them again. He could not immerse himself in its castles, cities, temples, and wilderness without recalling Cora's fingers, feeling the air for a gateway. The memory had spoiled the joy of Thera for him and closed a door. This magpie trash washed to shore came only from

Earth. But he liked spreading the debris with his hand, hunting for a treasure. Surely these fragments told a history that he could read if only he knew more.

The jet bead and nubs of "garnet" he and Otto had used for their jewels came into his mind. With a fingertip he touched the little moon of opal, hanging at his throat. He remembered hardened drops of blood, brilliant as rubies. It seemed to him that his brother's body with its neck drooping like a flower's stem was as good an emblem as any for human suffering. The outline could have been engraved on a shield or chiseled on the door to a tomb. Then the image could stand for something besides itself, could be the image of his own trials and those of all the floaters who were roving North America with no place to lay their heads. Perhaps the violent Dutch Pete was more akin to the child Otto than to anything else—more like a boy in anguish than like his murderer.

"Even the killer," he said, pushing grains of sand aside and picking up a shard painted with single blue leaf. "Maybe he's more like that than anybody else is. Suffering. And I hope he *is* suffering. Because he's not innocent like Otto. And he did wrong." But he felt uncomfortable, knowing that he, too, had failed. He was being carried farther and farther away from what his brother remained: unmarred in stainless purity.

The wind off the water made him shiver, and he hunched his shoulders. The hills opposite were dissolving into the mist. In the hush of descending dusk, he felt a pang of desire for the tintinnabulation of a Georgia summer. Strange, he thought, to long for the rasp of day- and dusk-singing cicadas and the night singers, katydids.

"I don't know," he said. "I don't know what's to become of me."

Closing his eyes, he thought again of that long-ago morning, irretrievable, and it seemed to him that his brother's face had subtly shifted and was more sorrowful than before—an emblem of loneliness. He knew loneness. In memory, the fencepost and its burden seemed magnified against the sunrise, the way a harrow or plow abandoned in an upward-sloping field sometimes seemed weirdly significant set against the burning sky at sunset.

"Time to head back." He looked at the blue and white china in his hands. Till would have known what to do with such crumbs of the world. He slipped them into his pocket.

On the path to the house he met Mr. Fairbairn, a shotgun over his shoulder. His cheeks and bulbous nose were bright red.

"Seen him?" The farmer was breathing heavily.

"Didn't look," Pip admitted.

"I hunted, and it didn't do no good." He mopped his face with a handkerchief. "He's long gone, poor devil. How's the hand? You staying with us a while? I got some odd jobs when this is done."

"Okay. I might."

Mr. Fairbairn tapped on the boy's chest with his forefinger. It was a habit of his that always got Pip's attention. He did not like to be touched by a man, but he did not flinch the way he might've done when he was younger. The farmer seemed in tune with the wanderer's mood, almost echoing the question he had asked by the lake. "What's going to become of you, hey?"

"I was—I don't know. Just keep moving, maybe."

"Well, what do you like to do?" He balled up the handkerchief and shoved it into his vest pocket.

"I like history. I like it a lot."

The farmer nodded. "That'd be a good subject for a thinker. You can go to teaching or else work in a museum—you seen our museum in town? They got all kinds of curious old mess in there. Or you can be in the government. You got to do what it's in you to do. And you need to get your education."

The boy stared at the earth, not sensing that he might really have a future but wondering whether such a thing could be.

"I recollect that your parents are dead, ain't that right?"

Pip nodded.

"See, ain't there somewhere that if you go, they have to take you in? Ain't you got an uncle or a great-aunt or somebody?" In the fervor of the question, Mr. Fairbairn took hold of his arm and gave him a little shake.

Pip stood with jaw clenched as if to keep in the words. If only he knew what had happened to Opal—if only he had jumped from the train and found and seized her and not let go.

"You think about it. Maybe there's somewhere. I bet there is. Here—let's hoof on home."

The two paused in the side yard where Mrs. Fairbairn was unpinning clothes from the line in the twilight. White shirts glowed in the darkness, and a breeze was catching the sheets and belling them outward, pressing against the curve of her breasts and belly.

"My Bideth's going to have a baby," Mr. Fairbairn confided. "She's only a bit of a girl, but she'll do fine."

Pip was taken aback; he had not known. He thought of her white legs and arms that had reminded him of the trunks of trees. She had not seemed "a bit of a girl" to him.

The older man stood beaming in the gloom, waiting until the boy remembered to tender congratulations. "You go on up and have a fine time with the other fellows," he said, but Pip halted to watch from the trees as husband and wife went in the house, carrying the baskets of clean clothes and linens.

When he reached the shack, the pickers were hunkered around a log fire, talking and smoking. That was the night when Pip took up the habit, having harvested currants all day off some no-account road in upstate New York. He and Otto had smoked pipes of rabbit tobacco, back in Emanuel County, but it had been a game. At the shanty he became a regular smoker and learned to roll a cigarette. It was a matter of determination and practice because he had never been dexterous.

He held an image in his mind of a silver spoon and a hand-rolled cigarette set on a linen napkin beside a Staffordshire teacup—he had bumped into a book called *Marvels of English China* at the village library and liked the look of the elegant place settings. He had enjoyed that hour wandering along the main street and finding his way to the stone building with the white Corinthian columns. The library had been only a room tucked behind the portico, but it was airy with long windows and high ceilings. He had run his hands along the spines of the books as if looking for the right grab iron on a boxcar. That was how he had found the book with its illustrations of Staffordshire tea sets and place settings. For an hour he had sat in an upholstered chair to read, unnoticed by the librarian.

Perhaps someday he would have a table with silver and plates and cups and the slender stemware he had seen in the black-and-white photographs in the book. Perhaps it was possible to have a future. Perhaps it was possible for his life to be like a stay at the lake with no crazy floater and no working for pennies—with a white cloth and marvels of English china.

But at the berry farm, he and the other fellows cooked and ate from cast-off tins. They washed down their food with cans of tea swimming with rancid leaves. Never was a word of tea-leaf fortune left to read in those containers because the floaters gulped down each jot and tittle of their bad luck.

14

Balling the jack: Pip witnesses the blood
Of innocence; raw anger gives him wings;
A piece of unexpected news arrives.

One morning in October of '41, he nailed a hot freight moving east on the Missouri Pacific. It was a rotten day; a kid had trotted alongside the looming black shoulder of the train and jumped for the grab irons at the rear of a freight car, though Pip and the others had shouted at him to stop. Helpless as a piece of wind-thrown laundry, he flapped between the cars for an instant before his hand was ripped from the ladder. There was no sound from the watchers, who glimpsed the body as it tumbled onto the couplings and was jerked under the train. The scream lingered in the air like a ring of smoke, weaving through the noise from the steam whistle and the pistons and the driving wheels.

"O," Pip whispered, instinctively feeling for the shell as the other boys shrugged or protested, each according to his nature.

"Too damn hot to nail," one of the boys said.

"Crazy."

"Balling the jack."

Pip walked to the rails, drifting over slowly though none of the others followed him. It was not a bit of use; anyone could see that. But he had to go and see for himself. He had to witness what the express had done. It was a compulsion that could not be fought. In some obscure manner, he felt that obtaining a sight of what had happened was his duty. A road kid was more than a moth caught in a fan's blades and sprinkled in pieces on the floor. He had to be acknowledged.

Why, a man might be nothing but a mote in history, but he could look and store the news up and perhaps make his scratch of a story on the wall of the cave. Pip had begun to think of himself as someone who had to know everything about the past and present. But that would mean education as Fairbairn had said. Sometimes he thought his self-taught learning out of public libraries and the school of the rails was enough and perhaps even better than what a gently nurtured citizen of the world could have. Other times he felt certain that he had to find out the rules by which people played—the ones that were historians and curators and whatever else it was possible for a young man who loved history to become. In the meantime, his eyes were wide open.

Some of what was left lay by lines smeared with blood. It was unbelievable to Pip that this poor kid had tried to nail the train—the cars still shuddered past him, ripping by, going who-knows-how-many miles an hour.

"Well?" One of the 'bos stepped forward to shout.

"Greased the rails," he called over the clack and roar of the train, half-turning to the knot of boys. "Dead. There's his leg and arm. It's bad." At this the others seemed faintly interested, hoisting their bindles and milling about as if they might come over. He didn't say anything about the kid's head and neck and a piece of a shoulder connected to a rope of muscle, strung together on the ground, the sparse snow beside the tracks christened with red. Pip still found it hard to judge expressions, but it seemed to him that it might be surprise on the face. The kid was just green. Even the side irons could've killed this one, but he had not known any better than to catch hold at the rear.

The boy had been in no marked way different from the others, now moiling in unease as the knowledge of death entered in. Pip glanced at them and turned away.

"Blood matters."

He had not meant to speak, but the words had slipped out. *Blood matters.* The familiar ache for his mother and Otto and the old daddy who had read them stories came over him. But all he had now was this aimless tribe of young men, an unconnected troop who had banded together out of a fear of wandering in a world without bounds and with no end to danger. It was not what he wished for. He wanted to be with people who had a meaning to one another; he wanted somebody who cared. He wanted to catch a glimpse of Opal hurrying away. He would seek her, leap magically from car to car, plunge through the dark until he could call her name and see her turn, his name in her mouth. But he knew that was a dream.

Wasn't he just as entrapped as ever, as far from finding a spot to call his own, despite his years of roving? People said the heyday of the 'bos was over, and it would be harder and harder to stay on the road. How long could he keep on as a roamer, living hand to mouth, fighting when he must? Although he had found no trace of Opal, Excelsior Tillman might be ready to welcome him. Surely he would never leave Roseville. Till's Countess-Princess had likely caught the westbound train by now unless she proved to be, as he had sometimes suspected, something uncanny and immortal.

Blood matters. He glanced down at the kid.

What was left of him was olive-skinned, with a faint penciling of moustache above his lip. The noise and the hot air forced from the wheels and thrusting pistons pushed against Pip, but he knelt, looking into the brown eyes, thinking that it was easier to look into dead than live ones. And he had done it before; he knew how. Imperceptibly the look that might be surprise bled out of the kid's face until it was simply a face, neutral, known to somebody, who maybe mistreated it or simply could not afford to feed it. Whatever his past, he was no longer anybody's problem. Raccoons and coyotes would come for his bones. He would be a grain of lost history, sliding into the abyss. No one knew how many children had been killed somewhere along the rails in hobo camps and boxcars. No one wanted to find out.

The train, smut black and triple headed, hammered against the line.

"Cerberus at the mouth of hell," Pip said. But that was not it. It was not the mythology he loved.

"Just a damn kid. Nothing but somebody's brother trying to hop a freight and get somewhere he can work." The sight wavered, made tremulous by unshed tears. Pip felt a grief for the dead kid that was as crude and simple as an iron blade struck with force to the heart. He had never felt so much for a person he did not know. It was a mystery. When he touched the jaw of the boy, his fingertips glistened with blood. Then, lifting up his fist and shaking it at the dawn light seeping from behind a host of small symmetrical clouds, he called out, "Damn you, damn you, damn," and he began to chase the train, galloping in the fierce shadow of breath cast by the cars, charging forward without watching for switches or ties that had dislodged from their beds, the sparks striking his calves and heels. Hot and tasting of metal, words the orphans had memorized for Pastor Bell shot from his mouth: "Who will, who will—"

Shouting, the others started to lumber toward the tracks as if they thought he might be about to throw himself after the unknown 'bo. He could hear them cry out his name, but he did not pause. None of them mattered in the way he longed for someone to matter. The cobwebs strung between them tore away instantly.

Pip churned the air with awkward arms, his eyes fixed on the train that was crashing forward like barely controlled wreckage, faster than any freight he had ever caught. More words scaled his throat: "Who will deliver me—"

Raising his hands, he brushed the cars with his fingertips until a grab iron touched them, and he dived against the metal, fingers seizing hold. Slammed and bruised against the boxcar, he held tight, the memory of the kid's stare making him grip down on the bar as explosive jerks snapped at his arms and threatened to unsocket his bones. "From the body," he choked out. The train seemed as malignant as a giant blackjack, beating at every inch of his hips and ribs and shoulders, the clinkers and rocks sucked up from the bed pelting his legs; his feet swung and groped, and he found a step and clung close, the boxcar's jouncing unearthing a quake, an eclipse in his head. "Of this death?" he spat. He turned his head and in a blur of landscape remembered Otto, the preacher's yellow peaches, and the pearly eye in the well. His marrow seemed to have been replaced by a trembly water as he rose slowly toward the deck.

A hand reached out and hauled him onto the rocking top of the boxcar.

"Man, did you ever nail her," an admiring voice called, "in a real pretty style."

"Damn." Pip crawled forward and collapsed at full length.

The voice and a second one laughed together, and a cupped hand offered him a cigarette, which he dragged on.

"Dead," he muttered, sliding one hand under his cheek to shield himself from the jolting metal.

"Too wild for a smoke."

"Too wild to sit up. But I sure had it lit for a second."

A fissure in his brain felt about to crack open, and so he lay quietly without looking, imagining that the chute of wind with its cinders and smoke and occasional speckle of fire could catch up the ache and whirl away, tossing the hurt westward until it fell apart over the Pacific Ocean. Two years ago he had washed Otto's shell in those waves, and for an instant he recalled waking on the shore north of San Francisco, seeing a girl canter across the beach on a white horse. Sea-drenched pillars of stone had jagged up from the smooth sand behind her.

"My dadgum head is going to kill me," he murmured, pushing himself upright and sitting cross-legged, hunching over with his back to the blast of wind. It made him anxious; facing forward was a cardinal rule of the hobo.

Lying at full length, two boys not much older than he grinned at him. He smiled, seeing that they were unmistakably brothers, long-faced fellows with green eyes and topknots of springy hair. Gusts tried to hurl him into the air, and in another instant he lay down possum-style, pressing his belly against the car.

"What were they hollering at you?" The older one spoke almost in a scream, his words striving against the gust.

"Pip. My name."

"That's an unusual kind of a name. Where you from?"

"Nowhere."

"How about before you got to be from nowheres?" The younger one shouted, his voice raw from fighting the air. "We're all from the same dratted town if you're just from nowheres."

"Say, I ain't from nowheres. Speak for your own durn self." His brother laughed and wriggled closer to Pip. "I'm from Hicksville, U. S. of A., and proud of it."

The younger boy yelled again, "So where you from?"

Pip dragged himself forward until he was so near them that the wind couldn't toss his words into oblivion before they could hear.

"Georgia. West of Savannah. Pretty much nowhere there too. You talk about the sticks, the cotton-picking boondocks—that's where it's at." Pip rubbed his forehead and lightly fingered around his eye, ringed with pain. Seeing the blood dried on his fingers, he rubbed them with a rag pulled from his pocket.

"All my brothers and sisters had names like mine—turn them around like in a mirror and they're just the same, backwards, forwards, inside out. It was a mad freak of my daddy's to name them that way. Old Gilead Tattnal. I guess he was a God-crazy man. Thought the alpha and omega of a name had to be just the same. But it makes no sense to me. *God's* not the same backwards and forwards. You turn it around, and you're not looking at much but a cocked leg."

"Hoo, you have sure got a mouth on you. Evil, man—"

The boy crossed himself.

"You thinking what I'm thinking?" His brother elbowed him in the ribs.

"A durn sewer."

"No, the name—"

"Maybe—"

"You got guardian angels working overtime in the fields." The boy let out a whoop as he tugged at a scrap of blanket, pulling it tight around his shoulders. "The paper—Tom, you still got that thing?"

"Dunno. It was in my safe deposit." The one called Tom
rummaged about in the lining of his jacket, turning up a stunted
pencil, some coins, a sack of loose tobacco, and a handkerchief
embroidered with pansies.

Wind ripped the tobacco into the air, batting the little bag end
over end.

Tom frowned, leaning to watch it dance and be jerked out of
sight, and then turned back to Pip.

"Got a sister named Lil?"

"Maybe. And every other name you can think of that starts and
ends the same. And some you can't think of. But I don't have any
truck with my brothers and sisters." Bemused, Pip gazed from one to
the other.

"It's him. Gotta be him. Came to *us*."

"Here," Tom said, unfolding a railroad timetable. The worn
paper curled around his hand, fluttering rapidly against the wrist.
"Best not let it flap off."

"You're one famous 'bo. People know about you. I mean all *over*
the map." The brother nodded at him.

Gripping with two hands against the wind so that the page beat
against his fingers like a wild bird's wings, the one called Tom passed
it to Pip.

"You hang on now—or it'll be miles gone, and that'd be sad.
That lady gave us the best feed we've had all year."

"She was sure one nice lady."

"They don't make women like that every day."

Pip stared at the worn sheet, creased with squares. He knew the
names on the schedule, but it was the penciled scrawl that caught his
eye. He did not recognize the handwriting, had probably never seen
his sister Lil's writing, but there were the words, *Lil Tattnal Tattnal*,
and the name of a road near Lexsy. He barely remembered Lil,
though he called to mind a photograph in a pot-metal frame. She
must have been about the age he was now, standing slim and
barefoot in the dirt yard, three or four chickens close by. He had

thought the picture funny because the hens were cocking their heads as if looking up in surprise at the person holding the camera. Lil would be a lot older now. She must have married a cousin to be twice a Tattnal. *They don't make women like that every day,* the boy had said.

The brothers were staring at him, waiting for him to respond.

Abruptly he recalled how the Dwarf and the Throat had talked about somebody looking for a brother named *Pip*. Perhaps she was better than the rest of his brothers and sisters—perhaps as kind as Till or Swain and Irisanne or Mr. Fairbairn. Even at the orphanage, those Hookses had tried to do right. And Mr. Sam, who had come along when he and Otto had nowhere to go.

The younger brother could not wait any longer. "That yours?"

"Maybe—"

Shifting his gaze away from the writing—did he really want, ever again, to see the piney woods and cotton and tobacco fields near Lexsy?—he stared at the horizon. It gave back no answer. Ducking his head, Pip peered at the cramped handwriting. As if the page had been perfumed by a local aroma, the hot, slightly fetid exhalation of the swamp with its festoons of snakes came back to him, one of those peculiar scents that other people disliked.

"Sure would've been funny if it went scooting away." The younger brother laughed. "Give you a scare. Wouldn't matter though. If you'd lost hold, we'd have done good enough. That lady told us all about how you run off from the orphan home about the time when her old man got killed, how she's been hunting for you. A little girl died after you left—drowned, maybe—and the county shut it down. So nobody's looking but her."

"Something, huh? It was *us* to find him." Tom tried to light another cigarette butt.

"Seemed like the one that started it all's dead."

Tom shrugged. "I don't remember any of that. Just ask me about the feed…"

Pip drew the sheet closer to his eyes. It was no surprise to find that they knew things about him. What kind of privacy did any of them have, working stiffs without a hole to lie in? He hoped that "how you ran off" did not mean that she'd been talking about Otto with strangers. They had liked the food she dished up. And he would not mind being fed, having some ham and biscuits and fried chicken and okra with a big serving bowl of lady peas all to himself. He missed the sight of women on the porch steps, talking and laughing while they shelled butterbeans or crowders and black eyes into a metal bowl: a musical tingle of beans and peas bouncing against the tin sides.

"Mrs. Lil Tattnal Tattnal. L. J. Tattnal Farm Road," he read aloud.

"You going? You're headed east."

He shook his head. "It's not me. Must be some other Pip." He offered to return the timetable.

Tom let out a hoot. "You said your daddy's name was Tattnal, and your sister's name was Lil. Your name is Pip. You're from west of Savannah, Georgia. It ain't you. Huh."

"Yep," his brother said. "You just keep that paper. You might change your mind. Be a crying waste not to."

The timetable still struggled to pinwheel like tumbleweeds across the prairie. Pip ran his eyes over the schedule and then folded it into a tiny square that he forced inside the conch until there was only a faint line of paper showing.

"You going? She sure wants you home."

He looked blankly at the boys.

"He don't know, Tom. He just found out. But it'd be good to have that lady cook for you at suppertime."

Pip's stomach growled, and he contracted his belly muscles.

"Any woman," Tom replied. "I don't guess there's a down side to a regular soup bowl. We been flying light for a while."

"If I get any hungrier, my belly'll start to button through my backbone," Pip admitted. He was remembering the doll, Buh, back at the orphanage, and wondering which one of the girls had died. Where could she have drowned? The well, he supposed. Hadn't the sheriff had cautioned Mr. Sam and Mr. Jimmie about the rickety slats fencing the hole on the afternoon when Otto lay under a cloth on the porch? And Mr. Sam was dead too, it seemed! He'd meant to do right even if the Orphanage had failed to save all its children.

He lowered his head, thinking about Miss Versie's club against snakes, the whine of insects, and the wash of heat that could come on you like sickness. He felt a jab of hatred for the lane shimmering with August and the barbed wire buried in the cedar uprights. A fence post could last longer than a child…. Yet even after the many miles that should have ripped all linkages, he was entangled with that landscape as if the very clay of him had been scooped from the Georgia fields. Bondage and bonding, the tie to the place held strong.

Was this a piece of news that could be a help to him? His head ached, and he could not decide, teetering between *yes* and *no*. Perhaps he had run too far and reached another world where he was nothing but a tramp, lowdown and unfaithful.

"What's it like to have a nigger for a brother?" The unnamed boy was smoking again, his hand making a shelter against the pummeling of the wind as he nursed a cigarette butt.

Heat surged behind Pip's eyes as he jerked up his head, and a star of sunlight, like the spark from a biting-down flange of a brake, struck him straight-on in the iris. He bowed his head, covering his right eye. His sister Lil was talking too much, telling private things about the orphanage and Otto, maybe even how he died. His brother had been parceled out and dispersed like an item of gossip. It made him feel nauseated. Or maybe that was the pain that came after the start of an eclipse, making him sick.

No, I'll never go back, never.

Picking up the shell on its string, he held it and squeezed until the spikes of the conch punched through his skin.

Never. Even if she does want me. Unless maybe I go shut her mouth. But it's strange. That all this time she's been wanting me.

His skin twitched as if his sister's thoughts plucked at him from thousands of miles off. He remembered a curious book he had skimmed in a library, a set of case studies about the tribulations of European mental patients. The writer, a doctor, had guided them to examine their childhoods in an attempt to adjust themselves to the world. Pip did not like it by half. Because who could be anything but askew and maladjusted to the ways of this globe, spinning through the aimlessness and darkness of space?

No. Never. He shook his head, dashing a cinder from his cheek.

Across the fields he could see a coyote, his legs twinkling along, a burden in his mouth. For an instant he thought of the dead kid, wondering if it might be an arm bone. But the three-headed train was still slinging its cars way too fast for a coyote to keep up. Probably a rabbit had been zigzagging in panic across the ground until the coyote had scooped it up and relieved it of hope and fear. Wind battered Pip's shoulders and twisted his hair back and forth like long grass until his scalp was sore.

"It was the best damn thing in the world," he said, raising his eyes with an effort to the boy's face. "Just the best damn thing in the whole world."

Picaroon's return

15

A shock of Pearl, a bindled wanderer —
Lil Tattnal Tattnal and the prodigal.

The flurry of rumors in the days following Pearl Harbor was the reason Lil Tattnal Tattnal and her sons, Roiphe and Alden, heard neither the disconsolate cry of the whistle nor the slowing of the train near the water tank nor the footsteps on the porch. Pip just walked right in. Finding no one's attention on him, he might have turned around and trudged back down to the tracks. To make an entrance and find that no one is waiting is hard, especially if you are prickly and certain that the day's event is you.

Much later when asked why he had stayed, he recalled a creamy yellow pitcher standing on a table in the room, beaded with drops of moisture that occasionally plunged along its curve. A puddle of water shadowed its foot. His eye rested on the vessel first and foremost; he was irrationally convinced that it was filled with milk fresh out of the icebox and had cream floating on top, and he could almost taste it. He hadn't had any but canned milk in months. Although he knew the others were there, his eye took comfort in the roundness of the pitcher's belly, the tears clinging to its sides. He shivered, wanting milk's coldness and freshness. The pitcher spoke of home more clearly than the three figures in the room and seemed to shape the chamber around itself.

Unseen and feeling a pang of loneliness, he might have wheeled away from family. But it was not what he did. The yellow pitcher sang a pure and milk-lit song to him, and cornbread and a bowl of winter greens simmered with ham made the air fragrant and drew him; after all, he had been hungry for years. At last he surveyed the big-hipped woman in a dress printed with tiny salmon and black triangles on cloth of robin's egg blue, her hair crimped. Between her widow's pension and her garden and a little seamstress work, Lil Tattnal Tattnal was doing fine, at least by the standards of the day and district. She was bent over a parlor table, fiddling with a brand new radio that sputtered and popped as she twiddled the knobs, and the words of an announcer flared in bursts through the chamber. At each side of her leaned a boy, well-nourished and dressed in ironed shirts and pants. The younger one was fair-haired and sturdy, but the slim boy with the intense hazel stare was the one who drew glances. Pip was home, or as near there as he could ever get.

One of the brothers caught sight of him, standing in the middle of the room with his bindle.

"Mommer—"

He tugged at her sleeve.

"Caught it!" Lil straightened up as the voice, powerful as an angel, soared into the room accompanied by attendant flecks of static.

She turned, saw him, exclaimed, "For crying out loud!" and stood up.

"It's me," Pip said. "I got the address. A while back."

He reached for the shell as if he might pluck the folded name of *Lil Tattnal Tattnal* from the whisperings of the sea in its heart.

"But that's not why I'm here," he added, feeling a need to assert himself. "I came because—"

Three bird dogs that have stumbled on unexpected quarry, the others had frozen, their eyes fixed on him as he fumbled with the string around his neck. The import of his words was felt before it became clear. Then, like the covey of grouse kicked out of a thicket, they broke toward him, clamoring his name, grabbing him, embracing his soiled jacket and the bony limbs inside, rubbing his hair, shaking him, whooping. Lil Tattnal Tattnal pressed her face against his unwashed cheek. It was more family hugging than Pip could remember from his whole life, but he suffered it, along with a battering-ram noise of triumph that hurt his ears.

"*Look* at you," his sister exclaimed, holding him at arm's length. "If you ain't purely Tattnal, I don't know what is."

The older boy spoke up. "She always thought we'd find you. She never gave up on it."

"The Japs bombed Pearl Harbor day before yesterday," the other one said. "Bombed the Pacific fleet to hell. Did you know that? Have you been to Hawaii? Have they got a trestle that goes out to the islands?"

Lil wiped her eyes on an apron printed with minute green and yellow polka dots on a red background.

"Turn off that radio, Roiphe," she said. "They'll be scaring us with news about more blackouts and Japanese attacks all evening long, wait and see. You, Alden, don't even mention that mess. It'll keep. The prodigal son don't come home but once."

She beamed at him and the boys.

"I'm a bit ripe," Pip confessed. "I'm sorry."

"I don't care what you smell like or what's crawling on your nape, I'm that glad to have you," Lil announced. "You, Roiphe, fire up the stove till it roars. We've got us a tub but not any hot water. You ever take a bath with running water?"

He had not.

"We're going to get us a heater. Some day. Right now we boil a pot or two and dump it in with some cold. Roiphe, put on four—fetch the canning pot—this is going to be a genuine deepwater bath. Alden, you go for the jug of kerosene and my sewing scissors."

"Can I have—"

Lil Tattnal Tattnal brought him the pitcher, holding it out with both hands, and he saw with an intense pleasure that he had been right. Still standing on the braided rug, he drank at the cream and milk, tipping his head back, his throat working until his belly hurt and the pitcher was drained and the Tattnals were staring at him as he gasped for air—the three surprised, half-smiling, young Alden with his mouth ajar and the proffered glass still held up.

Then the boys were set to chopping wood and ferrying pots of water while Pip was transformed, his hair clipped short and soaked in kerosene, half of what had seemed a tan swirling down the drain of the porcelain tub. Cauled in a light quilt, he sat down at the kitchen table. Behind the house, jeans, shirt, and jacket smoldered in the burn barrel, raising the ghost of a plume: a goodbye to the rails.

"Dadgum," Alden said in an awed voice as Pip, having wolfed greens and cornbread, held out his plate for more.

"Roiphe and Alden, go chop some wood and fill the firebox, you hear? I'll be having to bake for four now."

They went, protesting, looking back over their shoulders.

Afterward, a mirror hanging from a nail above the kitchen sink startled him: the shearing of his hair had left a band of pale skin high on his forehead, and he was drawn irresistibly to stare at the face beneath.

"You're a good-looking young man, and that's the truth," Lil said, her reflection nearing his in the mirror. "Daddy was the same way when he was young. They say his eyes would just stop you, just as sure as if he'd put out a hand, and he had just such a jaw as yours. I like a man to have a strong face, with no piddling chin hiding under his nose."

"But he covered it up with a beard," Pip said, still staring at the unfamiliar face that was his.

"And what a beard it was! That was a bush for the birds of the air to build their nests in. A sure-enough bountiful beard." She moved away, pausing at a tin cabinet. "You want something else to stow in that belly? I guess it'll be a long time till you're worn out from eating. How about a slab of velvet cake? I've got plenty."

"Yes ma'am, I'd like that."

"You've got some nice ways still. More than I'd guess. Your mommer was a bug for manners and wanted you little boys trained up right."

Pip's eyes burned as he accepted a fat slice of cake and began to eat, listening to Lil as she wiped the table and remembering his mother, the glass of the jar flashing in the light and shattering. Little by little he noticed what he was eating, tasted the deep red of the cake against his tongue.

"Best cake I ever ate." He scraped up the crumbs, and she brought the cake plate and tilted the last piece onto his saucer.

"I thought you said that you had plenty," he protested.

"Plenty more where that came from." She held up her hands and smiled at him. "I'm real fond of baking."

He ate the second piece slowly, looking out the window at the smudge of smoke from the barrel.

"That's the end of that." He nodded slightly in acceptance, though his voice sounded rueful. A light rain began to leave pin-fine tracks on the glass.

"You've gone and swapped your free nights and days for a home. It's not such a bad trade," she told him. "I sure hope you won't think so."

His sister appeared very tidy to Pip, and he thought that the window before him was so scrubbed of dust and grease that without those streaks of raindrops, he would have thought it only air.

"No ma'am," he said to her. "Not so far, anyway. Though that was quite a boil-up."

"The bath, you mean?"

He nodded and then reached up and felt the clipped edges of his hair and did not much like the way it felt against his hand. *Graybacks*, he recalled. Like the hobos, his granddaddy, that powerful old man in a serge suit or overalls, had called lice *graybacks*. It was good to get rid of those free riders. He sniffed at the smell of kerosene that still haloed his head. It reminded him of the pleasant stinks of the road.

For the first night in years, he got into a bed with clean sheets, sliding down into cool, crisp whiteness. The borrowed nightclothes felt strange against his skin, their much-laundered softness like a caress. He was not used to their texture, was not sure he could get used to the flimsiness of the cotton and go to sleep.

He could hear Lil talking to her sons.

"Don't you bother him now. There's all the time in the world to find out his adventures. You hear me? Don't mess with him. He looks dead tired, and you just let him sleep. You listening to me? Look at me, Roiphe...."

When Roiphe and Alden came bursting out of the kitchen and raced to the bedroom, Pip sat up and looked at them. They stopped in the doorway, breathing hard, their hair damp from a wash in the sink. Until now, Lil had kept them busy, but now they were let loose, rife with curiosity.

"Hoo," Alden shouted, leaping onto the smaller bed.

"Did Mama say you'd have to share?" The older boy hesitated in the door, his eyes going to the far side of the bed. Outlined against the light from the room beyond, a resemblance became clear. A kind of commonality with Pip showed in the squared face with its straight nose and high forehead. "With me because we're the closest in age. Alden's only twelve. Really because he won't give up his bed for anybody. He just won't. He used to wet the bed—"

"I never did any such—"

"You did." As he spoke, a dirty balled-up sock smacked Roiphe in the face. "Ow! Phew—you stink. What you got loaded in there, stones?"

"Aggies." Alden grinned, ducking as his brother slung it back across the room. The marbles jangled against the iron rails of the bed.

"Missed me—"

"So did she say?" Roiphe looked unsure of himself, here in his own room.

Pip shrugged. "Get in."

"Ever kill anybody?" Alden got up on his knees in the bed, staring intently at this new relation. They were used to uncles and aunts of all ages, but this one was the closest they had seen to their own.

"What a bloodthirsty kid," Pip remarked, lying down and pillowing his head on an arm. "Is he always like that?"

"Yeah. But did you?" Roiphe waited, seating himself on the opposite edge of the bed.

Pip stared up at the ceiling. "Your mommer must be the cleanest person in the entire country. Would you look at that? Not one wisp of cobweb in the corners. All just as white as can be."

"Aw, shoot." Alden bounced on his bed, and the metal frame bucked and squeaked in protest.

Lil's voice floated in. "Don't you jump on that mattress, Alden Tattnal!"

"There you go," Roiphe told him. "Getting Mommer down on our heads."

"Ain't," his little brother retorted. "Uncle Pip, how'd you get so scarred?"

Pip rolled over on his face, laughing against the coarse linen. He was weary enough that once he got going, he could not stop, and uncontrollable gasps pumped out of his mouth.

"You nit." Roiphe lay down and pulled up the covers. "Don't go calling him *Uncle*. He's just a year older than I am."

Alden ignored him, hopping off the bed and running to inspect the shaking back and peer at a glimpse of the face.

"He's gone punch drunk."

"So talk to him in the morning, why don't you? Let him sleep." Roiphe raised himself on an elbow and frowned at his brother.

"He ain't sleeping," Alden retorted.

"He's not sleeping."

"I know that! Hey, Uncle Pip—"

The boy jigged in place with excitement, but laughter kept shaking the bed. He lifted a flap of the chenille spread and saw an ear. "You get laid, out there?"

"You foul little rat—"

Roiphe erupted out of bed and chased Alden from the room, howls spiraling behind them.

In a minute the younger boy crept back in. His new uncle was still laughing but had flopped over on his back and begun blotting his eyes with a handkerchief Lil had given him.

"Anybody try to shoot you?" The boy's voice sounded wistful, and that set his uncle off again.

"Would you just leave him be?" His older brother came in, a glass of water in his hand. He paused between the two beds to drink, his throat pumping. After gasping a moment, he set the glass down and murmured, "How on earth did he gulp that whole pitcher without a stop?"

Meanwhile Alden jumped about in irritation. "He won't quit cackling! Like a durn hen laid a jillion eggs. I wanna talk to him!" Mirth billowed in the room, and the brass bed trembled and squeaked.

"Well, did they try? And why'd you go?" Alden shouted at the mummy-like form wound in chenille, but it only quivered in reply.

Lil appeared in the doorway, wearing a muslin nightgown and a shawl.

"Boys, boys—Alden Tattnal, get in the bed—"

She peeled the spread away from Pip's face and laid a hand on his forehead. It felt cool to him and smelled of dusting powder, dish soap, and the kerosene she had used to rinse his hair. After a minute his laughter slowed and came to a stop, though he could feel a faint vibration inside, waiting to break out again. He listened as she said a prayer of thanksgiving for his safe return, all the time still sensing the taut string within him that could at any moment be plucked and resound with fresh hilarity.

In turn she kissed the boys, tucking the covers around them, although Roiphe protested. He could hear her telling them that she loved them and their low-voiced replies, shy because of his presence.

Once again she touched him, her fingers brushing against his temple and shorn hair.

"I'm glad you came home. I sure wish Roiphe and Alden's daddy could've seen his day." She withdrew her hand. "I hope you stay with us. I love you, Pip Tattnal, my brother."

"You don't know me." He breathed in the scent of her, staring up at the ceiling. Again it struck him as being the most pristine swath

of world he had ever seen, showing Lil's care in its utter
marklessness. "Not hardly."

"Well, I saw you now and then when you were a baby and a
shirttail boy. And I cared about my children before they were fetched
into the day and when they weren't but something that made my
belly poke out and gave me kicks. So I guess maybe I can love
somebody that I've been praying on for years." She bent and kissed
him, a fringe from her shawl brushing along his cheek.

"Alden and Roiphe, you get to sleep. He'll be here in the
morning. You hear me? The Sandman better be coming or else I'll be
marching you out of here pretty quick."

"It's not me, Mama, "Roiphe said, turning on his side to face the
wall.

Alden kept whispering in the dark, but Pip was emptied out and
unable to speak. The jag of glee had depleted him, and he felt as if he
had been gulping at some fine mist of drowsiness. Perhaps it was the
Sandman's crystals, flung by the handful into the air. For a long time
he lay caught in a no-man's-land between waking and sleeping until
he opened his eyes and saw that a delicate and glittering rain was
falling in the room. It came to him that he had seen many wonders in
his travels, had gone north until he met the midnight flares of the
aurora borealis, had waded through the high prairie grass until he
knew it to be endless, and had crossed a western beach piled with
agates and inset with pools of pink and green stars, but that now he
had come to what might be home and this sight was the strangest of
them all. In its in-between realm, he struggled to name the peculiar
snow but could not. When he realized that he had felt no surprise, it
occurred to him that he must be asleep. But yet he could feel the
flecks against his skin and piling in the bedclothes though not
moistening them. He closed his eyes.

Opening them again, he glimpsed Lil bending over Alden, her
shoulders and hair glistening, and when she left the room he saw that
she vanished into a dazzle of light.

"I am asleep," Pip said or dreamed that he said, his tongue laggard in his mouth.

Was this some new state—was the fine slippage also falling over the ruined water tower at The White Camellia Orphanage and over the Madonna in her shell and over Opal, wherever she was? Perhaps over her grave and over all he had known who now lay in the bone orchards of Earth. He could feel warmth at his side, and he remembered his nephew Roiphe and how he had stood uncertainly in the doorway.

The shining silt made a faint hissing sound. It pressed on him, insistent, and he felt uneasy.

Stay.

Yes, he thought in answer, *I will. I will stay. I will try to stay.* The glinting fall increased, and when he looked up at the ceiling, it was a sky of staring white into which he looked until he forgot.

16

In which Pip is a schoolboy once again —

Camellias were in bloom in front of the schoolhouse. Pip had not remembered how deep a red could be set against the shining leaves and how sweet it was to the eye in winter. The ones with white petals, cold in the January air, seemed an impossible purity. They drew his gaze, and he could hardly look away, so different were they from the unraked sand of the yard, littered with needles and flecks of bark and pecan shell. He had seen them in the twilight, looking like soft stars; they remained luminous in the day. Across the street stood the gleaming tower of a persimmon hung with fruit, the tight smooth skin orange but flushed with red and glowing inwardly.

But it was the flowers that made him forget what was going on around him until somebody shoved at his chest.

"My ma says that she's crazy—"

Stumbling back a step, catching himself, Pip stared at the boy— what was his name?—a heavyset fellow with hair so fine and thin it looked like a baby's over the round face. The mouth, too, was infantile, a mere bud that never blossomed into a smile. If not for the broken nose and the pox scars on his cheeks, he might have changed little from the day of his birth.

"What did you say?"

"Crazy. Roiphe's ma. She's crazy. Feeding every tramp that came through here. Ma says she's made us the prime station for all the hobos and con men in the country—"

"You don't want to insult my sister. Is that your lookout? Trying to rile me?" Pip's glance drifted along the neck, corrugated by acne, and the limp shirt collar. *Johnny. His name was Johnny.*

Alden had run up to see what was happening. "You better not mess with my uncle," he offered. "He really likes to wrastle. He knows all kind of ways to fight that he learned on the road. Wrastling to him is like catnip to a catamount."

"She's got no more sense than a goose. That's what my ma says." Johnny ignored the advice and leaned forward, jabbing at Pip's chest as he spoke.

"Don't touch me." Pip's voice was lazy, seemingly unperturbed, but his eyes flicked to Johnny's face and away. He had lightness on his side, for even after a month of Lil's cooking, he still looked boiled down to bone and muscle. And despite the years living hand to mouth and sleeping close to strangers, he still did not like to be touched unexpectedly. Not unless it was a girl—his girl. Then it would be all right.

"Touch you if I want." Making a fist, Johnny drew back his arm, shaking it lightly in threat. "You damn Pip. Pip the pip-squeak."

"Back—get back." Now the voice seemed to crack in the air, quick and harsh.

Alden was watching, and he yelled to his brother. "Roiphe, Roiphe, Pip's gonna fight!" He was jumping in anticipation, the aggies in his pocket clacking together.

As about a dozen older boys began to gather, Johnny launched a punch, but it was blocked with snakelike swiftness. In an instant, the attacker was on his knees, throwing up on the sand.

"Sweet taters," Alden said in surprise. Then he leaped in the air. "I tried to tell you, I tried. Didn't I? Now you puked your supper, didn't you?" He waved his arms. "Did you see that?" He was shouting as he acted out the scene. "Boom! He stops the arm. Ka-pow! Right hand to the face. Pow! Pow! Left hand to the gut, right hand to his ca-rotch."

"Some kind of a wild man you got there, Roiphe," said Lengie, a boy who lived down the road from the Tattnal boys. His pale eyes looked out of a cloud of freckles. "Believe I'd be scared to cross him. Man alive, you'd be doomed." He pulled his jacket tight around his body. "Just what we needed—another Tattnal. Busting with big words. Knowing all kind of nonsense by heart that nobody would ever have call to know. Only this time he's a fighting man."

"You said it," agreed one of the others. "What you got no use for and never will."

"I ain't no walking dictionary," Alden declared.

"Yeah, you're no Tattnal. Just a dumb clodpole like the rest of us," Lengie said.

Still doubled over, Johnny let out a moan.

"Pip's not afraid of getting hurt—not afraid of pain or cold or pretty much anything. Which is good because I guess he'll have to beat up every idiot in Emanuel County before he's done." Roiphe went over to his uncle. "You all right?"

Pip nodded, looking off at the persimmon tree. He rubbed his knuckles lightly. His face was as composed as if he were sitting in the classroom.

"That kid, Johnny, he shouldn't have said what he did."

His eye settled again on the crimson and green of camellias. He was restless, but the flowers made him feel calm: they were peaceful, lying on the glossy leaves. This afternoon he would break off some of those red ones to take to Lil. He flexed his hand, letting the pain disperse. He was glad that the first afternoon lesson would be history; at least in that class he had been bumped up into Roiphe's year, the tenth grade.

The girls had drifted out of the trees at the edge of the yard. Roiphe's girl, Addie Mae Latimer, was standing with her friend Lavadera.

"Hey, you boys want to come down to the river this afternoon?" Addie Mae smiled, putting an arm around Lavadera's shoulders. "We thought we might go swimming."

"Swimming in January? There's an idea." Lengie clapped his hands together. "But I don't think she's asking me."

"Why not swimming? It's warm enough," Alden said, indignant.

"Not so many snakes in January, Lengie," Roiphe said, ignoring his brother. "Good time to hit the sandbar."

"Oh, the sandbar, I get you." Lengie tilted his head and inspected the winner of the fight. "I thought you were talking about *swimming*."

Pip's eyes traveled up Lavadera's dress and lit in the tangles of her blonde hair.

"It's a little early in the year for my nephew here to go swimming," he said. "But maybe we could do a little ornithological observation. I have a devotion to ornithological pursuits."

"Is that right?" Lavadera gripped her friend's arm.

"What's orny-what's-it?" Alden spoke shrilly, grabbing at his brother's sleeve.

"Get off, Alden." Roiphe pulled his arm away.

"Bird-watching, son," Pip said, giving him a light cuff. "Don't you know anything?"

"I guess somebody would see a bird, one way or another." Lengie looked up at the sky, but it was empty.

"What's been going on here?" Mr. Mangum was standing on the steps, shielding his eyes.

"Guess you've got some explaining to do," Roiphe murmured. "It won't be much. Johnny's been a bully from way back."

Mr. Mangum nodded and sent Pip on to class, where he shared a desk and a book with his nephew. Lengie had said that Mangum liked both the older Tattnals, that he was proud of the way Roiphe always needed extra work. He could do any kind of problem in his head, never needed paper. Lengie had overheard him telling Lil that Roiphe and her newfound brother could burn right through the curriculum in a year if the teachers were up to it.

"Real Tattnals," Lil had said, "like my daddy, Gilead. It's my brother that's most like him. He's a demon for dates and history."

Pip watched as Mr. Mangum set the ninth grade to writing an essay and then gathered the tenth grade for a history lesson. He was a little disappointed to find that the man did not tell him anything he did not know already, but he was used to the idea that most people did not share his obsessions.

He listened with a stray portion of his mind while his thoughts floated elsewhere, detaching themselves from the room and the fight and the way Lavadera's pink dress fitted close along the bodice before flaring outward. They sailed past the windowsill and the camellias and the house where Lil Tattnal Tattnal was up on a ladder, scrubbing the kitchen ceiling. Skating the rails, they flew west, following his longing. What was it he wished for, he wondered. Was it simply to lie in Opal's arms? He did not know, but the desire was familiar, a twisting together of pain and joy—something unappeased. The not yet harvested wheat was making a light sifting noise, the stems catching on other stems and on the bearded seed heads as the wind blew. He closed his eyes. The fields made the sound of hissing, and he realized that the harvest was not grain, and the music was not from its tossing. Thousands upon thousands of flimsy golden snakes were singing, standing on their tipmost tails, their thready tongues high in the air. The grasses parted and bowed down so that Opal could pass through, the bright child in her arms, and as Pip looked up at her from where he knelt in the gold, the day-moon made a halo around her head—

"Who can tell us something about the Constitutional Convention?"

The teacher's question echoed in the room. Most of the students ducked and looked intently at the book before them as if scouring the page for an answer.

"Pip. Pip Tattnal," Lengie said in a sepulchral tone. "The history bug. He can tell us."

"Stand when you have something to say, Leonard."

Someone jeered, and back in the ninth grade group there was a snort as Johnny, who was repeating another year, lifted his head from the desk. Using a nail, he was digging his initials into the soft pine surface.

"How about it, Pip?" Mr. Mangum tilted his head.

The boy jumped up, knocking a book from the desk and eliciting more laughter.

"The Constitutional Convention," he repeated, brushing a hand across his eyes as if to see more clearly.

"Yes, can you tell us—"

"Well, it was called by the Annapolis Convention of 1786 and by the Continental Congress, and it was to meet in Philadelphia on May 14, 1787, but only a few delegates had arrived by that time. By the 25th, delegates from seven states had arrived, and the convention began. Only 55 attended, and not all of them signed the finished document on September 17th."

He swept a glance along his row of desks, noticing that Lengie was grinning at him, goggle-eyed, his brows lifted in mock surprise. He felt a stab of annoyance.

"Good," Mr. Mangum said. "Anything more to add?"

Pip shrugged, looking out the window toward the pines. "George Washington served as president of the convention, and he and Benjamin Franklin were the most notable delegates. Eight of the delegates had signed the Declaration of Independence. Some of the most important ones there were Charles Pinckney and Charles Cotesworth Pinckney of South Carolina, William Richardson Davie of North Carolina, George Mason, James Madison, Edmund Randolph, and George Wythe of Virginia—"

"That's first rate, Pip." Mr. Mangum was smiling and did not seem to mind that some of the other students were laughing.

"Want me to tell about the competing plans for government and taxes and the argument over how to count the slave population, or was that enough?"

"Drive me stark mad to hear it all," Lengie called to Roiphe. "Is there anything he don't know about the U. S. of A.?"

"Ask him about China or Japan or Europe or whatever. You'll see."

Pip frowned, unsure if he should sit down. He heard Johnny hooting, and that was pretty damn bold after what had happened in the schoolyard. They would learn; he would learn them.

After assigning a set of questions to the class, Mr. Mangum called him over to a side door and stepped outside, standing where he could watch the students at their desks.

"I've been teaching for a spell, and I'd say you're about the most curious student I've met." He dragged on a cigarette as though hungry for smoke. "You're all lopsided, you know—heaviest on history by anybody's reckoning. Delinquent in mathematics, ahead in rhetoric. A fine and often surprising sense of words." The teacher leaned against the doorframe.

Pip's indignation was quieted by the praise. He liked the man's accent and his energy, tempered by manners.

Everybody knew that Mangum had grown up on a ruined rice plantation in the low country near Charleston but married a local girl. His words seemed more elegant than other people's, and there was a devil-may-care flash about his quick movements. Roiphe had said that all the girls were in love with him—the way he flicked the hair from his forehead made them go dreamy and still. He was as foreign to the place as a peacock, but that could not make Pip like the teacher less. They were both foreign now.

"You were riding the rails, Mrs. Tattnal says. But you know quite a lot of facts."

"I used to borrow encyclopedias and history books from libraries." Pip's eyes met the teacher's and then slid away and settled on the man's temple. "I had a lot of questions. So I might take a volume of the Britannica in Denver and drop it in a mailbox in New York or some bugtussle town in the middle of nowhere. I'd fasten on a note to tell the post office that the book was public property and should be returned home."

"Stole an education, you might say." With a jerk of the wrist, the teacher cast the stub of his cigarette to the dirt.

"Yes sir. I've got a pretty good memory. It's like I have a roll-top desk in my mind, with different sizes of drawers and pigeonholes."

Mr. Mangum laughed. "Most of my students don't have such luck. Squirrels are always frisking in their mental desks, tossing everything around."

The teacher lit another cigarette, and Pip noticed a scattering of stubs tossed behind one of the brick pillars that supported the schoolhouse.

"Smoke?" The teacher held out a gold case.

"Sure. But won't you get into trouble?"

"Don't worry about trouble. I'll bet you know a lot more about that article than anybody teaching school in backwater Georgia." He tapped ash from his cigarette. "Here—light it from mine."

"Yes sir. Thanks."

"Just don't let them see." He nodded toward the classroom. "Or there'll be a smokers' riot."

"Why did you—"

"You might like to do something a little more demanding than what the others are doing. In this class, I mean. Harder reading, maybe a presentation or two." Mr. Mangum sucked smoke in through his nose and afterward blew a ring toward the doorway; as if just realizing what he had done, he snatched at the circlet.

"I'd like it fine."

"We'll talk about it after school. It would be good for me too." He stepped onto the slab of fieldstone below the door and glanced inside. "You know the boy they call Pud? Tall, red-faced, boil on his neck?"

Pip was not quite sure. But Alden or Roiphe would point him out.

"He's going to be laying for you on the way home. But looks like you can take care of yourself just fine from what I saw." The corner of the teacher's mouth tugged into a half-smile.

Pip nodded. "Thanks."

Despite the fights at noon and on the way home, despite the hours Lil and the boys spent around the radio as if around a hearth, listening to urgent wartime voices, the words made even more fierce and dangerous by the sparking and crackling of static, Pip's residence with Lil Tattnal Tattnal was about the most peaceful, happy era of his growing-up years.

Lil was as much a teacher to him as Mr. Mangum; she fed and clothed him well and she listened. "Some hankerings have to be met," she explained to Alden. "Some people just have it in them to say what they know and think." His obsessions—a family trait that marked him and Roiphe as "surefire Tattnals" at school and in their community—were strong, his mind intent. "You go a mile a minute," Lil Tattnal Tattnal would say, but she heard him out.

Pip suspected that his time with Lil might have saved his life because he might not have survived another year as a 'bo. The time for tramping the country was ending, and fewer and fewer boys were staying with the rails.

Still, he often made his way to the train station in town, sitting on a platform bench and scratching the ears of the white-muzzled Special or idling away an hour in the office with the depot agent, listening to the news from overseas. Somehow he had earned the freedom and the right to do those things by journeying north and west. He did not have to abide by the unwritten laws of Emanuel County. As the months passed, it appeared that it might be too late for Lil to tame him completely, and his sometimes unusual ideas about right and wrong were Tattnal solid. He believed in treating other people well unless they deserved thrashing, and he believed in justice and pleasure wherever he could find it.

On any given Saturday afternoon, he might spend an hour or so visiting at the station, waiting but lacking an immediate goal, his limbs pent up and eager.

Picture him lounging on the platform bench but with one foot tapping the floor in a way that looked tense and jittery. His thoughts pulsed in a rush; he had a slight headache, which he rubbed with the heel of his hand. It was 1942, and he could not stop thinking. He was reading about the travels of the fourteenth-century Moslem tourist, Ibn Batuta, who saw the great seaports of his time—"Zaiton in China,

Calicut in India, Soldaia on the Black Sea, southeast of Kiev, and Alexandria, on the Mediterranean"—in a book that lay flopped open on his knee, and in a series of intrusive bursts, he was pondering the extent of the Japanese empire. Gnatting about his head was the image of Lavadera Collins in a black bathing suit. Already he had picked up signals of the approaching train by the hum in his feet and legs and barely heard notes of a warning. In a minute he shoved the book under his arm and paced, considering the Japanese tactic of infiltration and wondering about the exact shape of Lavadera's breasts, the noise of the locomotive pistoning in his mind like the name of a rapidly approaching traveler—*Ibn Batuta Ibn Batuta Ibn Batuta Ibn Batuta Ibn Batuta...*

His rampire and his stronghold

17

*Pip goes on pilgrimage to Roseville's streets
And to The White Camellia Orphanage.*

"Good news from far away," Pip muttered, wading knee deep in the Canoochee.

"What's that?" Roiphe frowned, trying to follow his half-uncle's leaps of conversation.

But he was gone, daydreaming the rails in the heat of early spring. He felt the faint touch of homesickness for the camps and the rushing wind on the decks of trains. Why? It was strange to miss the brawls that he had learned to win by being light and fierce and dancing his older and burlier opponents into weariness, or else to evade by taking to his heels. Strangers from all over the world had taught him how to defend himself. He did not miss the illnesses endured in boxcars, shacks, and open air or the stabbings from knives like the one he still carried, a great, easily fanned blade pillaged from the body of a tramp. With all the accidents of fire and kerosene and locomotive, it was purely a wonder he had survived and come home to Emanuel County.

Lax and faintly cool, the Canoochee lapped against his legs.

"Good news," he whispered, remembering the days when he had slipped through subway stations and along crowded sidewalks without glancing at the faces. The city was another kind of river, dense and crammed with life, with its own fast currents and deep pools. He had learned to keep his mouth clamped tight, a good method for dealing with the problem of not knowing what other people were thinking. He knew no one by name, and no one knew him. He had been a no one for a long time, almost long enough to forget who he was and how to get home if one could have called the orphanage a home.

But in the end there had been news from faraway: Lil Tattnal Tattnal had been as obsessed with hunting him down as he had been with flying from his own history and starting over. And she had proved faithful. Her bountiful hugs left no doubt that the half-brother had been claimed as her own, equal in standing with her sons. She was as fearful of war for his sake as for theirs.

"What was it?" Alden raised his voice, damming the flow of memories. His voice was not annoyed; he was accustomed to somebody shutting him out. He went on peeling the skin off a catfish.

"What was what?" Pip asked but didn't listen to the little boy's reply.

It had been a bad time, hadn't it? Maybe it would have been better for Roiphe and Lil and Alden if he'd never come back. Maybe it would have been better if he had been flicked aside by the *Silk Train*.

He stood in the low water, staring off to the east.

"I need to ride out to Savannah. And after that, Truetlen's in Swainsboro. Ever heard of it?"

"Sure." Roiphe tossed his line back in the current. "The far side of Swainsboro from here. What for? It's crazy—nothing but clocks and fusty old doilies and glass. Mommer had a watch fixed there once."

"They have a photograph." Pip bent, jerked at a piece of grass growing close to the water, and bit down on the crisp pale stem.

"What kind? Naked ladies?" Alden hardly ever teased his young uncle, who was able to quell him with a stare.

"Brazen weevil." He spat out the blade.

He and Roiphe had recently begun coining obscure epithets and thus avoiding the wrath of Lil, who could not stand to hear the three cuss and would go for a bar of Camay, threatening to soap their mouths.

"Why should I tell you, rampire of ignorance?" Pip waded over and climbed aboard the sandbar, not even sure why he was telling his nephews about his plans. "It may be a picture of my brother Otto. A photograph of a boy at a fence..."

"Hellfire—somebody's going to shoot you for poking around." Alden cocked his thumb and aimed his forefinger at his uncle.

Roiphe cuffed his brother. "What do you mean, *hellfire*?"

"Shoot me for poking around?" Pip winked at Alden. "The red ball express is going to grind us under its wheels, one day or another. Only a poltroon of the first water would even mention the risk. I'll get that photograph if it's—if it's genuine."

"Who told you?" Alden demanded.

"Man named Durden Pooler if you must know—"

"Durden—aw, that piece of—"

His half-uncle broke in. "Pernicious polecat."

"Dissembling slime of a catfish," Roiphe added.

"Steaming black-boiled okra pod."

"Backhouse hunkerer."

"Dumb shit," Alden finished.

Pip frowned, thumping his nephew on the head.

"Camay, son."

"You ain't Mommer," Alden said.

"And I admit," Pip said, "that Pooler is a pail of night slop, a mawed chaw, and a weak-hinged Lexsy scantling."

"Miscreant chitterling," Roiphe added.

Alden sighed, knowing that the two older boys would do what they would do. "That's a bad business," he protested.

"Thou lousewort, thou mop pot," his uncle said idly, his thoughts roving elsewhere.

"Why y'all got to talk like that?" Alden tossed the shucked catfish skin. It caught on a branch and flapped for a moment before hanging still.

"Boredom," Roiphe said.

"I ain't bored," Alden said.

Roiphe ignored his protest. "Same reason we don't let you swear. Because it's more fun for us that way."

"It ain't fair."

"But it's just."

Hardly hearing his nephews, Pip hunched on the sandbank, summoning the rails to mind.

Once on the roof of a boxcar at sunset, he had squatted and kicked out like a Cossack dancing the kazachok, hands in his trouser pockets. The purple- and ochre-colored desert with its mesas and plugs of stone had spread for miles on each side, the colors and shapes sifting through him, the openness of sky and plain widening him with the emptiness of the West. He had not felt the cold except as a different kind of touch against his skin, one that he did not flinch from—he had relaxed in its grip.

"Ai, yi, yi, ai, yi, yi!" he had shouted, letting his chant mix with the thunder of heels, sending the message of himself in waves across cacti where birds and animals nested and across the burrowed darkness where snakes coiled, torpid and cool. Antelope sprang to the tune of his song.

The world in which he had spun was a kaleidoscope of color and repetitive noise and rhythm, but even in its flurry and shift, a white shard sprang into view, a rectangle under which memory slept. Behind a jumble of cloud rails painted rose and violet, the sun had sunk like the roundest O and eye in the universe, and the boy on top of the car knew that its burning sphere was peering at him, beaming a syllable to him alone. The star had meant one thing: *O*, and *O* was Otto, forever and always, in every scene, in each wrenching turn of the kaleidoscope.

"Savannah," Pip murmured. "I didn't fathom how rare Excelsior was, and I'm going to thank him. Then White Camellia and the Truetlen store."

"All right," Roiphe told him, "fine. But there's not much left of the orphanage."

"What about me?" Alden dumped worms onto the dirt and stood watching them wriggle.

"Nope," Roiphe said.

"You soft-headed yam, you can't cut out on school—"

216

Pip stopped, seized by the sunset's armory of spikes and lances, rose and orange.

Alden picked up the cane poles and the bucket of catfish, lugging them the length of the sandbar and then jumping to shore.

That simply, the expedition was arranged.

With a rail orphans' pass, the older boys rode for free to Savannah, sitting on slippery upholstered seats that made Pip restless. The air was close, the car jammed with a party of young soldiers. He liked seeing the men in their caps and uniforms, but he had always hated noise and bustle and felt trapped in any crowd that was not flowing forward on foot. From his seat, he had a view of several enlisted men, one sitting with a woman wearing a crown of braids and toting a basket of yolk-smeared eggs; two girls who eyed the military caps and shirts and giggled behind their hands; and a mother with a fat-cheeked boy who kept escaping from her clutches and patrolling the aisle, his mouth so open and his eyes so round that Roiphe named him *the goggle-eyed minnow*.

Though he wanted nothing more than to shimmy up on the deck, Pip kept to the promises he had made to Lil Tattnal Tattnal.

"My son isn't going to ride in boxcars or prowl around hobo camps. You understand me, Pip Tattnal?" She had seized him by the shoulders and stared into his eyes until he said that he did, and he would not take Roiphe where he should not go.

"No ruckuses, either. Not when you're out of town." She had untied her apron, snapped the cloth free of wrinkles, and hung it on a peg. "There's been enough uproar—you had to go and scrap with every dadblame boy in the school."

"They asked for it," Pip had protested, feeling a quick flare of anger at his schoolmates.

"You didn't mind. Don't tell me you did because it would be a flat-out lie."

When he had nodded, she laughed and put her arms around him. He had looked down at the little whorl where her hair insisted on having its own way and felt sad, discovering something about her that she could not know—as if it bore some secret importance.

"My boys don't know the rules of the road the way you do," she had reminded him. She was a good woman, his sister; she could not keep him from the occasional hitch to Metter or Lyons or beyond and didn't try.

On the train with Roiphe, he jerked open the window and leaned out until the man collecting tickets told him to sit down. Fresh air made him feel better. He had awakened too early and rolled out of bed, tired and jittery. Roiphe told the conductor all about the father who had worked and died on the railroad and how Pip had run away from home and waded in the Pacific Ocean before he came back again.

"Boxcar tourist," Pip murmured.

"Is that so?" the trainman kept repeating, glancing at him and nodding.

At the next station, the fellow let them come forward to the engine where Roiphe got to shovel coal with the fireman. Shaking off an uneasy memory of running from bulls after a night spent tucked inside the diaphragm of a head-end passenger car, Pip laughed to see his nephew sweat. The whole incident struck him as amusing—to be invited to pay a social call on the engineer while the train was stopped rather than, say, leaping from a swaying passenger car to the ladder of a steam locomotive tender! *So ladylike*, he thought, his mouth quirked in a half-smile as the train pulled away from the platform. He lolled in the open door, chatting about the California coast with the engineer and enjoying the collision between the cool rush of wind and the blast from the furnace.

The run to the city seemed shorter than he remembered, with fewer stops, and in the afternoon the boys searched for the place where Pip had lived with Excelsior Tillman and the Countess Casimiria and Clemmie. At first they passed through streets and neighborhoods. Later on, the houses appeared haphazard in arrangement as if they had sprouted where the wind had blown seeds, some in patches and others standing stray and alone. They wandered through pockets of scrub and on dirt roads overhung by oaks and Spanish moss, guided only by an uncertain memory and the river's course. Hours passed, and Roiphe complained that his arms and legs were sore from the bout of shoveling.

"You'll never make diamond cracker."

"What's that?"

"The fireman. The one who bails black diamonds into the firebox. Look here—I think this is—"

Pip recognized the familiar rutted lane above the Savannah River and began to run, loping parallel to the river as Roiphe lagged behind him. But as he reached a place that seemed familiar, he slowed down, looking for but not finding the shape of what had been home.

Then he found it at last.

A scattering of pecans and oaks led the way to a slope of bare ground and the broken foundations of Roseville, looking like the lines of an enormous jaw with crowns of teeth jutting from the soil. The two shacks were gone. Blackened spars and irregular chunks of coal marked the sites where they had been. Only the trees held fast in their old places.

"What happened?" He looked around, bewildered, as his nephew caught up.

"Was this it? About like what's left of the orphanage," Roiphe said. "Nothing left but trash trees."

Pip didn't hear him. He stared at a pecan tree that had stood close by the house, trying to convince himself that this site was wrong and the true Roseville lay just around the corner. But the slats he had sawn from cast-off boards and nailed to the trunk snaked up to a height that had made Clemmie dizzy as she watched him scramble up and shake the limbs with a pole.

"They were good to me, Clemmie and Bill and Excelsior Tillman. Even the Countess. She used to sit on her throne of plush and queen over us all." He tried to conjure their faces, but he had never been good at capturing the look of a person. Now they had all been swept away. He supposed Clemmie was living in the mountains. She probably had at least one more child now.

Bill was young and strong; he would be fodder for the war. He knew a woman's dread, for it was Lil's great fear that her young men would be carried off by the tidal wave of destruction that had begun in Japan and splashed up against Pearl Harbor. Soon Pip and Roiphe would be old enough to fight, and already they talked of becoming pilots.

"Thought I could see Till again," he said. "I meant to—"

"Sounds like he was a nice old fellow."

Roiphe was gathering pecans. He had stripped bare to the waist and tied the straps of his undershirt together, turning it inside out to form a sack. He chose the plump ones, tossing any that looked lean and thin-hulled.

"It was a good year for nuts," he said.

"He fed me," Pip said, "and bought me clothes and made me go to school. When I made a little bit of cash, I offered it to him, but he wouldn't take it. Said he had not helped me for money and was not going to start. He took care of the Princess, too—or Countess, or whatever she was—and I don't think she ever had a cent."

"Was she real royalty?"

"He acted like she was." Pip shrugged. "Maybe that's the same thing. One time Casimiria started hooking her finger at me, crocheting at the air—meaning for me to come over. 'Yes ma'am?' I say, trotting right across. Then she puts it to me. 'My nearest and dearest,' she tells me, 'have considered the services to our family— that is to *me*—and the loyalty so wonderfully exhibited by Mr. Tillman.' She pauses to take out her fusty old reticule and pries open the clasp. I make out a macaroon lurking in its nether regions, decked out in lint, and a thimble. She plucks out the thimble and holds it out like she's going to make a toast. 'My beloved Pulaskis,' she goes on, 'have determined on an act of true condescension: that this artist and man of the people should be knighted.' 'Is that so?' I say. She jabs a narrow, beady look at me as if she suspects I might be about to tell a Polack joke. Maybe I *was* about to tell one.

"After that she often called him *Sir Excelsior* or *Sir Till*. And I never heard him let out a hoot at being appointed Knight of the Polish Court-in-Exile. Never heard him laugh at her either. Though she could be a gaudy old peacock."

Roiphe was stooped, scouring the leaf litter for more pecans. "She sounds dadgum curious."

"You know, sometimes I forgot about the Countess and Till and even Clemmie for a long time. Maybe the old ones are dead."

On the remains of city streets, Pip bent to retrieve a shard of tabby studded with shells and a flowered chip of blue-and-white porcelain. "And Roseville's no more. Was it worth all that mixing of tabby and piecing together the china and glass?"

"If he was always planning new parts of the city, he must have got his fun out of it," Roiphe said.

"I still wonder if it was worthwhile. Maybe I just wonder if anything is worth it when you just end up a stiff in the end."

"You're loony," Roiphe told him. "You need to listen to Mommer. She'll set you right."

"Maybe it was plain old joyfulness to him, following some dream in his head. Roseville was his glory, he told me once. He has to be dead to let this happen." Pip scraped the dirt from a flow blue flower. "Till had it in him to make something new in the world." He stopped, examining the ground. "Like wanting Thera," he added slowly.

"Who's she?"

Pip did not notice, his eyes on a bit of white. "Excelsior Tillman saved me." He bent to pluck a star-like shape from the dirt: a tiny china hand from the Garden of Lost Dolls. Now even the garden itself was lost. "Lanie. I wonder whatever became of her."

"Who was that?"

"A baby." Pip looked toward the river's edge where Clemmie's shack used to stand. "She was sweet, didn't cry all that much. Not like some. Rail babies, they can fret and weep to beat the band. A baby needs to stay home with its mommer and daddy and not go gallivanting. I found that out. It's no good in the cars. Not even any good in the fields. There's danger, sun and men and animals. And bees."

Squatting, he surveyed the ruin.

"At sunset I used to think Roseville was downright lovely. That old man put his heart into all these little alleys and miniature shops and churches and gardens. Children used to come to see it. Grown-ups too. Somebody must have used a sledgehammer to knock it down."

Roiphe was kneeling in the stubby grass, picking up more pecans.

"I couldn't stay. That's what I said, but I could have. I could have saved them from this." With a pang, Pip remembered how close he had come to betraying Bill. "I suppose we all left, the younger ones anyway," he said slowly. He felt like a child again, inconsolable.

"I lost out." Pip seemed to whisper this discovery to the open china hand on his palm.

His nephew shook the undershirt and jammed a few more nuts on top, tying it roughly. "Mommer always thinks it's a win when you get to understanding a thing you didn't before. Maybe you didn't know what you had—that's a misfortune—but now you do, and that's good."

"How could it be good? When they're all gone, and I wasn't there to help." Pip looked down the lane. "Let's see if anybody else is around."

No Miss Ruby Looner was in residence with her cats. Nor did they find any old people, immured in afghans while the rest of the family scampered off to work or errands. Finally they found someone at the house of a retired farmer—the very man who had loaned his wagon on the day that Pip the wanderer left Till and the others behind. But the old man was dead, and the new daughter-in-law knew nothing about Roseville or Excelsior Tillman. She stood on the porch and stared off at the spot.

"You can write my husband—he's not much of a hand at letters, but I'll help him. He might know. Maybe the old people moved away." She fetched a pencil and a scrap torn from a calendar and jotted down the name and address. The two thanked her, and a smile flicked to her mouth. She wasn't much older than they, but she was married and settled. When a child howled in the rear of the house, she waved them goodbye and let the screen door bang.

"Dadgum babies are taking over the world," Pip said.

Roiphe had walked over to a stump topped with a fat-bellied planter, stuck about with garish shards of glass.

"What *is* this monstrosity?" Crown-topped, it spilled over with aloes and blue-gray hens-and-biddies. "That is the goofiest thing I have ever seen."

"You may be right. It's powerfully goofy." Pip inspected the pot, searching for and finding a star-shaped piece of glass that he had once pushed into the damp surface.

"That's an Excelsior Tillman creation—he called it an urn for a circus elephant."

"Big enough," Roiphe said.

"The old man who lived here was proud to get it. He wanted gussied-up gaudy, and that's what he got. Might be all that's left of Till's making."

Roiphe hoisted the knobby, filthy bundle of pecans onto his hip. There was nothing more to do but head back down the lane the way they had come. Pip slid the scrap of paper into his pocket, crumpling it into a ball. Till was dead, and Roseville with him.

As they walked away, the young mother came running after them with an astonished-looking infant tucked under one arm and a burlap sack in her hand.

"Here, take this—"

She held the bag out to Roiphe, who was grappling with the undershirt bulging with nuts.

"Thanks, thanks a lot," he said.

"You won't look so peculiar now, carrying that funny-shaped—well, it's your underclothes, ain't it?—all smeared with pecan soot." She nodded, giggling at her own boldness and holding up the baby so they could see its round eyes and open mouth.

"Nice little minnow you have there! And thank you, ma'am." Roiphe grinned at her as he dumped the bundle into the sack.

Pip leaned over to help and murmured, "Another goggle-eyed minnow."

They alternated trotting and walking on the way back to the station, the burlap swinging between them. By the time they arrived, the boys were sweaty and tired.

"Dadgum pecan-eater." Pip said.

"I'm keeping them." Roiphe pushed the damp hair back from his face.

"You just might be the most pigheaded, obstinate mule of a nephew a man ever had. I knew you were crazy about numbers, but I never knew you were such a nut for nuts." Pip grimaced, half amused, half irritated. "You still have that pass?"

"I do." Roiphe flopped onto a bench.

"Wouldn't want your mommer in a rampage because I'd brought you home on top of a boxcar. She'd skin me for sure." Pip spat onto the pavement and wished he had a smoke.

"I'd like that. Not the skinning but riding under the stars." Roiphe's voice sounded hopeful.

"Yeah. That part's pleasant. Till you get tired of the gusts trying to throw you off." For a moment Pip considered scrambling onto a deck with Roiphe, letting him feel the wind ruffle and then tug at his hair as the engine pulled away from the station and the stars emerged, fire by fire. This nephew was less than a year from him in age; he was something new, someone who put up with his moods, listened to his ideas: perhaps a friend. But Pip felt that he owed his half-sister a kind of fealty that was different and perhaps even stricter

224

than what a son would owe, and it kept him faithful to her and honest.

"Whew, I'm thirsty. I'd give a nickel for a dipper of water. Gimme a co-cola, Uncle Pip," Roiphe teased. He stretched out his legs, using the bag for a hassock.

"Beetle-brained nut smut," Pip murmured, leaning over to loosen his shoelaces. Sitting up again, he watched the yardmen swinging their lanterns in the early dusk. He could almost hear the crack of the stick against Gandy's head, off in the shadows beyond the station. If he had not been so young and so hurt, he might have thought to see if the man lay dead or if the bull had just dragged him into the weeds. But he still thought Gandy had been a goner. The brother and sister—what were their names?—she had thrown the baby, and he had caught it as neatly as if were a pigskin ball arcing across a schoolyard. That minnow was *Harbert*.

"You got to hold on to people because they're sure not going to last." Pip said it aloud but maybe to himself, or else as a cautionary warning cast out toward his sister's son.

When the train pulled from the station, he yawned and said that he felt a headache coming on. The cars slid away into the night, the window glass reflecting the faces of the Tattnal boys, along with a scattering of other passengers. Long accustomed to the rocking of the cars, Pip soon fell asleep. His nephew pressed close to the glass to watch for the firefly clusters of hamlets, glimmering in the night.

Some ninety miles later, Roiphe had to wake him when the locomotive whistled once as it neared the water tower.

"Did we change trains? If we did, I must have been sleepwalking," Pip said, rubbing his face. "And shoot," he added, "I never even thought to look in the churchyard. I'll bet they were there all along, Till and Casimiria. The Princess for sure. She was as old as the hills—*all* the durn hills."

He jumped from the steps, landing in the soft dirt beyond the rails.

"Maybe we'll go again some time." His nephew yawned mightily, following along the edge of the track.

As they neared the house, Roiphe carrying the burlap package like an awkward child in his arms, the boys could see Lil sitting up, reading her Bible under a dangling bulb. She was so used to the passing trains that she had not even noticed the whistle.

Pip stopped, watching his motionless sister, her head bent. Annoyance flickered through him and vanished. He was not really penned up, he reflected, by a woman hoping for his arrival. And it seemed so precious to him, that image. No one had ever waited up for him, staving off sleep because she needed to know that he was all right. She would have kept vigil even if Roiphe had not gone with him.

The window before him hung in the lower corner of the night, its glow diminished by the rich panoply of the stars. Their sparks were little more than hydrogen and helium, he thought; they had been set alight with no visible pattern, yet they all had names and were parts of constellations that long-ago people had discerned in the sky. It was a thing he had wondered about, out on the rails—how even a ball of gas could have a place and a name when he had no place and no one knew his name. And now here he was, belonging to Lil, to whom the world and stars made sense, and to Roiphe and Alden. But sometimes it seemed that the other Pip, the floater, was still out there, rolled in a blanket and looking up at the brilliant sky. He remembered the sense of losing his very self in the distances of the universe as if he were melting, thawing, and rising like dew toward the morning sun.

The train whistled two long notes in the darkness, hailing him with its mingled joy and ache. Its tune sang in his bones, and he was tempted—for years he had felt that its whoop was best met by running away to a new place where longing might at last be answered.

"Cruel and profitless," he muttered. Stone-hearted tramps and men who would not pay a living wage roamed the far expanses, possessing the rails and the land around them, leaving no cranny of peace. Long ago, one of these lion rulers of the universe had taken his last human connection from him. Yet what had been left for him but to let his heart shiver into pieces and hold his tongue?

Lil stood, going to the glass and looking out. Pip stared at the silhouette, backed by yellow light. Everything in him was alert to the cry as a far whistle sounded the notes for a crossing.

"You coming? You sleepwalking?" Roiphe spoke from the porch, letting the burlap down with a thud. "Wake up. We're home."

His nephew slipped into the room and his mother's arms, and Pip could hear her laughing in relief. For an instant more he remained a spectator and caught a glimpse of Gilead in her face, something about Lil Tattnal Tattnal's straight nose and the reading glasses and the shape of the head. Perhaps he imagined the look. But it was good to be met by a reminder of the old man. The glimpse helped a little with what he thought must be a lingering childhood heartache—was it for his parents or Otto or a lost seamlessness that felt so far back in time that it might as well have dated from before his birth? It was as if he saw a door, long closed, standing ajar.

The light from the house spilled into the darkness, and Pip followed it across the threshold as his sister called his name.

18

*And "burningly it came" to Pip that this
Drab, unlikely spot was the very place.*

"Don't you boys dare stay out all day and half the night," Lil warned the next morning. "I can't handle another one of these long outings."

She was busy shunting from stove to table, dishing up grits and scrambled eggs and ham and a hoecake, drained of grease on a brown paper bag. Gleaming slices of persimmon were heaped on green glass, the rim speckled with orange dew.

When her eldest answered, "Yes, Mommer, we'll be careful," Pip had copied him in the same monotone and made her laugh.

"I wanna go," Alden declared, standing with his legs wide. "I'm gonna."

"You aren't going anywhere," Roiphe told him, "because we're taking your bicycle."

"Mommer! Mommer!"

"Hush. Get back in that chair. I told Roiphe it was all right. Hasn't he helped you with arithmetic all week? Didn't he put up with your hollering every blessed night?" Lil rapped her spoon on the edge of the hominy pot to emphasize her words, and Alden sat down, scowling.

"I was a little bit afraid you would get homesick for the rails once you got to Savannah and just light out for California." She came up behind Pip, setting a hand on his shoulder. "Maybe Sunday afternoon we'll cut some poles and go fishing. We can have us a picnic by the river. It's pretty warm for this time of year—it'll be nice to cool off."

Pip was not listening. "We'll go out to the farm first," he decided, his eyes resting on the cabinet with its bright depression glass, fished out of cartons of soap powder. "I don't feel up to the cemetery quite yet. Not this early in the morning."

When they left, Lil came out onto the porch and waved, Alden lurking behind her in the doorway.

"That was a fine meal," Pip said.

He rolled the bicycle forward and hopped on, pedaling across the yard. He did not always thank his sister, but just then he had recalled the brothers on the boxcar saying what a good feed she gave and what a nice lady she was. They had said he was famous, Pip remembered, but Lil was the one.

"We're not flying to the moon, Mommer," Roiphe called.

"I know that. But be careful!"

"I hope you fall in a dadgum ditch!" Alden's shrill imprecation, flaring out of the shadows, made Pip wobble as looked back with a wave.

He rode the boy's too-small bicycle, but he had too little experience not to reel from side to side in the road. "Durn thing gives me the cramp," he said, but he felt cheerful, watching grackles cut across the sky. Occasionally he hopped off to stretch his legs and walk in the dust. Standing water reflected dried stems and the sky in the ditches by the road. It would not be all that long before the first little orchids bloomed in the muck. Pitcher plants would be sending up strange shoots, burgeoning into rose and green vases, their flowers hanging like weird parasols.

Once they stopped to ask directions of two fellows standing in the back of a pick-up with a pair of spotted dogs that snarled and lunged on their chains.

"Hookses? The Orphanage? Oh, you mean the old Lamar Truetlen place." The man yanked at his animal's choke collar—"shut it, Fell!"—and pointed. "Two roads down, take a left."

The cyclists could see nothing but patches of piney woods interspersed with swamp, but they thanked him and pedaled off.

"Smells about right." Pip sniffed the air, his eyes on a length of black looped over a branch. "Look at that. The snakes are partying in the trees."

"Did you take a gander at that farmer jerking on the dog? Probably one of your brothers, with the forehead and jaw on him," Roiphe said. "At least it looked like any number of my uncles. Might've *been* one, for all I know. I haven't seen but half of them in years."

"Nobody I know." Pip spat over the handlebars. "I wouldn't recognize my kin from Adam. Unless it was a choice of two and Adam had on a leaf loincloth. I don't want to know any of them, either. What did they ever—"

"Is this it?" Roiphe paused at a turning.

"That brute on the chain was sure plug-headed," Pip said. He peered down the lane. It was pot-holed but straight, unhindered by the least inkling of a rise in the ground. "He looked kind of familiar too. Like a speckle-faced prairie farmer I worked for once."

He stared some more. "Damn, this road looks just as scant and ragged as the others. But it feels right. Reminds of the poem: 'Burningly it came on me all at once / This was the place!'"

"That's 'Childe Roland to the Dark Tower Came,'" said Roiphe, who was as good at reeling off quotes as his uncle.

"You got it." Pip winced at the sun, shading his eyes with one hand as they ventured on. "I had forgotten that the land really belonged to Mr. Lamar. That was Sam Truetlen's uncle. A real skinflint. I'd guess those Hookses didn't make a cent sharecropping for him." He gestured to the cedar fence with its sagging strings of barbs. "Used to be blackberries along here. Looks like somebody tore them up. We'd walk a quarter mile to get them, they were so much bigger and sweeter than the ones near the house."

They came to a gate where two ruts headed off at angles from the lane. Pip stared down the fields. The scarred, tamped track and the rows of cotton seemed to point toward a clump of trees.

"Roiphe, you said there wasn't much left, but you didn't say there was *nothing*." He shaded his eyes, looking toward the windbreak. "Where's the rusted-out water tower we called a castle? And the house—it's just not there."

"I don't guess it was so much of a place," Roiphe said. "It burned right down to the ground. They got rid of the orphans, and the place was empty. Probably somebody torched it."

"Guess it was a hazard," Pip said. "There were rats in the kitchen house. Bugs and skinks in the shack."

"Alden and I rode out to see the fire with some cousins and Uncle Dod, and there wasn't much left. Dod said it was probably so old and greasy that it went up like Lucifer's match."

"Lit by some polecat like Durden Pooler."

Transparent clouds billowed behind the bicycles as they jounced forward over the cattle bars and onto the farm road, their tires printing seams in the paired ruts.

"We used to pick buckets of plums behind that field," Pip said. "Little yellow plums, some of them flushed with red. Translucent things with bugsucker marks on the skin: those were the best plums I ever ate. But the ground was rife with snakes down that way."

The fields were dun in the shade of tobacco leaves and white in the open, here and there shadowed pink. He climbed off the bike and picked up dark pebbles that he rubbed between his fingers until they turned to a paste of rusty grains. The little coolness gained from the breeze had been instantly swept away when he stopped; sweat made him feel clammy in his clothes.

"Early in the year to be so warm," Pip said, "but I guess it's always hot in hell."

"That stuff don't come off so easy, does it?" Roiphe watched as his uncle scrubbed the stained fingers with a pinch of soft dirt.

"Nah," Pip said. "Otto and I liked to use those reddish nubs for jewels. We had a game where we were city dicks in New York, hunting down treasure. And now I've been. I solved a mystery, too—never even thought about how it was like what we used to play."

"What mystery?"

"It wasn't much." Pip spoke slowly, rubbing his hands together as if their dryness bothered him. "I was in the city for a while. I used to slip along the sidewalks without looking at the faces. I learned pretty quick to keep my mouth clamped tight.

"I'd hang out in the parks when I wasn't scrambling for a job, see all these crazy fellows haranguing a crowd, maybe about the Reds or the A. F. of L., something like that. I always liked arguing or a good heckle. And I was fond of trying to catch the con men in their tricks. I used to spend hours watching shell games or cards.

"One day three men hung out on the edge of Central Park with a doll scam. And I figured it out. The ruse depended on shrubs and shadows. A tall, lanky sharper would croon to the audience. He'd say, 'Closer, closer, not too close! Give the little lady air! It's a marvel, a piece of fairyland magic, ladies and gentlemen, one of the tinsel-dusted wonders of New York.' He looked like a clown with his legs all akimbo, a package in his hand. Very gently he would tear open the wrapper and remove a doll and set her on the grass. Her arms swayed in the air, and then she stretched and stood on her toes. She'd start to jig and twirl, her arms and wings waving, her dance shoes bouncing against the grass."

Pip bent his head as if seeing the little ballerina in the dust of the lane to The White Camellia Orphanage.

"I followed them from site to site before I saw how it was done. The tall fellow would slide a hook into the doll's scalp. A short man nearby twiddled a line of black thread tied to a branch at one end and to the hook at the other. A third fellow would rush up to demand a doll. Like it was the most marvelous true thing in the world.

"After a while, I couldn't keep it to myself. I went over to the tall man when he was packing the dancers into a valise. He told me to beat it, but then he grinned and tossed me a nickel and told me, 'Keep your damn trap shut, or you'll get your arms broke.'"

Pip lifted his eyes to Roiphe's, a faint smile on his face.

"I went zooming across the lawn and leapfrogged a bench, scaring the pigeons, to where I'd seen a fortuneteller sitting in the cool spatter from a fountain. He was still there, rolling a bead of mercury under a glass dome and calling for customers to 'Rejoice in the benefits of foreign prophetic education! Distilled Eastern wisdom of the ages! Ten cents, one bare dime, for the Sir or the Madam. Twenty cents, less than one quarter, for a deluxe revelation. One penny for the infant baby. One nickel merely for those under ten years of age.'

"I didn't have the right amount, but he took it. For that coin, he let me tilt the glass with its dollop of quicksilver, and he examined my palms—'very dirty'—and he made me choke down a cup of bitter tea and shake the leaves left in the bottom. He told me, 'Reverend Child Sir, the worst has already happened to you. You will have many splendid women in your arms. Good news will come to you from far away.'

"The whole show impressed me at the time. I was so young, and it had the ring of something genuine because some of the prophecy had already become true—wasn't what had happened to Otto the worst that could be? I couldn't imagine a piece of fresh news. I didn't have an address. But I was thrilled by the aura of the thing, even when I discovered that he wasn't really from India—you could see pale skin near his collar."

The story had poured out of him, and already Pip felt a twinge of regret that he had spoken at all. Still, he kept on talking, more slowly now.

"I did get some good news from far away. But till now I never thought about how Otto and I had wanted to solve mysteries in New York, and how the solving a mystery there brought on the promise of good news. As if our game made something happen." He paused, looking off toward the creek and the grove of plum trees.

"What about the women?" Roiphe grinned at him.

"What?" Pip glanced at his nephew. "Well, there's Lil. She's always game for a hug, isn't she?"

"That wasn't what I meant," Roiphe shouted as Pip leaped onto the bicycle and pedaled away.

"I know," he called back.

A hundred yards down the road, Pip jumped off again and wheeled the bicycle along the brink of the fields. His steps slackened, and he turned as his nephew rode up behind him.

"Here," Pip said abruptly.

Letting the bike tumble, he paced back and forth. Why had he told that story about Otto and how they had wanted to be city investigators? It was nothing—nothing compared to the mystery that was Otto's death. His little brother had wanted to solve mysteries, but instead he had become one. When an eyelid fluttered spasmodically, he pressed a hand against his face. Right *here* he had found his brother's body; he could feel the spot drawing his iron ache like a loadstone. With a twitch, he freed himself and hurried toward the site of The White Camellia Orphanage. Roiphe dismounted and ran after him.

"There was a shed," Pip was saying. "Here was the gate. I can't believe the cedar isn't here. Maybe it burned. And the hedge that Mr. Jimmie called *gardenia* though it wasn't one, and the big shrub that was a real gardenia with limbs thick as a man's. As if they'd been anchored here forever. As if the roots went down to China—and vigorous—like something that can't be killed. I can't fathom the hedge being gone. It must have been ten feet high." He scuffed about in new growth and last year's weeds, gone as thin and light as old men's hair. "Not even a root sticking up from the ground."

"Must've been some camellias hereabouts," Roiphe said.

"No. Not a one. Not even a white one."

He hunted a little longer for the four corners of the house, but there was no trace. Even the rudimentary chimney had left no scar.

"That's about where I slept, I guess, and the fireplace and the girls' room were over there, with Mr. Jimmie and Miss Versie's bedroom in the back. I never did get my daddy's books, and now they're not even ash."

Pip wheeled about and pointed.

"See that rock? The outdoor kitchen was about twenty feet to the left. Nothing left but the barn, and it's small, nothing like what I remember. It seemed monstrous, bristling with rats. They'd get into the corn and fatten up like shoats. The little children were scared of snakes and vermin, but the big ones liked to chunk rocks at the rats—it took a hard lob to the nose to kill one.

"Look at all this dried-up dog hobble." Pip kicked at the brush. "Just rubbish, no good for anything."

Roiphe wandered toward the back lot.

"Don't go that way," Pip called. "Somebody must have closed up the well, but I wouldn't guarantee that stepping there would be safe. I'd hate to have to haul you out. Your mommer would have my hide pinned to the woodshed."

At the barn he reached out, paused, and put his hand on the latch, now padlocked. The names of the Seven Worlds flashed through his mind—Erath, Wrathe, Herat, Thare, Heart, Thera, Earth. For a minute he just stood there, staring.

"This is the only thing," Pip said, "that I am dead certain I touched and Otto touched. We used to fetch corn from the crib and bring out the mules if they'd let us. We were just little old boys."

Here and there like notes on the staves of time, Otto's small thumb had pressed the latch before wresting the door open. Pip touched the grip lightly as if feeling for a thumbprint. Otto would never have recognized him, not in those pants ironed and starched by Lil and the pale blue shirt, not with such a height on him, not with scars. Only the patch of damp between shoulder blades would have seemed like anything familiar. The hand dropped.

"My dadgum noggin is killing me," Pip murmured, his gaze on the scrub forest of chinaberry that had spired up by the barn. "Look at those trash trees. We had a few back then. Not so many as that. Around New Year's or so, we'd have a fight with the fruit. Of no earthly use whatsoever, I guess, except to fire from slingshots."

"They're not even American—from Asia, I think." Roiphe picked up a pebble, but it crumbled to grit in his fingers.

"Chinaberry, the yellow peril." Pip rubbed his eye again. "Miss Versie liked chinaberries, liked those purplish flowers."

"You okay?" Roiphe glanced at the barn, sparkling with silver-gray crystals of salt.

"If I don't get something for this head, it will surely crack open," he admitted. "Like last year's pecan in a vise."

He gestured to a crooked margin of trees beyond the field. "That gap in the piney woods is a path. Down that way, we distilled turpentine from pine gum. Hot work in the summer. I liked the smell of the fumes though. Beyond that was a field where hogs were let to forage and run wild. Otto was scared of them. Miss Versie had told him that they would eat him if he climbed the fence and fell in.

"Not much to see, is there?" Pip glanced at his nephew. "I guess we should go." He wished that Roiphe had not come and that he could be alone with the place and the past.

"I'm all right with this," Roiphe assured him. "We'll do whatever you want."

Pip imagined the geometric maze of back roads around the Truetlen farm. Probably there was not anybody around for miles unless maybe the two men had let loose their dogs and were hunting coons in the scrub and swamp lands between farms. It was lonesome with the bare long sky and the pines and the fields of dust. A nightmarish feeling crept over him as if they could be caught in a labyrinth of dirt lanes and trapped on the grounds of The White Camellia Orphanage forever.

Nearly forty acres is small to support a Depression-era family but a large area to explore and master. Pip recalled his small boy fears: being bitten by copperheads or rattlers, plunging into a gulley, being sucked into a sinkhole or crashing through rotten boards into the well.... He set off walking across what had been the barnyard. He battled through the weeds, trailed by Roiphe, burrs and briars catching at their socks, beggar lice sticking to the legs of pants. At least it was not summer, with the cicadas droning at his back as the sun clanged in the sky, shedding prickly heat. Nevertheless, his breath came quick and anxious; standing in the shade of the chinaberries, he could barely drag the air through his nose.

Without thinking he reached into his pocket and found the small pierced conch with a slip of paper wedged inside. When he glanced down, the chill of realization flashed up his arm like sudden damage—a burn on the cheek or a knife slash across his fingers. *The soul-catcher. Otto.*

"Fearless," Pip whispered, "on wings of horse."

19

In which cat-killer curiosity
Makes fatal inroads on a boy's resolve.

It took Pip and Roiphe hours to bike toward home, borrow the car from Lil's father-in-law, and ferret out the shop, a process made considerably more interesting by the fact that Roiphe had never driven an automobile. Mr. Louis Tattnal gave them a ride to the gate and back again, all the while spitting tobacco into a coffee can and hollering instructions as he pumped the pedals. There he got out, gave the yellow enamel a pat, and gestured at his grandson to slide over. Under Roiphe's hands, the Packard backfired, lurched, and took off as if shot from a sling.

The old man choked on his chaw and jumped backward, his face flushed. When he caught his breath, Louis Tattnal began to bellow as the machine whirled past the house, sending up gay streamers of pink dirt.

"Glory! Slow down. Stall out!" Mr. Tattnal roared at them, his short legs churning in the dust.

Pip had been tossed against the door and hung there, gripping on tightly and laughing helplessly as the old man sang out as if he were calling hogs.

"Sooee! Sooooee! Soooooooee!"

The car's owner cajoled enticingly, but the auto failed either to stall or stop for Mr. Louis Tattnal. Under Roiphe's hands, it whipped through the sand yard, scattering chickens, upsetting cans of succulents, and knocking down a clothesline hung with a drooping union suit and overalls. A clutch of sows lurched toward the barnyard fence and stared, blinking their eyelashes at the little red turkey cock of a man.

"Hoo boy!" Roiphe screamed, jerking at the wheel just in time to miss toppling a pair of children riding in a bull cart.

Pip's hands shot to his face; after a few seconds he spread his fingers and peered between them.

"Son, I thought those perishing boys were goners!" Leaning from the window, he saw Mr. Tattnal shrinking in the distance, his legs jigging in the dust. Arms waving, he appeared to be agitating for their return.

Pip sat back and wiped his face with a handkerchief.

On the straightaway Roiphe did a little better, occasionally rollicking into what might have been oncoming traffic had there been any cars on the road.

Once in town, he made frequent use of the horn to indicate both green ignorance of proper navigation and the urgent need for flight on the part of cars and pedestrians alike. Children whooped, scurrying onto the nearest porch. Dogs barked, and the elderly broke into shallow runs. A woman scuttled into a doorway, leaving a delicate edifice of millinery in the middle of the road where it was promptly flattened by the Packard. Roiphe took corners wildly as he screamed warnings to the universe at large.

"We're just about there," he called out, hurtling onto a narrow street.

The car skipped by the store, the boys jouncing on the upholstery as Roiphe worked the clutch.

"There it is!" Pip shouted. "Dadgum! You missed it!"

"Whoa, whoa, whoaaa," his nephew yodeled, swinging around in a u-turn and making another driver tootle his horn in indignation.

"There it is again! Roiphe, slow down—damn! Go gee or go haw but turn her head around before we smack into—"

"I don't know how to—"

"Stomp that pedal, boy!" Pip's voice veered into a shout. "The other one! Stomp it!"

At last a foot crashed onto the brake, and the car rocked forcefully to a stop. They had landed a fair ways into somebody's yard, straddling a rut that served as a walkway.

"Not bad. Next time, maybe you could try a smidge harder and make this thing lift off the ground." Pip stared his nephew full in the face, marveling at the fact that the two of them were alive. It felt fine.

Roiphe's voice trembled as he laughed. He stuck his head out of the window and breathed deeply while Pip climbed out of the car and slammed the door. A girl with pigtails and a small boy so recently out of babyhood that his scalp shone pink through fine white hair were looking at them, goggle-eyed, their fingers still snared in a cradle of string. Pip waved, grinning wide, glad to have his feet on bare earth. The earth rocked a little as if he had been out sailing and had not yet unpacked his land legs.

A mere three doors down was their destination.

"You were right. Not bad at all," Roiphe noted. "I was afraid I'd overshoot and be out in the durn boonsticks before I got her grounded." *The boonsticks:* it was one of his uncle's phrases. They were rubbing off on each other, the two boys.

"*Overshoot* is a fine term for what you were up to. *Catapult* is another." Pip stopped in front of the shop. A homemade sign in the window read *Cotton Gin Shop & Clock & Watch Repair.* He had expected the place to be a gin, but it turned out to be a remodeled filling station from the prior decade with a lean-to at the rear.

"Seems like it ought to be *Gas Clock Shop.* Wonder who he thought would be fooled by *Cotton Gin*? Or who would like the sound of it?" He stood looking at the store, suddenly unsure, and then turned toward Roiphe, who said, "You're my blood. You're my friend, dadgummit. So. I go where you go." Roiphe gestured at the entrance as if to usher in his uncle.

When they pushed open the door, a row of sleigh bells stitched to a leather strap jingled, but no one appeared. From the rear of the building came a strident voice, hortative in manner but obscured by static.

"Look at the jingle bells," Pip said. "I saw some like those hanging in a Yankee barn once. Some year we'll go north and astound the natives with how you handle a sleigh. I bet you could make one of them fly. Get you a present for Alden and soar home—come sliding in to Lil's, claw down a chimney or two and crash onto the porch. It'd be a regular Christmas treat."

"Hah. Me and Old Nick." Roiphe looked about for the owner, but the shop was empty.

The boys walked around the space, their hazel-eyed glances traveling over the sideboards, the rewired lamps, the ticking mantle and wall clocks, the framed documents and photographs.

"Bunch of old ladies clearing out the knickknacks." Arms akimbo, hands shoved in his pockets, Roiphe leaned over a case to examine a group of pocket watches and fairy lights.

"Can I help you?"

A man of about thirty, his hair dusty and his overalls stained with oil, emerged from the back. His drowned eyes blinked sleepily at the two young men.

"That your name?" Pip jerked his head toward the door. "Jempsey Truetlen? You related to Mr. Lamar and Mr. Sam and their kin?"

The fellow nodded as if in answer to all three questions, his pale glance slipping from one to the other. "You got a timepiece to repair, boys?"

"No," Pip said. "I wouldn't mind if you could repair a piece or two of time. But I don't guess that's in your line of work, is it?"

Truetlen gazed at him. "What's your business?"

"You bought a photograph of a little boy from The White Camellia Orphanage," Pip told him. "The time of day seeming to be almost sunrise or almost sunset, the picture probably lit by a lantern. You were showing it off to somebody I know. I'd like to take a look-see."

The man acted hesitant as though he might not fetch it.

"Who told you?"

"Can't quite remember." Pip leaned onto the counter, smiling with only one side of his mouth. "Maybe I've got a bad memory."

The no-account Durden, a pest and a bully from his days in the Orphanage, had told him about the image. The mockery in that voice ignited a fight, from which he had emerged the victor though decked out with a bruised jaw, a shiner, and a swollen hand. It had been a lowdown, dirty scramble that had given him no pleasure.

And now he felt reluctant to be any more obliging than he had to be in order to reach his goal. His fist was gripping the tiny conch, pressing a spike against his palm.

"Who're you?" As Jempsey Truetlen turned his head, the boys saw him swipe a cobweb from his cheek.

"Just somebody who wants to buy a picture," Pip assured him. "I'm not going to grab and skedaddle—I'll give a more than fair price." He shrugged, raising his hands to show that he meant no harm.

At this, the shop owner gazed at him, then nodded and vanished behind a raw-edged quilt top tacked to a rear doorway as a curtain.

"Fool gizzard," Roiphe muttered.

Pip did not reply. The radio filled up the silence between them with twittering voices. He stared at a funeral parlor fan, one common enough around Swainsboro and the outlying region: Jesus lifted his chin to the skies while a flock nosed about his feet, bare on the grass and flowers. The sheep were unhealthy-looking creatures, their heads small and the fur a yellowish green. After a few minutes the gizzard came shuffling back.

Roiphe peered over the counter. He raised his eyebrows and signaled to his uncle, pointing surreptitiously. The dealer was wearing women's homemade bedroom slippers with crocheted flowers on the toes.

Jempsey Truetlen held out the envelope without speaking and watched as Pip examined its manila, creased and worn to the softness of much-laundered fabric and labeled *A Death at the W. Kamelia*

Orphanege in straggling letters. Pip straightened the brad, opened the flap, and slid out the contents.

He was breathing through his mouth as if afraid he could not get enough air through mere nostrils—as if it might not be safe to take in oxygen by the usual way. Inside was a frame, face down. He opened the wire tabs and shook out the protective backing together with the picture. The photo was pale gray, slightly out of focus, with a turquoise water stain in one corner, but its subject was clear, illumined by artificial means. A flotilla of low clouds was barely visible in the background. In the foreground was what might be the only known close-up of Otto Tattnal, face half shadowed, neck flopped to one side like the stem of a flower. Perhaps it was not broken, as children often sleep so when propped upright, their necks crooked at an alarming angle. Barbed wire crowned his head. Blotches discolored his arms and naked side. The cheeks were still a little babyish in their roundness, the eyes large and features pleasing, framed by uncut, tangled curls. A pair of insects nestled against one eye.

That last detail determined him. Pip picked up the negative, which had been clipped away from its fellows and tucked into the reverse of the frame, and held it toward the light. The same figure showed, its bruises looking burnished and metallic.

"Were there more of the same scene?"

"No, the rest of the pictures are hanging up. Over there." Truetlen pointed to the wall. "They're just mules."

"Mules." Pip paused. "You don't know whose?"

"No," he said, his eyes flicking away.

"You sure?"

Pip wondered if Jempsey Truetlen lied occasionally or often and easily, or whether he always told the truth.

"Don't even remember where I bought the envelope. I buy a lot of old clocks to fix up and other used stuff to sell. Estates, mostly."

The fellow toyed with a crystal paperweight in the shape of a slice of watermelon, but he dropped it with a bang when Roiphe burst out, "Swainsboro estates! What a concept!"

"How much?" Pip reached for his wallet.

"I don't get this." Truetlen mumbled when he talked as if he did not like what was in his mouth and wanted to spit.

"There's nothing to *get*. I just want to buy the picture and negative," Pip said in a low voice. "You take the frame."

"How about ten bucks?"

"What? You're crazier than—"

Roiphe paused when his uncle pressed his arm. "But that's too much," he protested. "He'll pay a buck."

"Five," said Truetlen. "He seems to want it mighty bad."

"One," Roiphe insisted. "It's not worth anything."

"Two, then." Truetlen smiled at them.

Pip leaned closer to his nephew and whispered, "Blood money."

"But why—"

Without a word, Pip produced a pair of crumpled bills, and the envelope was pushed across the counter.

"Now." He picked up the manila envelope. "Have you got the rest of the negatives? The ones of mules?"

"Somewhere in my storage." He waved a hand toward the back room. "I was maybe going to make some more pictures. People like mules."

Roiphe laughed at that idea. "They do? Really?"

"Show me. I'd like to examine them," Pip said.

Jempsey Truetlen cocked his head and stared at the name embossed on the wallet in Pip's hands. Lil had given him the wallet with his name in gold. The boy held it out so that he could get a good look.

"It's *Tattnal. Pip Tattnal.* Mean anything to you?"

The seller shook his head. "Lots of Tattnals around here."

"So can I take a look? The negatives?" Pip leaned on the counter, casually tapping the envelope against the glass.

"Well, it might take a time or two," the man allowed, shoving the dollars into his pants pocket.

"Me and my little nephew here, we'll look around," Pip said. "We've got time. Maybe we'll find something we like."

Roiphe whistled a minor tune, catching his uncle's eye.

"Okay, I'll see what I can roust up—"

Truetlen's face was attentive, his head tilted as if trying to catch a distant piece of news from his radio.

Pip thrust his hands into his pants pockets as if to affirm that he would not be pilfering any treasures from the remains of Swainsboro estates. He began wandering through the shop, his eyes drifting from clocks to an opaque glass shoe to a chamber pot painted with forget-me-nots to a wheeled bell toy, rusted but still whole. The owner followed him with his eyes.

"Watch him for me," Pip said in a low voice as he brushed up against his nephew.

After Truetlen vanished from sight, Roiphe tiptoed to the curtain printed with dots and arrows. When the scuffling of slippers could no longer be heard, he gave a wink, and Pip hopped onto a chair and started unhooking photographs of mules from the wall. Several of them had a backing held in by a few bent nails. Working the cardboard loose, he peered at the reverse of the first photograph: the word *Beulah* was scribbled in pencil. Feeling a thrill of panic, he moved on to the next, dragging the chair along the floor. Often a series of prints would be stacked inside old frames, and he hoped to discover something, perhaps even a hidden glimpse of the killer. The second piece of board he tore, hands trembling: nothing. But the third slid free easily, held by a single tack. Roiphe whispered that he could hear the gizzard shutting drawers in the room behind them. Pip swallowed as he lifted the soft backing from the frame and was again disappointed to see that no prior image lay tucked beneath. Slipping out the photograph, he made out the traces of two words written on the margin of the picture, the letters gone blurry, perhaps erased, the inks seeping into the abraded edge. *D—SY BE—E.* It was impossible to make out fully.

"Daisy-be-good. Daisy-be-something," Roiphe said in a low voice, coming up to see. "Hurry up. The gizzard's coming soon."

"*Daisy Belle,*" Pip murmured. "That's what it is."

He managed to loop the wire hanger over a nail just as Jempsey Truetlen's crocheted slippers slapped into the room. It pressed on him, the need to leave this ticking room of clocks and watches and the graveyard clutter of glass and souvenir knickknacks.

Arrested by the sight of Pip stepping off a chair, Truetlen stopped. "What the devil—"

"Just a little close-up art appreciation," Pip said. He shoved his fists into his pocket. "You were right. People do like their mules."

Truetlen closed his mouth; he had a white packet in his hand. Opening the flap, he scattered the negatives. Pip moved back to the counter and slumped against the glass. At first it appeared that he was only gazing at a watch and fob on the top shelf of the case.

Then he eased his hands from his pockets and shuffled through the strips of negatives, trying to still the tremor of his fingers, all the time thinking how the photograph of Otto had been taken before the sun rose. And he had seen the sun vault over the horizon line.

"There."

Pip tapped a pair of odd-sized pieces that meant a strip had been cut, and when he held them up, they could see the shapes of mules, eyes bright in negative. Pip laid the two on the counter top and fished out the cut-away square of film; they fit precisely with the negative of the dead boy, making a dark puzzle.

"There's Beulah, Goshen, Otto, and Daisy Belle. You got any more of Mr. Sam's estate?"

Truetlen stared at him. "I never said these were his."

"Daisy Belle," Pip said. "I rode on that mule when I was a little boy."

"I buy a lot—"

"Of so-called *estates*. You said that already. But these were Mr. Sam's mules and his pictures."

"I couldn't say."

Pip snatched at his collar, yanking the man forward.

"Yes, yes, Mr. Sam," Truetlen gasped.

Roiphe whistled. "That was mighty easy."

"What a piece of work is a man." Pip let go of Truetlen, who rubbed his neck with both hands, looking from one to the other.

"I could have you arrested," he muttered.

"For that little tug? I doubt it. Besides, my nephew and I could tell the truth about Sam Truetlen," Pip said. "I'll bet your family tales have an interest for people round about here."

"They sure interest me," Roiphe said. "I just relish telling a good story." He slouched against the display case and winked as he caught Truetlen's eye.

The man held quiet, waiting.

"No sir, I just don't think I need these mules," Pip said, returning his negative to the manila envelope. His voice was quiet, ebbed to whisper. It was the only way he could control the shiver that had lodged in his throat.

"Sure." Truetlen shook the strips into the packet, his glance shifting from one to the other.

The world traveler recognized that look from rail time. No 'bos were ever wanted in a store. The shop owner might be afraid of them—and certainly feared that they were tramps who had stolen something while his back was turned.

"Look at that. I bet he's scared we took a five-finger discount." Pip jeered, his voice wavering.

"No, fellows, I—"

Roiphe grinned and turned his pockets inside out. The white cotton linings stuck out like nightcaps.

"You'd think Mr. Jempsey Truetlen would know by now that we were buyers," Pip said. He pointed to a gaudy wind-up toy box. He did not want it. He did not even really see it.

"How much?"

"Two dollars," Truetlen proposed.

"Way too high."

"I can do better," the shopkeeper said.

Then, seeing the toy for what it was, Pip picked up the carton. *Alabama Coon Jigger.* The cardboard crumpled in his hand. "I'd like to break it," he said softly, slowly raising his eyes to the man's face.

Roiphe approached his uncle and tugged at his arm.

"You're confusing the gizzard," he said. "You got what you wanted. Let's go."

A wild desire to laugh glanced through Pip.

"No sir, Mr. Truetlen. I think one purchase is enough for today, sir," he said, mimicking his sister Lil's good manners. "Bless your heart, I don't really need a thing more." His tone changed and became severe. He pointed at an ashtray with a folder of matches neatly centered in its bowl. "The book of matches? How much?"

"Free. Take it and go." Truetlen lunged forward, flipping the pack onto the counter.

"Amazing. Free," Pip said. When he palmed the matches, the slick cover clung to his skin.

"There's a rack of cigarettes by the door." The shop owner nodded toward the exit.

"We don't smoke. It's a foul habit. You should stop immediately." Pip's nostrils flared, and he peered at the man's stained fingernails.

"It's not any of your business," Truetlen protested.

"Oh, but it is," Pip replied. "Isn't it, little nephew of mine?"

Roiphe was watching him, not saying a word.

"Am I not my brother's keeper?" When he received no response, Pip repeated the question.

Truetlen looked toward Roiphe, who began to whistle a tune.

"And look at those nicotine hands," Pip said. "I wouldn't be a whit surprised if you spontaneously combusted one afternoon. See, you're just going to blow up some day, mixing cigarettes with those foul oils and chemicals you mix up and daub on all these helpless clocks. Fixing them up for people so they're like new. Some morning you'll be in the Savannah paper, listed with all the other small-print goners. The floaters with their skulls cracked and the little girls who fall down wells. You'll just be fried to a frizzle. Nothing left but a smear of tallow on the floor." He tossed and caught the matches. "Come on, little nephew. It stinks to high heaven in here."

Truetlen looked blank as the two walked away. As they reached the door, he seemed to wake up and called out to them: "If you don't smoke, what did you want with matches? Hey, you're not going to burn that—"

Jangling the door shut behind them, the two sprinted to the car. Broiled by an unseasonably bright afternoon sun, the automobile had become a cauldron, and as the ignition caught fire, the sunlight's dragon heat made the air quiver. Roiphe caught a glowing vision of red crocheted slippers padding down the walk as he gunned the car and, to his own surprise, swept easily from the yard and the faded blue eyes of Jempsey Truetlen.

"Daisy Belle and Goshen."

Pip hardly knew who had spoken, and his own words startled.

His nephew's fingers were cramped on the steering wheel.

"You want a smoke?"

The new owner of a one-of-a-kind photograph rolled a couple of cigarettes and lit them with a match from the store, passing the first to Roiphe, who shot a glance at him and murmured, "It's a foul, filthy habit, they say."

Pip pictured Sam Truetlen riding to the gate of The Cottage on Daisy Belle. He wore a white short-sleeved shirt and khaki work pants pulled up high with a belt, the way the farmers dressed if they were not wearing overalls. A hat was on his head, or else in one hand, fanning his face in summer. He and Otto were proud to have a ride; even now, Pip could feel Mr. Sam's warm, secure arm around his waist as the mule paced to the cattle bars and back. Otto's curls tickled his cheek. Everybody was watching the boys, up so high with

Mr. Sam. He felt proud as though he stood on a tower at the top of the world. Everybody knew Mr. Sam Truetlen, a dignified, clean old fellow with his chin in the air as if he were Jesus on a funeral parlor fan. Well, perhaps he had not been old then. Going on fifty-five or a little past, say. He was the kind of community pillar who stood up in church to make an announcement or passed out fans to the ladies on summer days.

A cluster of sharecroppers on a bench downtown would holler when he stepped out of his Cadillac. Every one of them knew the cotton gin and Mr. Sam, and they all wanted a car like his. A few of the men owned a tired old Caddie, parked in the shelter of an open shed of unpainted boards.

Pip and Otto had never been invited to go anywhere in Mr. Sam's vehicle. Goshen carried the brothers to The White Camellia Orphanage, but Daisy Belle, the white mule, was Mr. Sam's favorite among the four or five on his farm. So maybe he had wanted pictures of his mules. Almost certainly he had taken the one of Otto at sunrise. If so, then he had arranged the child's pose for the photograph. He had killed the boy he once meant to rescue and later found someone who would develop the film without asking questions.

"Did you get everything you wanted?" Roiphe unbuttoned his shirt and blotted the sweat from his neck with a handkerchief.

Pip did not reply but leaned out the window of the Packard and let the breeze rip through his hair, recalling how he had classed even Mr. Sam with the mass of burning-eyed men. Were there two of Mr. Sam, one who had summoned the eyes of his community, white and black, and sauntered through town as though he possessed it—and another who had delved in secret? One a Mr. Sam for whom a child could feel respect and a kind of awed fondness? Another one to dread and hate? If the second Mr. Sam became known, his kin and all the people living near Lexsy would shun his memory, first worrying his reputation for honor and faith and probity like a hound worrying a hambone until it was chomped and shattered into splinters. None of the facts of the matter could save the murderer from that fate. Not even the puzzle of race would stop their mouths.

Pip could picture Pastor Bell, scorching the congregation with coals and brimstone, one hand clamped on a child's shoulder: "Woe be unto you, O sinner-man! Get thee a millstone to dress thy unholy neck and hide thee in the deeps of the sea with the sharks, the electricals of fish and eels, the Jonah-gulping whales, the fearless Leviathan who is Master King of the sons of pride—yea, with all manner of things too wonderful for thee. Do that afore you hurt a one of these little ones."

Mr. Sam had always dreamed of being weighed in the gin scales and found wanting. The man thought this was funny or at least choked out a laugh when he told the story. But perhaps he had been telling the truth about himself the only way he could. Maybe an older evil, even more primitive than race hatred, drew him to the little boy. What about the other child who died later, a girl thought to have drowned?

He was guilty: Mr. Sam who liked to toss pennies and laugh from his saddle on Daisy Belle as he watched the orphans scramble and fight in the dust of the road. Their Mr. Sam! The wind could not make the thought stream away out of the shell of Pip's head. His mind echoed with one name.

Tears rose in his eyes as Pip remembered the sky above The White Camellia's farm: once he had believed that lion-maned angels cast their molten swords in a fiery furnace just overhead, tempering the weapons in a cloud. Hadn't there been a single blade hanging in the dissolving brightness that morning? He imagined reaching for that instrument of flame and thrusting it into a wraith that was the last evil wisp of Mr. Sam, utterly annihilating the vestiges of what had been a man. He leaned farther out the window, cursing and crying into the raking gust until Roiphe slowed the car and seized his pants leg, jerking him back.

"Let's fetch Lil and Alden and ride out to the Tattnal plot," Pip said, rubbing his eyes.

He thought of himself and Otto, each leaving off where the other began, one spooned against the other in the hammock-like beds of The White Camellia Orphanage, their dirty little boy smells twined in that moist nest. One had held the bucket of poison for the other in the fields. Roving together, they had scampered down the lane to the sweetest berry patches, their sun-darkened hands grabbing at the selfsame twigs, their fingertips still dusted with poison...

20

Where questing ends in sacrifice to fire.

"I can't *believe* Louis let you drive his Packard. He has babied that thing for years. The poor old coot must've lost his mind. Been rocking and spitting too long in the sun." Lil Tattnal Tattnal stood smiling at them with her muscular legs planted wide, a stay against wild teenage boys who borrowed cars and roared up on people's lawns, knocking over pots and rocking chairs and water barrels. "If you've nicked the paint, he's going to have your hide, Roiphe Tattnal." The white blouse and the leaf-green apron and the red skirt printed with tiny yellow violins and bunches of flowers tied with blue ribbons whipped in a gust of wind.

She reached up and began pulling the crossed bobby pins from the tiny wreaths that began on her forehead and looped around the back of her neck. Lil had been letting her hair grow long ever since Pip had suggested it, though Alden complained that he did not know why—she had never paid any mind to *his* ideas. Short spirals dangled from her head and swung in the breeze.

"Mommer, would you go comb your hair? You look like a medusa." Roiphe climbed out of the car, staggering a little as if the ground were a foreign medium.

Her fingers moved nimbly around her head, collecting the crooked pins into a small dark sheaf, which she bound with a rubber band and dropped into her apron pocket. "You could have been killed, the pair of you, or landed in the county jail with a pack of misfits. Roiphe Tattnal, you don't know the least thing about driving, no more than a fresh-laid egg."

"He does now. The boy proved himself a driver of ingenuity and downright verve." Pip clambered from the passenger seat and leaned for support against the side of the auto. He was not sure he could walk away yet, having recently been startled by a close call with a straggle of cows in the lane.

"Lil, that was a dadgum shattering experience, but I believe—I truly believe that he could have done a powerful sight more if he had put his unthrottled genius into the thing. If he survives, Roiphe Tattnal has some kind of a future in transportation." With a wrench, Pip yanked a bushel basket off a headlamp and surveyed it.

"First man on the moon," Alden crowed.

"First idiot on the moon, more like. Y'all better pluck those chicken feathers off the front before Mr. Louis sees it," Lil advised. "That's all I've got to say."

"Would that it were." Roiphe rolled his eyes dramatically. "All," he added in case she had not understood.

"I got your drift, bud." She started combing her hair out with her fingers.

"Pip wants to ride out to the cemetery," Roiphe announced.

Lil gave her brother a quick glance, half screened by hair, and then turned back.

"Is that so," she said, no hint of a question in her words.

Roiphe continued, his voice coaxing. "I thought maybe we could have us a picnic. Remember you said a picnic and fishing? We could still go fishing tomorrow. But we could eat out there—maybe rake and clean up the plot. If we run the car by after that, Granddaddy would give us a ride home."

"Did he really say you could take the Packard? Or did you boys foozle him and tear off with it?"

"Mommer, we'd never do a thing like that—"

"What about when you and Alden stole the goat cart out of his barn and wrecked it on Anna Tattnal Road?"

"Mommer! I was little, and Alden was nothing but a baby—"

"I was not!" Beside the pomegranate trees, Alden was pelting some chickens with handfuls of dried kernels.

"Big ears!" Roiphe shouted.

"I was *never* a baby," his little brother yelled.

Pip came up with a pinched-together bouquet of feathers and down, which he presented to his nephew with a low bow: "My compliments. At your service, my bandit prince of the road."

He climbed the porch stairs and settled himself in a rocker, where he sat watching mother and son argue. It was an entertainment better than plenty he had seen. He did not want to think anymore and so he lay back, stretching his legs. They still felt a little wiggly. He might have just hopped a ride on a train that looked too fast to catch.

After a few minutes, Lil shaded her eyes and looked toward him. "Did my daddy-in-law say that Roiphe had to bring that car back by nightfall?"

"Before dark. Yes ma'am."

"Well," she said, "then let's get to packing a picnic basket."

"Hooray!" Alden whooped, throwing a cob into the air and watching as it hit the ground and chickens skittered off. An instant later the hens made a bobble-headed rush for the half-shelled cob.

"Roiphe, go find us a basket that's not got tire tracks all over it, and let's go have us a picnic. But I'm doing the driving." She smiled at them. "Nobody much goes down the cemetery road. Maybe I'll even teach you boys how it's done."

At the graveyard it was not as bright and pale as Pip remembered from the day he had planted the can of ladies' hatpins and zinnias on Otto's grave; the year was younger than before and the hour growing late in the afternoon. Otherwise the boneyard was the same bare ground like a scald, framed by pines.

"Makes you think the dead live in a country that's all white." He had stopped to survey the place, standing beside his parents' graves.

"I don't suppose that's it." Roiphe jingled a few stray pennies in his pocket. "Some people get buried in ice and snow, and some tumble into volcanoes or tar pits. Some sailors drown in the sea. You could just as well say that the dead live in salt water or lava."

"All fire and snakes," Pip muttered, not listening. He nudged silt into a hole near Gilead's grave with the toe of his shoe.

When he looked around to check for his sister, he saw that Lil and Alden were already spreading a quilt at the edge of the plot and unpacking the dinner. There would be leftover cold fried chicken and cornbread and sweet potatoes, with jars of pickled okra and beans and egg custard pie and Japanese fruitcake.

"Last time I was here, I would've given a lot to find some nice lady with a picnic under the pines," Pip said.

He stood up and crossed the bleak soil and the coping dividing it into plots, trailed by Roiphe. Outside the last of the polished stone, Otto's mound was no more—the sand had blown away and the ground had begun to sink, shallow beside the deeper groove of the neighboring grave.

"Some year I'm going to put up markers here, and I'm going to have rosy marble all around so it's not just bare." Pip sank to one knee, running his hand across the dust. "And I'll put on names and words to tell something about Otto and his mommer."

"What would you say?"

"I'd cut the letters and the dates deep and bold, so the rain can't wear them out," Pip said, glancing from the grave to Roiphe and back again. "On this one I'd have them carve, *Thou'lt come no more, / Never, never, never, never, never.* I read at Shakespeare on the road, but I never got to the end of him. Those words hit right at me like they were taking aim—shot a bolt through all those centuries."

"What was this one's name?" Roiphe squatted beside the deep depression.

"That's Otto's mommer," Pip told him. "She was called *Nan.* Sometimes I guess that name like a ring was what attracted my daddy because he was drawn to things that kept going forever. Maybe that's why he liked to build bridges. Old Gilead, my daddy, he was a sport."

"He was a real night wanderer." Roiphe gave a low whistle. "Mommer says he was a God-fearing man, but he must've been one holy hopper."

256

Pip was engrossed in his plan. "I'll have something pretty here. I'll have the tablets be tall and arch-topped like some gravestones I saw up north. I'll get a carver to do something fancy and different. An angel with tobacco leaf wings. A conch shell or maybe a bottle with a woman's ghost inside. They'll make people stop and look."

When his thoughts settled back on Roiphe, he found that his nephew was kneeling on the ground next to the graves, his eyes closed and hands clasped. It made Pip feel suddenly far from the living as though he had been left entirely alone on the bleached ground. He reached in his pocket and palmed the little conch. It was nothing but idle fantasy to picture the soul of Otto spiraled inside a whorl of calcium, but the old idea occurred to him. He rubbed its silken body and tugged the paper from its heart. Then he blew lightly on the horn, making a stray note.

"Let it go. Let him go," he whispered into the waves of heat.

Roiphe's lids fluttered, and he opened his eyes and looked at Pip across the graves.

"Aunt Mem took a box of pictures from Granddaddy Gilead's house," he said. "I remember seeing them when I was little. They were in a wooden tea chest, tin nailed on the inside to keep out the bugs. She probably never threw them away. Mommer says she's a packrat, sure enough. She might have some pretty good photographs of Otto. Maybe your parents and you and Otto and Chach. She might even know what became of Chach." He paused, and his gaze settled on his uncle's shoulder. "It's not far. We could drive out there and see."

Pip hesitated. Long ago he had decided to turn away from his remaining brothers and sisters, and he had sworn never to retreat from that stand. But Lil and her boys had won a certain amount of his loyalty—how much, he was not sure. He imagined Otto's living face looking out of a photograph or a snapshot of Otto clinging to his hand.

"I'd like that."

Hadn't he known he belonged somewhere at last, watching Lil through the window, her head bent over the book on the neat kitchen table with its wiped oilcloth and the salt shakers molded in the shape of thatched cottages, although there was not such Cotswold quaintness in the whole state of Georgia? It was fine to have somebody wait up. Good to have somebody like to cook meals for three boys and get some satisfaction out of their pleasure. And it was sweet to be scolded for being out late—he, who had tramped the continent! His hand went to his neck, and he fingered the cracked opal stone, the two halves hugged tightly in a hoop of silver. As he thought about Lil's intent face, a tendril of feeling uncurled inside him, winding upward like a ghost gyring through a shell.

The feeling was pleasing, though it had no name and was something he only dimly recognized. A memory of his mother standing in flowering fruit trees drifted into his mind as if to help him learn what it might mean. He shut his eyes and let the vine come to its leafage and blossoming. He could feel the bright tint of pollen suffusing his body, and he could feel the air going gold with sunset. He remembered riding through fragrant peach orchards in a boxcar and longing for his nonexistent home, the garden place denied when he had been banished as surely as if an angel with a sword of flame in its hands barred the gate.

"The King's horse, with a kind of contempt of the enemy, charged with wonderful boldness and routed them in most places." The words, forgotten for years, sprang from his lips like a banner.

He lifted his hands to his closed eyes, shielding his face and darkening his sight. Then he dropped them again so that the light through his lids brightened. For some moments he felt the simple aspiring of a flower for the sun: as if he had gone past everything he had known and even past himself until he was nothing human but some radiant other. In that instant everything he knew about himself from the beginning and everything he hoped to be was lost in one burning sphere of longing. No syllable could bear the huge freight of his dimly felt purpose. Desire spilled its nameless treasure of gold like a maypop under a child's stamping foot.

Opening his eyes, he glimpsed Roiphe drifting away and then slowing to stoop and read the words on a marker. Unfallen tears blurred the boy and the stones. The scene wavered and seemed about to buckle, perhaps to reveal some world behind their own like a glimpse of the kingdoms of Roseville and Thera and the old man and the child who had sought them.

Now one word was in his mouth like a magic coin—a fee for the ferryman so that he might cross over to the land of the living. *Love.* That was what other people called it. Lil had it in spades. She had no trouble letting him in, putting her arms around three big boys who messed up her neat rooms and sparred with one another and ate her pies straight off the rack where they were cooling for the next meal. She sought and loved him when he was hardly more than the faraway mourning of a whistle. Mr. Fairbairn had been right after all; there was a place where if he went, they had to take him in. Home had cost him though. The price had been the death of his freedom, the halt to his long running away, and the end of ignorance about his kin and about how Otto had passed into the sunrise and disappeared.

Lil.

If he could care about and be loyal to one earthly person after Otto, maybe he could manage such a feat with another. Perhaps it would raise him from that long-ago death at The White Camellia Orphanage to a life of people and ways he could not imagine now, as distant and as seemingly closed as another dimension. As if deciding all over again, he told himself that he would stick with Lil and the boys—at least for the lull between the red-hot years on the rails and the fire that was burning in Europe and Asia, blowing sparks and soot their way. Where and how it might carry him could wait.

He slipped the photograph with the turquoise water stain from the creased envelope. While he hoped there would be another picture of Otto somewhere, a better image, he knew that even if no other existed in the whole world, he would not preserve this one. As

Roiphe meandered across the Tattnal cemetery, pausing to read tablets, Pip studied the face of his brother Otto until he had memorized its shape and bruises and the look that should have been betrayed innocence but was only emptiness.

He stared and took the little boy in until his eyes ached with pent tears. If this meant love, perhaps it was easier to live without it, just as it had been simpler to turn his back on Excelsior Tillman, just as time and again he had caught the death-dealing red ball express and let the train hurl him away from somebody who was fond of him and might have held fast. He might still be striding the Lilliputian streets of Roseville. He might be resting in the heart of some eucalyptus wood, telling a never-ending story to Cora. Or he might be living on the brink of the prairie sea with Opal and their child of dreams, an Otto bright as the moon.

But he had chosen to live without love for years.

Was that how Mr. Sam had lived, hard by the gin and the farmers' wagons, each one holding a cumulus of cotton to be made into stacked bales of lint? The heaped pickings looked snowy from far away but held stones and the bitter dark tears of seed.

"No," he said to the pebbles and the soil and the bones of his ancestors, not even knowing entirely what he refused.

"Pip! Uncle Pip!" Alden was dancing under the pines, calling his name in hungry shrieks. Roiphe turned to gaze at him, wordless, waiting.

"We won't start without you!" His sister was standing beside the cloth loaded with food. She waved when he looked her way.

Mine, he thought, *my bulwark and my rampire.*

For an instant he was unable to utter a word, staring toward the three of them as the tears swam into his eyes. Then he blinked and called out strongly: "Just a minute—I'm coming. I'll be right there."

He knelt on the ground, hurriedly reaching in his pocket for the book of matches. Arson had taken the shacks by the Savannah River and The White Camellia Orphanage, and it seemed fitting that there should be a third sacrifice—that it should be an offering wholly consumed by flame. Ground hallowed by bone would be his altar. One by one, he lit matches and held them to the negative and the heavy stock, adding final fire to a long-ago sunrise. The burning took the remaining matches in the book.

In a moment he would fly across the graves to Lil and the boys and into the harsh, glittering light of his life to come. But for now he waited until the very last corner of the photograph was given over to death. Blackened pieces caught on the depression of Otto's grave, falling like impossibly soft shrapnel through the air, with edges glowing and dangerous to the touch.